The Sorrows

stories by
GARY FINCKE

For information about permission to reproduce selections from this book, contact *permissions* :

Stephen F. Austin State University Press
P.O. Box 13007, SFA Station
Nacogdoches, TX 75962
sfapress@sfasu.edu
www.sfasu.edu/sfapress
936-468-1078

Edited and designed by: Jerri Bourrous
Project Manager: Kimberly Verhines
Typset in Garamond

The views and opinions expressed in this book are the authors's own and do not reflect the views and opinions of Stephen F. Austin State University, its Board of Regents, or the State of Texas.

ISBN: 978-1-62288-311-0

First Edition

TABLE OF CONTENTS

CLIMBING TO THE LaBIANCAS'

RYAN GIFFORD STOOD in his mother's tiny kitchen listening to her praise him for finishing rehab and coming straight her way so she could help him through the first tough days. "You'll be fine," she said. "Starting tomorrow, I'll drive you to your meetings. I'll go for long walks and wait for you to come out so we can mark off another good day."

"I can walk, Mom. It's only a mile to the church." Ryan opened and closed each of the kitchen cupboards without touching anything inside. "I put everything away," she said.

"You can say liquor, Mom."

"I didn't mean to make it sound like anything."

"I'm on my feet now."

"Good." She lit a cigarette, and when he didn't say anything else, she added, "That's good. Maybe a week is all you needed."

"That's what they said. It sounds crazy—the one-week rehab, but the place was crowded. One week is a start. A push in the back."

"For the right person, for sure, enough to get your feet under you. You look good."

"Better maybe," he said. "Good's a stretch."

THEY WALKED TOGETHER just after lunch. He'd picked afternoon meetings, filling in the time of day when he always felt like cracking that first cold beer. Almost thirty years he'd been drinking, but always from lunchtime forward, taking pride in that small discipline until a few months ago, when he opened his first beer as soon as he was on his feet and keeping a cooler in his car so he could keep his buzz on during work until those habits had gotten him fired.

The church was in Silver Lake. The meetings held outside in the small amphitheater behind the building. "So many people," his mother said. "I bet it's more than they get for church." She sat in the only adult chair in a room where children had Sunday school and shooed him toward where the bench seats were filling outside. "Enough walking just getting here," she said, but he knew she was going to watch through the window, making sure he didn't leave early.

Ryan climbed six rows up and sat where the crowd thinned. Close to a hundred, Ryan guessed, relieved. He could work his way toward saying something. Nobody would pick him out among all these people, some others fresh out of rehab, for sure.

Afterward, they went to the PinkBerry across the street, both of them loading up with strawberries and chocolate syrup before they walked back to Los Feliz.

Just before six, she cooked spaghetti with hot sausage to eat outside on the patio. "You did good today," she said. He noticed she'd eaten a sausage link but left half of her spaghetti on her plate as if she were in a hurry to light her after-dinner cigarette.

"It's one day, Mom. You have to let me walk by myself or else it's all pretend."

"Next week," she said. "Let's do pretend for a week like that rehab."

"I'll be gone in a week if a job in Glendale or close by happens without any kinks. Let's do one more day and stop kidding ourselves. And you don't need another mouth to fill on your retirement pay."

She took a long drag and seemed to relax. "First, promise to help me do something special almost right in my own back yard."

"What's that?"

"I want to climb straight up to the LaBiancas'."

"After all these years? You've seen their house how many times by now? And you've said yourself it's too steep. And that was before you were in your sixties."

"That's why I have to climb now before it's too late. Straight up to the LaBiancas' like nobody else has ever done."

"Are you sure?"

"I've never seen anybody. Living here all these years, I'd have heard."

"Maybe the potential mountain goats notice there's a fence with barbed wire all the way across up top."

"That's for the priests next door up there. We don't have to bother them if we go up along that fence off to the left of the Yang's place. Regular people won't have barbed wire in their back yard. I don't care about priests, do you?"

"No."

"There, then. And that cyclone fence gives us plenty of handholds all the way to the top. The Yangs are gone all day. They'll never know we started in their yard."

"We can walk on the street. That's a hike by itself going up that hill on Waverly. Maybe test how you feel."

"It's not the same. Anybody can do that. Millions have, I bet, in nearly forty-five years since. I've wanted to do this since forever, even way back when I told you all about taking you up there with Lisa, so here it is time or never."

Ryan nodded. When he was thirteen, his mother had told him how she'd taken his sister and him with her to see the LaBianca house. "You were five months and Lisa was three, both of you in a double stroller. I had to stop six times on that upslope. It's not far, but it's hard going. And going back down? It was some struggle holding the two of you back from zooming away and crashing somewhere."

Ryan had listened like he was in history class because he expected his mother to test him later, asking what he remembered, whether he could find the LaBianca house if she sent him off with a camera and told him to come back with a photograph to prove it.

"I waited exactly one week to make that climb. Where Sharon Tate and her baby were killed, they had tourists forever, but the LaBiancas were just people, and sure enough, the traffic was gone, the police and the press moving on. The crime scene tape was still there. A few cars passed, not so many that maybe they all lived up there. I was counting on a woman with two small children looking like she was from the neighborhood. People have to keep living. They have to walk their own streets and not be thought awful for gawking at what's special even if."

She'd walked him out to the back patio and pointed up the hill through the trees and the browned-out undergrowth that always looked to Ryan as if it would burst into flames. "Almost exactly straight up," she'd said. "Lisa went to a couple of parties up there almost right across the street, the very same house Manson visited for a whole different kind of party before all the rest happened. It's in a book if you care to read it someday and learn how you were that close to history."

"Sleep on it, Mom," was all Ryan, now, could think of to say.

"You know what," she said, "why don't you, in the morning, make the climb to the house where the motorcycle gang actor murdered his landlady three years ago. See what it feels like to take a close-up look at something like that."

"It's not like that was last week, Mom. It's nowhere that close."

"So you know all about it? We weren't talking much back then. Close? Look right over there out across the boulevard and see that house if you know where to look."

"I know it was Johnny Lewis," Ryan said, "who was Half-Sack in the first two seasons of *Sons of Anarchy*."

"What he did for real was beat his landlady to death, killed and dismembered her cat, and then he jumped from the roof and killed himself way too late to help that poor old woman."

"Half-Sack was missing a testicle."

"He was missing decency," his mother said.

"It's half a mile straight over to that house, Mom. A mile or more walking."

"If you see it from my kitchen window, it's almost next door. You'll have something to do besides drink coffee and listen to me jabber." She crushed her half-smoked cigarette among the uneaten spaghetti strands. "It's a start, sweetheart. You know."

LOWRY, THE JOHNNY Lewis murder street, was as steep, Ryan thought, as Waverly, good practice, maybe, for the climb to the LaBiancas'. Every yard displayed a security sign, half with extra warnings that promised an armed response.

By the time Lowry spiraled up to the 3600-block murder site, the houses seemed to loom on the side of the street where the crime took place, each one built for height to guarantee a view. The short driveways were all steep, the houses fortress-like. A few houses had pulley systems for the luxury of delivered groceries and packages. The driveway at the murder site was pitched so steeply he saw at once how a head-first tumble from the roof or even the balcony could be fatal. What he was less certain of was that from her kitchen, his mother could look across Los Feliz Boulevard and know which house was a murder site.

He walked past and kept going, switchbacking up toward the border of Griffith Park, high enough to sit and yet still see all the way to downtown Los Angeles. As long as he was on foot, he thought, he'd be able to walk off his anxiety. It was another twelve miles to where his car was locked in place by a boot. His mother's car, though, was right there on the street below her house, and for now, at least, he was glad he'd found out, while looking, she had hidden her car keys before she'd gone to bed.

When he returned, his mother had lunch on the kitchen table. "A long walk can do a body good," she said, caution in her voice.

"I took your advice and went up Lowry past the Lewis house and then on up to the park for a while." He noticed that the ashtray on the kitchen table was full and remembered that it had been empty and wiped clean when he'd left after downing two cups of coffee.

"You need to get something into you, for sure. You can't live on coffee."

"I had a slice of bread with jelly. I'm not starving."

"I didn't see you stand up and speak yesterday," she said. "You plan on that today?"

"When I'm ready, Mom."

"You walked all over creation and back this morning. You're ready. I can feel it."

"I need to feel it, Mom."

"Maybe if I don't come along, you'll talk?"

"Maybe."

"So, you go and come back in one piece and tell me what you said and we'll climb tomorrow morning."

HE SHOWED UP just before four, over an hour later than they'd made it back the day before. He caught his mother glancing at the clock. "I talked, Mom," he said, "and then I met my sponsor and talked some more. I drank iced tea." Ryan felt her examining him, watching him move for signs of trouble, listening for a hint of slurring. "Tomorrow he's driving me to Glendale. There's a place for me to stay."

"A halfway house? You already have a place over that way."

"It's temporary. It's part of the rehab. My sponsor goes to his meetings there, so it's all good that way. They've given me some leads on jobs. One of them's even a tech job. Once I'm at work again, I'm back in my own place."

"There's always room for a techie like you."

"Let's hope that room's close by. There's riding the bus until I get my license back."

"You'll be good at an interview. They'll see you have a good heart."

"Whatever it is will be like starting over, Mom. It will be what I did fresh out of school."

"They'll be lucky to have somebody like you then. You'll be doing somebody a favor," she said, but he caught her glancing where the fingers of his right hand had been drumming the kitchen table. "This is your bad time, right? This is when you want to start in on the beer?"

Ryan pulled his hand back, thought about standing, but settled for crossing his legs to show her he was relaxed. "Sometimes even earlier, Mom."

"Your father drank nothing but the hard stuff with ice. Vodka by the quart. I always thought you were ok because you only did beer."

"All the beer, Mom. The whole case or when I passed out, whichever came first. On my good nights, a six-pack so I could sleep."

"I hope you didn't say awful things to anybody. Your father always had a mouth on him. He said 'cunt' all the time. I hate that word. He knew it. There should be sexual words you can't say aloud like they did with racial words. Cunt should be an N-word."

"I think it is, Mom. People call it the C-word."

"Not in my house, they didn't."

"He didn't say it the night you locked him out and called the police."

"But I could hear him thinking it."

"He just left and didn't come back for two days, like he was afraid."

"And then he was gone for good because he was a coward," she said. "I'm sorry you remember that. I wish I'd done it when you were half that age. If you had been four years old maybe you'd have forgotten all of it." She paused, etc. "I always worried about how your marriage would work out, and then I ended up worried you'd never marry."

"I wear out my welcome, Mom. Those women all had time to see behind the curtain."

"Don't you be putting yourself back there with somebody who's all mouth like your father. He's still strumming his cheap guitar and singing his mopey songs to the wind somewhere. I keep hearing him telling me how great we had it, how we'd only just begun. He'd sing it even, like we were the goddamned Carpenters."

"There had to be something, Mom."

"Oh, there was. He was so charming and handsome. It made him a wonderful waiter. It was the perfect job for him."

"Waiting tables is a performance," Ryan said.

"Yes, it is. Everything is an act, and look at me, I was mesmerized. You know the way you feel when you're watching an excellent magician? You know what he's doing is impossible, and yet in the moment you believe it's happening."

"Don't punish yourself, Mom," he said, but she kept on.

"Did I tell you I've read about somebody just like him, that I'm not the only one who figured it out way too late? People like that learn what pleases people and then they act like that, maybe even as far back as when they were children. They're sick with it."

"Lots of people are sick then."

"And all of them thinking it's the other way around."

"There's lots of churches for that talk, Mom."

"Oh no, not those places. They make you feel awful about yourself, and then they ask you to sing like you mean it."

"Didn't you go way back when?"

"Your father dragged me a few times before either of you were born.

He thought it made up for his foolishness, but he was all lip synch when he got there."

The next morning, they watched the Yangs drive away in separate cars before Ryan let his mother lead him across two back yards, sidestepping on the steep hillside until they reached the cyclone fence. Ryan's mother steadied herself, then raised both arms as if they'd already reached the top. "This will be a day to remember," she said, "a turning point."

"I hope that's already passed," Ryan said.

"This one's for me," she said, dropping her hands and reaching for the fence as if she'd felt dizzy. "Give me a second. It feels slippery."

"Yes, it does. It's close to straight up."

She looked back toward her house, and for a moment Ryan thought she'd changed her mind. "You know," she said, "your father adored your sister, but when you were born he couldn't stay interested, like he only had enough feelings for one child."

"Lisa used to tell me stories about happy things that happened when I was two or three years old. I couldn't remember anything from then, so it started to feel like all the blanks were filled with good things."

"She was good-hearted that way. That sounds just like her to be giving you the fairy tale side of things." She laughed and turned away. "Let's do this thing."

The climb was slow going, the fence acting like a tug-of-war rope that kept threatening to be ripped away by gravity. In a minute, he was sweating hard enough to stain his t-shirt. His jeans felt heavy. His mother's breathing was accented by a rasp.

When, panting hard after a few minutes, his mother stopped, the fingers of her left hand gripping the fence, what they were doing felt forbidden to Ryan. Even twenty feet up, hanging onto the cyclone fence just below her and fighting the urge to kneel to keep his balance, Ryan hoped his mother would say "enough" and begin to slide back down to the Yang's back yard.

"We tried," he could say, but his mother's breathing slowed quickly, and she smiled as if they'd already arrived at the summit, a signal to move on.

"I wish you still had a sister to talk to."

He nodded. The sensible one, his mother had always said, the one who would ask for an evaluation, whether he was doing anything about "problems." Somebody he would never tell about climbing, regardless of the outcome. "Well?" she said, "am I right?"

"Listen, Mom," he said. "Let's just concentrate on what we're doing."

"She wouldn't have made this climb, that's for sure," she said. "She would have told us it was dangerous. She was a little planner, from the very start always thinking ahead, and it turned out she didn't have much ahead of her, and yet here we are working our way up like those Sherpas in the Himalayas."

"Whenever you're ready, Mom," Ryan said, but his mother looked down at him as if she were about to let go and fall and carry them both to the bottom.

"I walked the two of you to Ivanhoe every morning. That school was wonderful with all those parents who loved music and art, some of them famous. Your father was all about going to the plays and trying to schmooze with ones he recognized, but he was never up in the morning, not once, and then it was just me and you doing the walking." She turned then, reaching for a new handhold, and tugged herself two short, choppy steps forward, keeping her balance. He heard her say, as if to herself, "For a while, when you were in fourth and fifth grade, I'd tell myself Lisa was over at the middle school," but she didn't look back, and he churned after her without speaking.

In less than a minute, though, a bare patch a few feet higher was terrible for traction. The soil reminded Ryan of the consistency of an anthill, more like ashes than the clay surrounding it. Both of them slipped, then slipped again. Ryan felt a familiar pain run through his left knee, the one he'd injured when he'd fallen down a flight of stairs at a party two years before. He saw that his mother was afraid to sit, afraid of more than stains ruining her clothing, afraid that sitting would prompt the irrevocable urge to descend. She lunged then, silent, her steps tentative and short until she reached grass and clover, not stopping again until she'd managed another twenty feet.

From where they stood now, it was clear that the fence and its barbed wire that could be seen from his mother's patio ended a few feet to their right, but so did the fence that had supported them. His mother put her head down and pulled herself up to where the fence stopped. Without speaking, she took her hands off the pole that ended the fence and lowered herself onto her hands and began to scrabble up. That she was wearing shorts, something she abhorred, made Ryan realize, at last, that she had anticipated crawling. For a moment, he held the fence and prepared to somehow stop her if she slid and tumbled back. Her knees were on the ground now, her shoulders hunched, and then she was on hillside that was weed covered and sloped modestly enough for her to slowly twist and sit before waving down at him until he let go and crawled.

They sat together for a minute before either of them spoke. "I can't get over it," she said. "Are you as surprised as I am that we made it?"

"More surprised."

She patted his jeans just above the knee. "There had to be some room here," she said. "They can't put a fence right up on the very brink."

"Like they do sometimes with guard rails," Ryan said, "and then you see them listing like they'd never even slow you down if you went off the road."

She turned and scrambled a few more feet on her knees, steadied herself, and stood where Ryan could see mowed lawn began. "These people spend a lot of money on water," she called down. "You don't have a lawn this nice in Los Angeles without money."

"Stop there, Mom. They'll have money for motion sensors and video cameras, too."

"I'd be more afraid if I heard good, old-fashioned dogs."

"They'll call 911 if they're home or else it happens automatically."

"Don't you want to walk right up and look inside like you're family?"

"Mom, no. We made the climb. That was the deal."

"You sound like somebody I knew once."

"Mom."

"Don't you dare," she said. "Don't you even dare."

Ryan heard himself breathe hard as if he were about to plunge into water, but his mother's shoulders seemed to sag. "Did I tell you how the new homeowners had the street number changed way back when?" she said.

"No."

"See? People still follow Manson and those crazy girls like they're stuck in time, but they've forgotten the LaBiancas. Like those that spout Kennedy, numbers one and two, and King, Jr. and take that for 60's history. They don't know the living, Manson forever still with us like Castro until he went kaput just when it seemed like he was going to make a run at Methusalah's record."

She took a step closer to the house, right to the edge of where the perfect lawn ended. Panicked, Ryan said, "Mom, tell me a story that I can't remember from when I was two or three years old."

She didn't turn, but she stopped and stood still. "One with your father in it?"

"No. One with just us, only I was little." He slipped closer to her, imagining hugging her and saying something kind while he guided her away from the house.

"It was the same, baby. You were sweet and quiet, and your father was always somewhere else even when he was home just like you remember."

He wanted to ask again, move the time back to before he was born, a time that Lisa wouldn't have remembered, too, but his mother, thankfully, had pulled out a cigarette and was lighting it, her hand cupped around the lighter's flame, her habit giving him the space to move close.

"Look, Mom, we need to follow the edge here and find a yard that's not gated in the front or else we'll never get to Waverly."

"I never thought of that," she said. "We don't want to be stuck out front there looking like fools, do we?"

"Or criminals."

He led the way, making sure they stayed in ankle-high weeds. Two doors down he could see that the yard was open all the way to the street, that if they stayed near the far edge and hurried, they might be able to walk along Waverly without the police arriving to question them.

His mother followed him onto Waverly without speaking. She walked slowly then, looking ahead where the boundaries of the LaBianca property began. When she stopped, he stood beside her and stared through the gate and up the driveway at the front door as if he needed to remember every detail, as if, years from now, they would have this to talk about, nothing more important than sharing a memory of the La Bianca house, studying the landscape, willing, right now, to concentrate until she decided to say, "Let's go home."

"Look how far those Manson people had to go thinking about what they were about to do. You'd think maybe some would change their minds."

"Some might have, but it didn't matter by then."

She turned away, and for a moment Ryan believed she was disappointed or angry and wanted to leave, but she pointed on an angle across the street.

"That house over there," she said. "Lisa was inside it twice, once more than Manson. For birthday parties when she was six and seven. See how close it is? I wonder if those people knew about Manson being inside there at a party way back before everything. Whether looking up the LaBianca driveway all these years spooked them."

There were three men doing yard work at the birthday party house, all of them Mexican, all of them young, in their 20s, maybe younger. None of them, Ryan thought, would know the history of this street. Or the street below, came to him then, history only as far as we can see and hear.

"There's always secrets," he heard his mother say before she turned to face him. "Everybody with their locks and longing," she said, and Ryan began to recast his future for his mother, choosing a job and a woman she would believe were attainable--tech support at a community college, seeing a woman who was an adjunct professor there, somebody struggling to get traction in academics—giving himself things she might accept because they were so ordinary there was no reason not to believe them.

"You're supposed to be safe in your own house," she said, close to him now, looking straight at him. "Those stone stairs down to the street you were always afraid of, they weren't in the house. I was afraid for you, too, but outside, that's a different story."

"I always held the rail," Ryan said.

"'Just a bump on the head,' your father kept saying. 'A good night's sleep was all she needed.' And then she didn't wake up. Your father put her to bed and watched television and drank his vodka right past when we got home, and all that time she was bleeding inside her head."

"You don't have to keep going, Mom."

"He said he held the chair for her. You know she would have been uncomfortable up there where she didn't belong just because he was too drunk to change the ceiling-light bulb in her room himself so she didn't have to feel around in the dark."

"I was six, Mom."

"Seven in a week. Old enough to remember how she was."

"You had to come get me because I didn't want to sleep over after David Moran's birthday party."

"Don't you be blaming yourself. It was a ten-minute drive, fifteen maybe, and a half hour of getting you calmed down before I got you in the car. David's mother had her hands full with you. She didn't want you to leave until she was sure you were ok. Everybody made the time longer, so it's not about you that hour he had alone with your sister."

"I was afraid of everything. Lisa was the one who always took care of me."

"Your father took his hand off that chair. He wouldn't admit it, but I told him I knew he did because no careful nine-year-old girl falls off a chair if it's steady. Not Lisa, absolutely not. Your father said I was being unreasonable. He said that out loud, but I know the truth, him not even paying enough attention to catch her. And then he made it worse by putting her to bed like he was hiding what happened." She waved her right arm toward the LaBianca house and took a deep, audible breath. "You know what forgiveness is for something like that? Something that happens after time runs out and the world has ended."

"There's no telling, Mom. That's what the future is for."

"I knew I'd never be happy again, not even for a minute. It was like I'd seen corroborating evidence there is no God."

She sighed, pulled out her phone, and began taking pictures. "Come on," she said. "Stand over there by the gate so I can look at our day later when I'm settled down. That's it. It's ok to look like a tourist."

Ryan eased into a smile at once, relieved to be back in the present.

In a minute, he thought, she'll pose and ask to have her picture taken, maybe even stand near the Mexicans in the front yard of Lisa's once-upon-a-time birthday party house. He watched a man approaching with a tiny, tightly-furred dog that excitedly tugged its leash until it stood right by his feet where the driveway entered the street. When he reached down to give it a quick pat, the man said, "Mr. Muggles likes you."

"Looks that way."

"I walk him for his owner. He's lived up here for quite some time, but doesn't get out much anymore."

Ryan noticed his mother listening. "Quite some time" might very well place that dog owner on this street in the summer of 1969, and the dog walker, as if he'd been overhearing everything his mother had said, offered, "After the Manson thing, the new owners of that house changed the number of the street address. Some people come up here and get confused."

"I can understand why," he said, happy that his mother only nodded and allowed the dog walker to have his way with what he believed would be inside information.

"Well, then," the dog walker said. "You enjoy your curiosity," and with what Ryan sensed was meant to be an ambiguous smile, he guided Mr. Muggles away from them.

"I'm glad we're going back down like regular people," his mother said. "My legs are killing me."

"You could sit somewhere, and I could get the car," he said, glancing away, awkward with remembering the hidden keys.

"Look where we are. Up here, a loiterer gives off a rotten smell. There's no place to sit except on the ground like a bag lady."

He waited, but she didn't give any sign she had a secret. She looked around again as if she expected never to be in a neighborhood she could drive to in less than five minutes. If a silent alarm had notified the police, both of them, Ryan thought, would be questioned and give entirely different versions of the past hour. He watched Mr. Muggles, in stop and starts, sniff his way up the stone walk to through the yard next to the birthday party house.

"This must be how those fellows who climb mountains feel. Even though you're freezing or exhausted, you want to stay up at the top as long as you can. You feel terrible when you start down."

"But we can go slow here, follow the sidewalk."

"I almost wish the police had come. This isn't how a big adventure should end. It makes us out to be barking dogs or maybe stray coyotes."

"That's what we were, Mom."

"I don't like the sound of that. And us slinking away like they do. Slinking is such a terrible word. It's full of shame."

Ryan tensed, but she was already shuffling away from the LaBianca's toward the long stucco wall that stretched in front of the Catholic estate that sprawled above his mother's house, so large the wall ran half way down Waverly.

"It's medieval up here," she said. "All those Brothers of the Good Shepherd in their fortress, and yet those Manson disciples came straight in from the front. I bet more than a few of those priests had some doubts about God after that. I bet they were reconsidering."

Ryan pointed at a plaque on the gate that divided the lengthy wall they began to follow. *"Cardinal Timothy Manning House of Prayer for Priests,"* he read. "I never knew the name of this place." Through the spaces between the bars he could see that Spanish style buildings stretched across much of the perfectly kept grounds. The Brothers of the Good Shepherd apparently hosted other priests looking to spend time on retreat. "It looks like a resort hotel for monks," Ryan said.

His mother moved so close to the gate Ryan expected her to grab it and try to make it rattle. "A vacation for priests must be they don't have to lie for three weeks," she said, but she didn't touch the gate, and when he didn't say anything, she pointed inside and added, "I've heard they're trying to sell the place. I bet nobody wants to be a priest anymore, and all the ones left in there are old and getting older."

"It must be worth a fortune."

"Then they better get to selling it and enjoy themselves for a few years."

The perimeter wall that lined the street stretched for such a distance that Ryan guessed it covered a couple of hundred yards. That's what even priests do when they have money, he thought, build privacy and insurance against danger. From here, on Waverly, it was all descent.

His mother gathered herself before she spoke again. "What do you imagine those poor people thought when their house was invaded?"

"They were being robbed," he said at once.

"They were being robbed, all right. Of everything. It must have seemed impossible."

"Yes," he said, hoping the word would be a period.

"Something like that never happens, and then it does. Those people inside there with the house number changed, they've learned that some other way."

"Mom," he started, but she was scanning the street, examining it like a neighborhood watch volunteer.

"And all those priests and their walls in case prayer doesn't do a thing to help."

Ryan waited, letting her decide when to start going down. "I wanted to move after Lisa. I threw that chair away and all the others like it. Some scavenger got a set of four, but then I knew that if I moved, she would disappear faster."

The air felt musty, like an attic. Ryan felt the need for the first cold beer, swallowed saliva, and fought it down.

"Well, all right then," his mother said. "I've said my piece" She looked his way, smiling. "Like those Mt. Everest people, right? They always say something when they get to the summit, don't they?"

"Top of the world, maybe."

"Yes. They celebrate. They shake hands and hug and kiss. They never forget."

QUEEN FOR A DAY

"YOU KNOW WHAT would make me happy," our mother would say. "I'd like to be Queen for a Day." It was what she repeated just after she declared herself good and tired with making ends meet and having my sister Jenny and me underfoot all-day long.

We didn't mind because saying "queen for a day" got her to smiling, and my sister and I to checking the clock above the kitchen stove because 3:30 was when Jack Bailey asked, "Do YOU want to be QUEEN FOR A DAY?" and the audience roared a great big "Yes" like the amen at the end of the benediction that always meant church was over for another week.

We'd had the television for three months now, and it hadn't worn off yet like our grandfather had warned it would when he had it delivered for our mother's birthday. What's more, Jenny and I could still see just fine even though when our mother was running errands, we sat right up close on the carpet where we didn't belong, our feet almost touching the television's wooden legs, ignoring the chairs she set up almost at the opposite wall to get them ten feet away like the eye doctor recommended. When we heard her on the stairs, we'd push ourselves backwards with our hands and pull ourselves up into the chairs where children sat who didn't want to go blind.

Dad had been dead two months, but the upstairs rooms we rented still smelled like the smoke from his Chesterfields that he didn't stop smoking even after his operation. Nobody ever said a word about that smell. If one of the frayed wires in our apartment shorted out, Jenny and I would know the difference between electricity and our Dad.

That smell always made me think Mom would win on Queen for a Day. Jack Bailey would place his hand on her head and ask the audience for their applause, and that needle would jump right over to the other side where the winners always went.

None of those women ever said they needed their husbands to come back from the dead. Mom would say that. She'd tell the truth instead of settling for a refrigerator or a washing machine or a stupid babysitter who couldn't do anything Jenny and I could do by ourselves if we had to.

ONE SUNDAY, AFTER we'd changed out of our church clothes, Mom told me now that school was going to begin, I had to learn to take care of myself. I was six and had to start first grade like everybody else my age. My sister made a mean face like she knew something I didn't because she was starting third grade. "Okay," I said, but I could tell Mom was just getting started because she was holding both of us by the hand.

"Plus," she said, "I'm going to work. Just for the afternoons, just four hours on weekdays, but that means you'll come home from school and I won't be here, not until after five o'clock, so there has to be some rules."

"Can we watch tv?" I said right off, and when Mom said, "Sure you can," I was ready to go along with whatever else I had to do—not open the refrigerator, not ever touch the matches above the stove, and don't be touching anything electric except that television set, including the lamp beside the couch because who knew, "for real," she said, when one of those old wires of ours would blossom with fire.

"And don't you be going in and out of these rooms because the door is to be unlocked once and locked behind you and nothing can change that, understand? You don't go out this door unless you see flames." I said "Sure" right off because my sister had the key anyway, and *Queen for a Day* was on right after we would be getting home. After that, I had a football game with three dice and a slick, big piece of cardboard covered with all the combinations of numbers and what they earned that I'd gotten for my birthday. I'd been moving the little plastic football up and down the "regulation field" every day for the past three weeks.

Jenny put the key in the little purse she carried in her pocket. It had beads that formed a kitten's face and a zippered pouch for coins and a bigger place that snapped shut where dollars would go if she ever had any. She carried Kleenex in there, and sticks of gum, the spearmint kind that I hated and would never steal.

"And never go in the attic and never go by the windows," Mom added, slowing down like she was getting close to the end of the list, ready for the thing she'd saved until the very end so we'd remember.

"Most important, you don't ever answer the door," she said. "Not ever. You don't tell anybody you're alone here. Not anybody. Not a peep."

"What happens if we do?" I said, and my sister made a hissing sound.

"We go to the poor farm."

My sister ran out of the room as if she knew exactly where the poor farm was and how terrible it would be to live there, and my mother, as if she knew what I was thinking, said, "There's no animals there, Benny. There's no corn on the cob picked right off the stalk."

"What's there then?"

"Poor people. Lots of them and nobody has a tv." She paused and looked around our apartment as if she was imagining what it would look like without the television. "I'll be home before dark," she said. "You'll be fine."

When Mom told us she was working at Isaly's, I clapped. "No, Benny," she said right away. "I don't do ice cream. I do meat and cheese."

"Why?" I said. Isaly's was the store we went to once a month for ice cream cones. The ice cream was always shaped like a tall, skinny teepee, not just an ordinary ball. If you weren't careful and licked too hard on one side, the ice cream would fall right out on the floor, but that hadn't happened since I was still five, and my sister had never lost her ice cream, even when she was four.

It turned out there were other things Isaly's sold that I liked. My favorite was chipped-chopped ham. Our mother got a discount on meat and cheese, ten cents off a pound, not enough to make her buy real ham, but it didn't matter because I loved how thin those pieces were. You couldn't use a knife and get it thin like that. It took the special slicer our mother used for four hours every afternoon.

The only problem was she looked as bedraggled as a queen for a day candidate when she got home. After she talked about her day at Isaly's, I felt like applauding and giving her my dessert. I was sure I could let her eat it without making the face I used when I wanted a bite of her ice cream after I'd finished mine.

When I brought a cold home from school in early October, Mom looked at me every time I coughed. "You can try harder not to," she said. "You don't have to cough so much."

Stifling my coughs was part of taking care of myself. You could get better by trying harder and using the power of positive thinking. "It's just like school," she said, "you work at it and you'll get an A. You'll feel better before you know it."

The cold went away in a few days. Mom said, "Aren't you proud of yourself fighting it off so fast?" But a week after that, she was home when Jenny and I got there one afternoon. She'd cut herself. "It happened so quick," she said. "I almost lost my thumb. Imagine that."

I curled my thumb under my fingers and held up my hand. She smiled. "Be glad you can pretend," she said, and she explained how she was going to be home for a few days, working to make herself better again.

She seemed happy. Jack Bailey came on, and she pushed the couch closer with her knee and her good hand until we were five feet away and then we started watching. "This won't hurt any of us for one time," she said.

"A new hand," I thought. "Nobody has ever said they needed a new hand."

Before we watched television at night, Mom always plugged in the lamp beside the couch. "You tell me if you smell something funny," she'd say each time. Sure, the wires might start to burn, but she was right there to pull the plug and put it out, and watching television in the dark was just as bad for our eyes as sitting up close.

On Sundays, we were only allowed to watch television after sunset. In the morning, we dressed up for Sunday School and church, and then we had the rest of the day together, but the television stayed off until it was dark outside just in time to let us watch Bishop Sheen.

His show was called *Life is Worth Living*. He was Catholic, Mom explained, but that was all right even though we weren't. He looked funny in his robe, like he was the Pope or somebody like that, and there was always a statue of Mary and baby Jesus to remind us this was supposed to be church. But all he did was talk and write words on a blackboard like a teacher. My sister watched like it wasn't the most boring show on tv, and we all sat ten feet away, which made Bishop Sheen look smaller on that seventeen- inch screen.

The best thing was the days were getting shorter, so now, before Bishop Sheen came on, it was dark enough to watch the *Wilkens Amateur Hour*. There were boys my age who could play the accordion and girls like Jenny who could tap dance. Everybody cheered for the youngest kids no matter what they did. If you were six like me and could play anything on the piano, you were worth two minutes on the show.

The commercials were all for the Wilkens Jewelry Stores, and half the time somebody sang the jingle: "EZ Credit, EZ Credit—Wilkens is the place where you can get it," it started, like all we had to do to get a nice watch or a necklace was tell them we wanted one because we didn't have to pay right away. "They're handing us a line," Mom said.

Mostly, though, old people won—a policeman who acted like he was going to cry while he sang, a woman who sounded like she needed to clear her throat the whole time she sang. Al Nobel, the emcee, acted like everybody was wonderful. He talked like Jack Bailey, but I didn't believe him because even I could tell that some of the contestants were bad. It was like somebody on *Queen for a Day* saying she wanted new furniture because it was pretty, and Jack Bailey going ahead and saying "Wonderful."

When the television went off after Bishop Sheen, Mom had us use the bathroom and clean up for bed before she unplugged that lamp. Without that lamp or the light from the bathroom, it got so dark in the living room you could see everything outside, if it had any light at all, more clearly, including my favorite thing to watch, the huge hump of stuff behind the steel mill that our Dad had called the "bony pile."

If I watched long enough, the top of the pile would flare up so brilliantly the light reached us from a mile away. I'd clap like I did on the Fourth of July for fireworks, and Mom would say, each time, "Those men down there are working on Sunday. Imagine that."

What was always disappointing was when, on the way to school on Monday, we'd walk close to that pile and nothing ever seemed to be glowing. "You're so dumb," Jenny said when I told her. "It doesn't stay hot just so you can see it. Nothing stays hot forever."

OUR MOTHER HAD a story she would tell when company came. That wasn't often, and always on Saturdays, another woman or two her age who would sip drinks and eat Planter's salted peanuts my mother would pour out of the can she let me open with the key that was attached to the bottom of every can.

I loved doing that, inserting the soft metal tab into the skinny hole in the key and then going around, making sure to stay level because if you didn't everything would snag and she'd have to shake the salted nuts out through whatever size hole I'd made before the key got stuck.

The story was about my father, who used to sleep in the attic above our three rooms. We didn't rent that attic, but nobody ever went up there, and because he couldn't stand the pull-out bed, he put a cot and a fan up there in the dust and heat. The door was always locked now because that was one more rule we couldn't disobey, going up there and maybe tumbling out the low windows to the alley forty feet below.

"Wally was a pip," she said every time, "and that last time he let the wanderlust get the best of him."

Word for word she said that sentence and the ones that followed until I could recite them myself, how our father had turned up in Alaska, sending each of us a postcard with the same message: "Hi there. I'm right here where you're looking." But the postcards weren't the same. My grizzly bear was in a forest. My sister's was standing in a creek. There weren't any animals at all in my mother's card, just the forest and the sun going down behind the trees. The women would nod and reach for more peanuts from the bowl that had a wreath of roses around its edge.

"And then he showed up like he'd been gone a week on a business trip. He didn't say one word about being sick. He had his cough with him like he always did. And a sore throat was nothing to worry about, just because it had hung on for a week or more. And he didn't waste any time getting right back to being a husband again."

If the women were eating or drinking, they would always stop here and smile like this was working toward a happy ending full of "sorry" and "welcome home." I wondered what they were thinking because anybody could see the story was pointed in another direction.

Two weeks, she'd say then. To the day. Like he'd decided he was giving that much back to me before he owned up to his misery and went to the doctor's.

Later, I found out he'd made the appointment the second day he was home, but I'll give him this—he decided he owed me and kept his own word to himself.

She'd take a deep breath then, and the women would reach for their glasses, giving her time. "That's it," she'd say. "That's all, folks."

THE THIRD FRIDAY in October a man came to dinner. He smoked as much as our father, but his brand was Lucky Strikes. He had a tattoo, a snake wrapped around an arm that started near his elbow and ended with a big fist on his shoulder where his short sleeve was rolled up tight. His name was Jerry Betters, and he worked on the road crew building the bypass.

Jerry Betters looked like somebody who might cause trouble for one of the queen candidates by dying in an accident. He didn't own a car, so I knew he would have to die at work, crushed by machinery.

Our mother asked us to play in the bedroom. She slid the heavy door shut between us and the living room, so we knew she meant us to obey. I got out the football game. There were three dice to toss to begin each of the thirty plays per quarter during that football game. The triple numbers had the best results—touchdowns, thirty yard gains—especially 111 and 666. There were fumble recoveries and interception runbacks, punts and kickoffs, all of them good or bad depending on how those three numbers turned up. I'd played that game so many times I knew right away that 246 was an interception, that 345 was incomplete, and 555 was a completion good for a gain of thirty-five yards

After I'd played two quarters, I looked up and saw that Jenny was wearing our father's jacket, sitting in bed and reading *Cherry Ames, Student Nurse*. I wondered if Cherry Ames was learning about throat cancer and how peoples' voices sounded after they were operated on. I remembered our father's voice. He sounded the way space men sounded on Captain

Video, a show I watched every Thursday after supper at my grandfather's until he'd given us the television two weeks after the operation, a month before our father died.

When we passed by the bypass work site on our way to the Sparkle Market the next day, I stared at each of the machines and chose one that went forward and back, scooping dirt and rocks before it retreated and turned and dumped it into a truck. A man wouldn't get run over by anything that moved in just one direction like a car on the highway, and maybe not even then, but that thing might take somebody by surprise.

"WHAT'S THIS I see?" my father said the third day he was home from Alaska. He'd been clearing his throat and spitting into the sink for two minutes, but now he seemed fine. I thought it was strange he hadn't noticed how the hillside above the mill had been gouged out, turning it into a cliff that swept toward the river a mile away.

"The barber shop is for sale," my mother said "but nobody's going to buy it. Once that road is finished, it'll be kaput. There won't be any parking half the day on that side of the street."

"They can walk," my father said.

"And they can drive to the mall, which is what they do these days if they want a haircut."

Anybody would take one look and know it's just a matter of time before they take that block too and run the road right out to where they're building a mall this minute.

"Let's go for a walk, champ," he said to me. He didn't look at my sister, which made me happy. I was going to be six in May. There was only two more months Jenny would be in school and I wouldn't. Beginning in September we'd be the same for a long time. My mother called Jenny to the kitchen table. "You boys have a good walk," she said. "We'll keep the home fires burning."

It was only two blocks to the barber shop where my father had cut hair. I remembered sitting on a board Louie the barber laid across the arms of the chair before he switched on his clippers.

Now that the shop was closed, it looked small. It had two chairs inside. My father shielded his eyes and looked through the window. For Sale, it said on a sign taped on the door. There was a phone number to call underneath the words and a sentence I read aloud: "The owner is retiring."

My father seemed surprised I could read.

"Your mother tell you what that says?"

"I can read," I said. "it's not that hard."

"Is that so?" He looked around like he wanted to find something to test me with, but all the words on the signs were easy: BAR. SWEET SHOP. SHOES. He flicked his finger against the glass and drew a cigarette from his pack of Chesterfields with his lips. After he had it lit, he took a drag, coughed, and started walking toward where the hill had been blasted and cut two blocks farther down where the mill was.

"How high can you count, champ?"

"I don't know. A thousand, I guess. And then you just start over again, so maybe forever."

"What's six plus nine?"

"Fifteen."

He smiled. "Ok then. What's thirteen plus twenty-four?"

"Thirty-seven."

"So what are you going to do in first grade if you can already read and do your numbers?" he said, his voice going hoarse.

"I don't know."

He squinted through his glasses and scratched the top of his head like he was thinking hard. "What's eight times seven?" he said.

"What does times mean?"

He winked. "Got you there, champ." He laughed a little and started to cough. He took off his glasses and set them on my nose, holding them in place with his hands. Everything turned smaller and fuzzier, and it made me wonder how he could cut hair or even find his way around. "You're going to need these someday soon," he said. "First Jenny, and then you. Mark my words."

I closed my eyes until I felt the glasses lift off. Wearing glasses when you didn't need them made your eyes go bad, our mother told Jenny and me once a month.

"It looks like that hill will come down some day," he said. "It looks like they've made themselves a problem."

I looked where he was pointing, but the hill looked like a huge wall.

"It looks like they scalped it, champ," he said. "You can't just take everything off like that and expect it to work out. They're in for it. Sooner or later, but they're in for it."

A flare of red and orange went off behind us, and we turned to see that a new load of hot scrap had been dumped on the bony pile.

"I wish we'd been watching," I said. "I never saw it up close when they're pouring it out."

"It's all scrap," he said. "What do you think they do with all that after it cools off?"

"I don't know."

"Maybe they dump it somewhere," he said. "Maybe there's places we don't know about that they're filling up with bony piles."

"Where?" I asked. I wanted to see a place like that, but I knew it couldn't be anywhere near Pittsburgh or else my father would know about it.

When we got back, Jenny was dressed in her pajamas and reading Nancy Drew. "We saw you," she said. "When you crossed the railroad tracks we could see you."

"We weren't sure," my mother said.

"Yes, we were. A man and a little boy. It had to be you."

"Yes, it did, sweetheart," he said. "You're right."

"The man wasn't holding the boy's hand when they were crossing the tracks," my mother said. "I thought that was strange. I thought that maybe it wasn't you after all."

My father stared at her and then at me. "Benny can read and do numbers," he said. "He can cross the tracks like somebody who doesn't wear diapers."

THE NEXT FRIDAY, Jerry Betters was carrying a six-pack of Duquesne beer when he came to visit, knocking on the door after dinner like the women always did. When Mom opened a bottle and poured it into a glass for him, I thought she might send me to the cupboard for peanuts, but she didn't start in on wanderlust and Alaska and never hearing another word these two years and counting.

The man acted like he'd already heard that story, like our father was long gone and out of the picture. The more he sat there, the more he acted like our father had been dead since the day I was born.

Our mother drank from the man's glass of beer. When he poured himself a second glass, he filled one for her from a group of bottles he'd put in the refrigerator. Already her voice was different, like she was being picked to be the winner, like she was somebody who would cry while she smiled.

Our mother had never left us alone at night, but Jerry Betters was already outside on the sidewalk while she told us to watch two shows and then go to bed. I could see Jerry Betters smoking and looking up at the window. My mother said, "Just this once," and hugged us.

When she closed the door, Jenny started to cry like a big bawl-baby, and I watched until our mother walked up beside the man, who put his arm around her. She looked up and I waved, but the man had her arm pinned. "Plug the lamp in," I said, but Jenny said, "No."

She put on our father's glasses to watch. "They make everything look dumb," I said. "You won't know what's going on." She turned up the volume as if that would help her see better, holding the glasses on with her other hand. Her eyes looked smaller, like they were sinking into her head. I thought she'd be nearsighted by the time two shows were over, and she must have too, because she kept taking the glasses off and putting them back on.

We watched *I Remember Mama* and *The Life of Riley*. When *Riley* ended, I wanted to keep watching, but Jenny turned it off. The room went so dark I thought of the show where a boy is stuck in a cave and lights a candle. He only has one and pretty soon it's short and he's trying to memorize the walls because he knows it's going out in a minute.

I thought it was a stupid show when I'd watched, but now, in the dark, I couldn't remember the way things looked, where the lamps were even if we were allowed to turn them on. I started to walk with my arms stretched out like in blind man's bluff, and I hit my sister in the face, knocking the glasses off and stepping on them.

She screamed, and I stood in one spot as if there was a hole in the floor. "You're going to get a spanking," Jenny said. I started to be able to see things, like it was getting lighter outside, like it was almost morning. I found my bed with no problem and got under the covers like I'd never done anything as awful as breaking my father's glasses.

After a while I added broken glasses to our mother's *Queen for a Day* story. I made them my sister's, a pair she needed because nobody had told her sitting in the dark to watch television would ruin her eyes. It wasn't a lie because my father had told me she'd be needing them soon. I didn't know how much they cost, but it couldn't be as much as a refrigerator or a washing machine or new furniture or any other stuff like that. Not asking for big things would make her story better. Everyone would clap louder if they heard about the broken glasses, something that would make the story of our father dying even sadder.

Jenny was lucky, I thought. I could have poked her eyes out if she wasn't wearing glasses. I could have made our mother a sure winner, somebody with all of her troubles with a blind daughter to boot.

A long time later, when we were supposed to be asleep, we both heard the key in the lock. I knew Jenny was awake because I saw her roll over to her side so she could watch the living room like I was doing and still pretend to be asleep. Mother took off her shoes before she closed the door. She tiptoed in her stockings and sagged onto the couch.

She's listening, I thought. She's trying to tell if we're asleep like we're supposed to be. I held my breath. She sat up and then stood, and I didn't breathe as she walked toward us, closing my eyes as the soft hiss of her stockings passed Jenny's bed and stopped between us. She made a sound like the boy in the cave did when his candle burned out, and I sucked in a gulp of air, making my own little boy's noise.

She stood there so long I thought she was holding the broken glasses, but finally her stockings hissed again, and I heard her take the cushions off the couch and pull out the hideaway bed. When I opened my eyes, I could see she was lying across the bed in her clothes, but in the morning, at seven o'clock, she was under the blanket in her pajamas.

"Your father wouldn't cut your hair," my mother said at breakfast. Because it was Saturday, she was taking her time drinking her coffee. "Isn't that the strangest thing? He said he'd get over it, but then he wandered off and we never found out, did we?"

I shook my head and my mother said, "Of course we didn't," she said. My sister was pushing at the glasses because the adhesive tape my mother had wrapped around the frame was working loose already. "Don't pick at it," our mother said. "If you leave it alone, it will last as long as you want to keep them."

Jerry Betters didn't come back to our apartment. A week later, our mother asked us what shows we'd watched while she was gone, and we sat with her in the dark to see *I Remember Mama* and *The Life of Riley*. When they were over, she said, "It looks like he flew the coop," and nobody said his name again except once, a month later, when we were walking past the bypass construction, and my mother looked things over for a long while before she said, "I guess they don't need Jerry Betters to get this road built, do they?"

By then I believed my father had made that doctor's appointment and hoped all his problems would clear up before the day arrived. That he was surprised by the cancer and must have wondered at how he'd been right all along even though he was wishing to be wrong.

I thought again about my father nicking my ear with the clippers, how he believed he'd get nervous somehow and carve away the top of my ear, making one more problem for my mother to add to her story while Jack Bailey listened. They always showed the audience, and there were just a few men scattered among the room full of women. None of them ever looked like they were clapping as loud as they could. If it was up to them, all of the contestants would get the same score on the applause meter, the needle swinging about a third of the way and steadying itself before scooting back down to zero. None of the men acted like they might know the contestants or be their husbands, the men with failing hearts, mysterious lumps, and coughs that never went away.

It seemed like there were more women than men in the world. In the Sparkle Market, at church, on the bus. My sister seemed to know this. She was going to live longer than I was, even though she was older. She'd remember me for half of her life, so I needed to do something she could use in her Queen for a Day story, the one she would tell when people were willing to listen for a few minutes. I was going to disappear, but so did a million other men. I needed to do something so her audience could tell the difference between me and a million other ghosts.

FILTHY

MY WIFE, SHE'S what my father and his three brothers used to call a mulatto. My father, at least, had said nothing about race when he'd met Jessica's father the night before the wedding. "If you're happy," he'd said and left it at that, but during the wedding reception Uncle Roy and Uncle Fletcher, his two surviving brothers, huddled up over by the cash bar as if they were taking a census for the KKK. Finally, a few glasses of champagne in me, my ears picking up that word while I waited for a glass of chardonnay for Jessica, I moved close to correct them, announcing, in a way I thought was hilarious that Jessica was technically a quadroon because she had exactly one quarter Negro blood.

That was 1987, over twenty-five years now, and I knew right away they missed what I was getting at, using the language of their boyhoods. "You think that makes a difference?" Uncle Roy said.

Uncle Fletcher slapped me on the back. "You keep track of those fractions," he said. "You'll need to have them handy for your children."

I thought Uncle Frederick, dead a year earlier from prostate cancer, would have uttered worse, but Jessica and I were already in our mid-thirties, so Uncle Fletcher's advice never was necessary. And those twenty-five years have finished killing off all four of them and half of their wives, that sort of talk buried with them. But if some with a like mind care to examine Jessica closely, they can see it in her hair. And a little around the nose and lips, if they care to dwell on things like that. But she's one fourth Italian, too, and half as German as my father and his brothers if you need to keep track.

WHY AM I telling you this? Listen up.

Late Saturday afternoon, just over two days until the election, Jessica came home from canvassing for Obama and started right in about her next to last visit of the day. "To start with, he answered the door with no shirt on."

"Really?" I said, but what I was curious about was how his shirtless body looked, whether he was fit or flabby or fat. "A big tub-o-lard?"

"A skinny fat guy," she said. "Soft, you know, but that's not the half of it. He couldn't talk. He had a tracheotomy and started in with his hands gesturing me inside like a traffic cop. I wouldn't have gone in except the house was right there on the main street and that hole in his throat made him such a sad sight I had to keep my eyes up on his hairline to keep from staring."

I didn't know what to say. She had me, though, and I was swallowing hard, thinking about what might account for that hole in his throat. "So we went into his kitchen where he had a notepad and a pencil, but I didn't get very far into my spiel before he printed out 'I WONT VOTE' in all caps, forgetting the apostrophe."

Jessica was practically fluttering as she poured herself a glass of wine. "'For Obama?' I asked him, thinking he meant that." She swallowed a mouthful of that burgundy while I snapped open a beer as if that would signal my willingness to sympathize.

"'FOR NONE' is what he printed when I asked that very question. I started in with the line about how everybody should vote, and he got excited. 'OBAMA—YOU WANNA KNOW WHY?' he printed." Jessica stopped and took a breath like she was thinking about that tracheotomy, too. "'You don't have to tell me that. Thank you for your time', I said, and I was heading for the door because he was all worked up, following me and scribbling and tearing off another sheet of paper and handing it to me and standing right up next to me while I saw it read 'HES A NIGGER!!'"

I didn't know what to do. I thought about giving her a hug or punctuating her story with a few well-placed curses, but instead I ended up just standing there and waiting until she finished by saying, "He was smiling, Michael. The fool was grinning, and I kept going with that paper until I was out on the sidewalk before I knew I wanted to go back and tear that thing right out of his throat and watch him gag like a fish on a hook."

"It's okay," I said. "You're all worked up about this, but he's just one asshole, and you can't go nuts on him or else Obama will get the blame."

"Who wouldn't be?"

"With the hole in his throat like that he's probably not long for the world."

"Every day that goes by is too long for a fool like that. Writing it out and shoving it in my face."

"He would have done it for any woman."

"The fuck he would. We should go for a ride out to Middleburg, see if he comes to the door with his notepad."

"The mice droppings we found this morning are a bigger problem than that pathetic man. I was more worried you were going to say he dropped his pants and showed himself after you said he answered in no shirt."

"The mice will get theirs. I should go back. I can't believe I just let him show me that and left without saying a word."

"You were trained by the Obama people, that's why."

"I'm thinking it was more than that. That shirtless fool. He needs an asswhipping."

"He's getting his ass whipped by something more than fists, it sounds like."

"He didn't look like he was dying. He looked like somebody who might drop his pants and show himself."

"Obama will win next week. You'll have the last laugh."

She looked at me then and shook her head. "You must have a hole in your ears not to hear yourself."

I WALKED AWAY to give her a glass or two of wine to settle herself. I sat in my blue La-Z-Boy downstairs and tried to pay attention to a football game on television. She'd see the mouse traps bought and paid for and come down and ask is what I figured, then there'd be something else besides a sick racist to talk about.

A couple of hours earlier I'd discovered that the hardware store had three shelves of choices, even what they called the "humane" type trap, a thing that made me think on just who would consider kindness as part of getting rid of pests. But right off I'd spotted the basic spring trap I remembered my father setting under the sink a few times. The brand name was Victor, and it looked so much like a replica of the ones my father used that it occurred to me some things actually do never change.

The company's location, I marveled, was Lititz, PA, not far away. The price was $1.89, two to a package, and it felt like a bargain. They weighed almost nothing in my hand. Like balsa wood, I thought, but the clerk said they were made from pine. The rat-sized Victor trap cost $3.49. It was identical except for its dimensions, and the increased size immediately made me uneasy.

The clerk, without embarrassment, said, "This is what I use," and for a moment I thought that the trap she was holding that looked like a little house was meant to capture mice alive, but she touched it inside and I heard a snap. The mouse, she explained, is out of sight when it's killed. For a few dollars more I could avoid seeing the dead mouse, but it made me consider how difficult it might be to clean if the kill was messy. Whether the people who bought it intended never to reuse it.

"There's some so expensive we don't carry them, but they can be ordered," the clerk said as she saw me decide on the cheap spring traps. I nodded, but did her the courtesy of reading the label on the Quick Kill Glue Trap. "Kill mice quickly so there's no waiting and possibly squealing for days," it promised, though using glue rather than the trusty spring seems to guarantee the opposite.

"Lots of people have mice around here," the cashier said while she rang up the traps. I felt like I was buying DVDs full of porn.

"Let's hope this is a one-time thing at my house," I said.

She slid the bag toward me. "You know what they say," she said. "Mice can squeeze through a space the size of the tip of a ball point pen."

"I've heard that," I said, moving toward the door, but she called out after me.

"Remember, when they're hungry enough, mice can survive on paper and soap or whatever is available."

BEFORE JESSICA ARRIVED with her story, I cracked a beer and looked up the Victor web site: The clerk was correct. If I wanted the high tech Victor traps, I could buy electronic killers for $199. A moment later I learned that if I wanted to capture them live, I'd need to pay $14.99. Being humane has a price, but what I noticed was the humane trap closely resembled my father's home made rabbit traps, the two he built and placed in our back yard garden from April to October. He would drive a few miles before he released the rabbits in a field. The one time I rode along out of curiosity, I listened to the terrified animal pawing at the box as we drove, pledging to myself to find excuses not to ride along again.

This is how we learn more than we need to, I thought, ready to log off just as I discovered that if I wanted to communicate with the Victor company, I could "like" them on Facebook where people with nothing better to do can ask questions and give endorsements. When I checked, I learned there were currently 4423 people who "liked" Victor. A few minutes later, just after I'd opened the package and laid out the two new traps, Jessica started in without even hanging up her coat.

I finished my beer, long enough, I thought, for Jessica to be ready to move on. When I came upstairs, everything edible from the involved cupboard was sitting on the counter beside the microwave--cereal, crackers, cookies, bread crumbs, coffee—as if all our dry goods began with C. "We have to throw all this out," she said. "You don't know where that thing has been."

"We should be able to tell."

"And you never wrap anything back up tight, so it has to have been inside the cereal and the cookies for sure."

"I'll finish everything," I said. "You can start a new stash up high until we kill it."

"That needs to be this very night," she said, but she barely watched as I put a knife to a wedge of cheddar, digging out two small bits

"Maybe you could hold this thing here so it doesn't slam down on my finger while I bait this."

Jessica pulled the bar back and held it. "It was the son I was supposed to see at that house," she said. "I don't even know the old fool's first name."

"Maybe that'll make it easier to forget," I said. I pushed the cheese into what I thought was the right place with the tip of one fingernail and smiled, feeling excited. "Killing a mouse is something I've never done. It's interesting to get to do something new."

Jessica frowned. "Interesting?" she said. "I could have let go with your finger in there and made it interesting. You know what? You're letting your whitey show."

It wasn't the first time Jessica had cautioned me. She knew all about my family. I'd told her about my uncles the day after the wedding while we were lying on a Bermuda beach, and she'd rolled onto her side and said, "If I didn't know that already you'd be married to a woman both blind and deaf."

She was so beautiful in her bikini, her trim body that light tan color that women envied during the winter, that I felt like I had to say, "My uncles' fat pasty wives wish they were half as beautiful as you."

"The fuck they do," she'd said, sitting up, then standing and walking toward the water as if she wanted to spare me saying anything else as stupid as that.

But there I was on Saturday thinking about telling her right there in the kitchen, the traps sitting by the sink ready to be baited, that she was as beautiful as ever, that I was happy she still took care of herself, keeping the pounds off, the both of us putting aside the red meat and the things that are full of sugar, but her tone set me off a bit, and I decided she'd have to do without any compliments from me.

Jessica, as always, fell asleep almost at once, but for half an hour, maybe longer, I lay awake, listening for a snap from the kitchen. I didn't even move, imagining that any sound I made would alert the mouse. By now the mouse had left droppings three nights in a row, and I was sure it had to be in the cupboard as I listened. I wanted to shake Jessica awake, get her to listen with me, but despite my excitement I fell asleep.

The first thing I did in the morning, even before I used the bathroom, was swing the cupboard open. Both traps sat where I'd placed them, the cheese gone from each. I closed the cupboard and took a shower. Jessica was sipping coffee when I came back to the kitchen dressed for church. "Our friend ate his fill last night. Now he'll never leave."

"It'll get careless," I said. "You'll see."

"Never in all my life has there been a rat in my house."

"It's probably a mouse. They can squeeze in like you wouldn't believe."

"Rat. Mouse. They're all filthy."

At church, the Methodist one near the university where she works, Jessica nodded and smiled at half a dozen families as we found seats half way up on the left. I recognized half of the women. Jessica's never socialized with my co-workers from WoodPerfect, but I have to with hers from something the school calls the Center for Civic Engagement where she helps out making up community projects for freshmen so the school can sell things like volunteering and diversity. I wondered whether the students thought everybody in her office was white or whether, when she was introduced, it was pointed out Jessica was African-American.

For sure, everybody sitting in that church was white, but after the service, before we even left the building, Jessica began telling her canvassing story to the woman from residence life who was her boss, starting at the same place with the same phrases. The more she talked the farther away she seemed, like a voice on the radio. I almost mouthed the phrases. I felt like I was being erased, wilted, and receding.

The woman sighed and placed a hand on Jessica's arm, but her husband spoke first. "And to think how much you've invested of yourself"

"You know you're loved," the woman said. "We so admire your courage." I'd heard this sort of talk at a few dozen dinner parties.

"That fellow could stand as a paradigm for local prejudice," the man said. He nodded at me in a way that felt like a sizing up, enough to make me greet someone passing by as an excuse to turn away

Minutes later, in the car, I opened up by telling Jessica that nothing that happened at her school would change anybody outside of it. "People have their minds made up," I said. "The world's full of hate and there's no sense adding another misery to your life fretting about one more example." When she didn't answer, I added, "And what the hell is a paradigm and how is that guy with no shirt one?" I'd learned two languages, one for my work, one for my marriage, but right then, with her staring straight ahead like she was considering on the deep significance of one asinine racial slur, I wanted to remind her I'd been to college, too. That was how we'd met, if she came back down to earth, associate degrees for the both of us the year we'd married.

"Look," I tried, "I've made kitchen furniture for thirty-five years where there's hundreds like him, but even though here we are living among the educated, you have to know those college people will talk and talk but will never lift a finger."

Only two minutes for the drive home, but by then, all that silence made me say, "You want me to burn his house down?"

Jessica didn't even turn to look at me. She opened the door and walked inside so quickly I half expected to find out she'd locked the door behind her.

I MADE MY own sandwich for lunch. I carried it downstairs to eat with the Eagles game, but Jessica was sitting in the La-Z-Boy, the one she'd moved to the basement with the television because one was ugly and the other stupid. And there was a notepad resting on the arm. "Okay," I said, sitting on the couch that ran along the wall, the angle so sharp from where I was that when she turned on the game without speaking, I could barely make anything out. "What's up?"

She turned the Eagles to mute and began to write on the pad, passing me a note when she finished. "I'm trying to feel what it's like to be you" it said.

We had a history of this, Jessica not speaking to me for two or three days until I said I was sorry for whatever displeased her—chronic sloppiness, chores left undone, or most often, using my family upbringing as an excuse for, as she put it, "dumbing yourself down." The notepad, though, was new, as if she meant to remind me of how this had all started or she was prepared to drag this out indefinitely.

I thought about sliding down the couch, eating my sandwich and watching the game and waiting for her to give up. From where I sat, the only thing I could tell about the game was when the commercials came on and went off. I didn't move, but I ate the sandwich and didn't say another word, and when she kept sitting there, I went upstairs and followed the game on the Internet until anyone could tell the Eagles would get trounced again.

She sat through the whole thing, turning the television off after three hours and coming upstairs to sit with a book in the living room. Her silence made me listen more closely to her—how her clothes rustled, each small cough and throat clear, the tiny sighs of discomfort or impatience that seemed just this side of disgust.

She kept writing me notes, but not many. "I get it," I said after two more. "I'm not the enemy," I said after three. And finally, "That's enough," which got me a note that said "You're as bad as he is."

I felt oafish, too large for the house walking from room to room. I tried to read, too, the local paper, careful with turning pages as if I needed to conceal what I was doing. She made dinner without speaking, and I finished as fast as I could, carrying my plate and silverware to the dishwasher.

An hour later I called her out to the kitchen to help me bait the traps again. Stuck for something to say, I told her all about how D-Con was the other main brand in the hardware store. "They sell a 'No View, No Touch' trap," I said, "a quality I imagine many people appreciate. Attracted by the bait, the mouse goes through what they call an 'entryway.' When the owner inspects the trap and the door is closed, he simply tosses the whole thing away."

Jessica waited, finger on the spring. She looked out the window as if that emphasized her silence, and I babbled on. It's because we don't have kids, I thought. We're alone together so much that we have more chances to pick at each other. Our faults were always available.

When the cheese had been gone early that morning, I'd hazarded a guess that I'd placed the cheese in the wrong spot. Now I said it aloud, but Jessica didn't nod or shake her head. She held the spring back the way she had Saturday night, but I put the cheese in the same place because I couldn't see any other place for it that made a bit of sense.

MONDAY MORNING, THE traps were emptied again. While Jessica was in the bathroom, I leafed through all of her Obama things until I found the pages of Middleburg names and addresses. She'd said the street name, and there were eleven houses on the list, but only one with "Nigger!!" printed in the margin. She had it written beside the name Caleb Heintzelman like a second address. Caleb's father lived at 303 Main Street, too. It didn't get much easier to memorize.

All morning at work I imagined Jessica at the college telling the story of the no-shirt guy, repeating the phrases exactly and accepting condolences filled with words like bravery and perseverance and paradigm.

At lunch I found a note stuck to my sandwich. "HE'S A NIGGER!!" it said, the letters all in caps, two exclamation points. I folded it and stuffed it in my pocket. "The old lady leave you a shopping list?" Naylon Wertz, another foreman, said.

"No."

Wertz laughed. "You that whipped you write your own and mail it to yourself?"

I didn't answer. Wertz was the kind of guy who repeated things like "The coloreds don't understand work," and thought he was being politically correct by saying "coloreds."

Charley Wolfe closed his cooler and said, "Mike can buy all the steaks and lobsters they have. He don't have kids and he's what, sixty something, free and clear when this place goes bust."

I shook my head and fixed a smile. Everything they said was wrong, but I couldn't think of one argument to say. Both of them were younger than I was by a decade or more. None had ever seen Jessica. Heintzelman pushed his chair back. "Charley has you pegged. A wife that works up at that fancy college on top of everything else. You could just walk away from all this and still eat strip steaks."

"I like coming to work," I said then, hoping that would stop things.

Wolfe shook his head. "One in a million is what you are."

"Or a liar like everybody else," Hientzelman said, and they both laughed.

The shift ended at four. There used to be a full-time second shift, but now, one reason why Heintzelman worried about his job, the company had allowed it to thin to barely more than maintenance. A Swede owned it. I knew that because he made a point of it the couple of times we'd had to listen to him. Twice we'd had supervisor's breakfasts—seven years apart, and both times he'd said he was there to congratulate us for a job well done. Ten and seventeen years ago now. Both times, before I'd finished a second cup of coffee he'd made sure we all knew what a success story he was, giving the same examples as if he'd forgotten he'd told the same stories seven years earlier. What I remembered was his telling us about his growing up in a neighborhood where the Swedes and the people from Norway lived right up against each other but everybody knew that one particular street was a boundary between them, that they didn't mix. I'd told Jessica about that, how the whitest people on the planet made sure to mark a difference between them. She hadn't laughed like I thought she might. She'd said, "It's in everybody."

The thing was, there wasn't one Swede or somebody from Norway who worked anywhere in the plant.

Monday evening, Jessica went upstairs with her phone and made canvassing calls for more than two hours. When she came downstairs, she handed me a note that read "I'M FINISHED!"

"That's all you can do," I said.

"What about that cracker?" she wrote, and I answered, "I don't think any white people care whether they're called that."

She hesitated a few seconds before writing, "That's why he needs to be punished."

"He didn't call you anything—there's no eye for an eye here."

Instead of writing another note, she tossed the pad and the pen on the dining room table. "Unless I'm a vigilante, you're done talking to me?" I waited for her to pick up the pen, but she didn't move.

Fuck your sensitivity, I thought. Fuck the paranoia of one-fourth of your ancestors, and the words, choked down, churned in my chest like heartburn, ridiculous and mine.

I went upstairs to the computer, but I didn't have anything to check. I figured I had to stay for half an hour, something to show her I had things to do besides beg her to talk. When I looked up the history of mouse traps, I found out that a trap like I was using had cost five cents in 1900. And in the late 1950s, when I first noticed my father setting traps, the cost had risen to only seven cents

I kept going, reading the rest of the on-line article. John Mast, the American patent holder, invented a trap that sprung in three milliseconds a few years before 1900. The design had remained almost completely unchanged, so it was no surprise when I read that he sold that business for a hefty profit.

I kept at it for a few more minutes. I learned that a humane mousetrap was invented during the 1920s. It was called the Kness Ketch-All Multiple Catch, but my father, despite feeling sorry for rabbits, wasn't interested in being humane with mice and rats, and neither was I.

When I came back downstairs I baited the traps myself, telling myself to change the location of the cheese. Without Jessica helping, there was such an intensity to setting the trap that I grew excited. I eyed the distance the bar would travel when it flew shut. I just barely moved the cheese from where I'd placed it the past two nights, hoping that fraction of an inch was enough to set things off.

For a moment, I thought Jessica was sitting up, alert and listening for the snap of my failure or the thunk of accident. I turned my head quickly but she wasn't in sight. Even so, I was so certain I folded a paper towel over twice and slid it between my teeth so that if I slammed my finger I would bite down silently like some old time Western hero getting a bullet extracted after a few mouthfuls of whiskey.

TUESDAY MORNING, I took a shower before I checked the traps. I made coffee and ate breakfast with that cupboard closed, finishing one of the boxes of cereal Jessica refused to touch. When I tossed the box away, I saw Jessica's notepad in the garbage. I lifted it out, saw that it had about ten sheets left.

At last, my coat on, and Jessica stirring, I swung the cupboard open and saw the dead mouse. A clean kill, it looked like, right across the back of the neck. I didn't see any blood, happy for that.

By then Jessica was in the shower. I touched the other trap with the tip of a pen and it slammed shut. I waited for a moment, listening, but she didn't call out, startled enough to speak. I wrote her a note on the pad. "Got it" and drew a mouse with Xs for eyes.

I carried the trap with the dead mouse to the garage and dumped it into the garbage can, thinking of the "no touch" trap I'd read about, the buyer directed to hold the trap over the garbage can and release the mouse before resetting it again. Some part of the world, it seemed, had turned squeamish.

I tossed the note pad onto the front seat of the car before I drove to work. I voted for Obama on the way home and showed Jessica my stub, but still she didn't speak.

She watched NBC election reports, wheeling the television close to the couch as if some sort of fine print ran across the screen to be read only by the alert. At 10:30, when it looked like Obama had the thing wrapped up, she switched to Fox where Karl Rove looked confused. She smiled for the first time in three days and I could tell she wanted to see everybody in that crowd squirm and fret.

When she came to bed I lay on my back, knees raised, to let her know I was still awake, but she didn't even sigh when she lay down, her back to me.

WEDNESDAY, AFTER WORK, I found two baseball sized rocks near the creek that ran behind the parking lot. I had masking tape from my office and plenty of it.

As soon as I turned toward Middleburg instead of toward home, I felt my pulse quicken. I was nervous, even afraid, but this was exciting. This, for sure, was going to be new. I was about to do something that could cause me trouble, get my name in the paper, ruin things. I concentrated on what I would tell the police until I saw the house and the rush of excitement returned.

I parked facing the wrong way on Main Street so the driver's side was along the curb, the door left open in case the son was home and available for sprinting after me. "Four more years," I printed on one note and taped it tight. On the other I taped the "HES A NIGGER!!" note from Jessica, two chances for him to understand where they were coming from, though I was sure he'd never remember her. A man of his persuasion would think she'd driven from a different neighborhood to stir up trouble. He'd think he was right all along not to vote.

There wasn't any chance of educating a man like that. All I could do was show him he needed to watch his tongue, even if he had a pencil handy the next time he came crawling to his door.

I heaved one rock through the window to the left of the door, then the other to the one on the right and hopped into the car and sped away. I turned at the next road, then turned again, nearly getting lost as I worked at being evasive.

After a few miles, with nothing in my mirrors, I began working my way back toward the road that led home.

It would be in the paper. That guy would call the police and say, "Niggers did it," and it was Obama's fault. He'd rant and rave on his notepad enough to land his story in the local section of the newspaper where the reporter would write "N____" in the quote as if the man had scrawled out a blank in an effort at politeness.

With a couple of miles still to go, I pulled over. "Got him," I wrote to give to Jessica. On a second sheet, I drew a man with no shirt and a hole in his throat. I gave him the same Xs for eyes that I'd given the mouse.

On a third sheet, the last one in the pad, I drew a house with broken windows, put the number 303 right on the front in case she needed it literal and figurative both

Sound bites, the news called them, enough to call up a pleasure in me

I was looking forward to getting home. I had to pay attention to keep from speeding. I hadn't felt like this in a long time, maybe years, finishing up those twelve miles to where, by the next morning, Jessica and I would talk to each other like husband and wife.

Pussy

"Grow up," my father said every time he disapproved of what I did. As if that could cure every fault. As if miracles could be performed by size and age.

For years. No matter the reason. I wet the bed until I was nine, and then I grew up. I had asthma, and then, at ten, I grew up.

And when I was eleven, I fought back when Ron Benko, a year older, called me a pussy for the hundredth time. I landed one punch and was swinging again when he stepped forward and pummeled me.

My father heard the story from my sister Beverly, who watched the one-sided fight after we all got off the bus after school. He looked at the bruise under my left eye and the welt on my cheek and said, "It looks like you're finally growing up."

At the bus stop the next morning Ron shook my hand and said, "I never hit anybody in the face before. I thought you were hurt for real."

"I bit my tongue," I said. "It made lots of blood." I didn't tell him the one punch I landed was the first one I'd ever thrown.

Ron Benko lived three houses away. That summer, before he and Beverly would start junior high school and I'd go to sixth grade and be the oldest boy at the elementary school bus stop, we were on the same Little League team, the Saxonburg Dairy Queens, wearing the logo of our sponsor on our uniforms along with the promise of free sundaes if we won our league championship.

The field was a mile away, a hike, but close enough nobody in either of our families thought we needed to be driven there. We could have ridden our bikes, but my mother wouldn't allow it, saying, "Never ever on that road with no shoulder," one of the many reasons Ron called me a pussy.

Ron's mother told us to walk together because "Isn't that what teammates do?"

Ron's father had left three years ago. Ron didn't have any brothers or sisters, and his mother stayed home. "Baseball's for boys," she said, as if no one else could play or watch, though I knew she kept track of the Dairy Queen's results because once, when I bounced two singles through the infield in one game, she said, "Congratulations."

My mother? The early evening of every game, before I left the house, she wished me good luck and said my uniform looked cute, but like Mrs. Benko, she never went to a game.

"WE SHOULD JUST get on our bikes and go," Ron said one afternoon a week after our fight. "My Mom doesn't care, your Mom never comes out of your house, and even your old man hasn't shown up to any of the games, so who would know?"

I was walking my bike in the rutted, packed earth beside the road, dirt that was mixed with the leftover crushed cinders the county used all winter to give cars traction on snow and ice. Ron pedaled, talking while I guided my bike toward BestView, the huge housing plan where we could ride six streets that intersected, some of them with dips and curves that made it seem like a racetrack. He pedaled away and waited for me, one foot resting in the middle of the lane for oncoming traffic. He turned around and pedaled back, his bike still in the center of the lane. "There's hardly any cars this time of day," he said, laughing. "What are you afraid of?" By then we were almost to the first side street into BestView, and I climbed up and pushed off, using the main road for fifty feet like I wasn't afraid of anything at all.

MY FATHER, AS if he'd been listening to Ron, showed up at the next home game. We won by three runs. I walked, rolled a single past the second baseman, and struck out. I caught a fly ball in shallow left field for the first out in the top of the sixth, but after I lobbed the ball to our shortstop, I noticed my father getting into his car as if he had to beat a crush of exiting traffic.

I walked home with Ron, staying in the weed-choked ruts while he bounced along on the asphalt, every car that approached swinging across the center line as he said, "See, Futhey? See that?"

My father, sitting on the porch with my mother and a glass of the ginger ale he drank at night since he'd given up beer, said, "You looked scared standing there at home plate. Like a little kid."

"You eat your Wheaties and you'll be fine," my mother said.

In the doorway, from behind both of them, Beverly, who hated baseball, pretended she was scooping food into her mouth, then stuck one finger in her mouth and pretended to choke.

MY FATHER WORKED graveyard shift—3-11 for the next two weeks. He didn't mind because it paid more by fifty cents an hour, but when he went back on day shift, he said he had to catch up around the house. "I'll tell you what," he said. "If you hit a home run, it's twenty dollars in your pocket."

"Really?"

"Maybe that will help you swing like a man when you have a bat in your hands. You'll be a professional ballplayer then."

"Twenty bucks?" Ron said. "Stop stepping in the bucket and swing hard."

I POPPED UP twice to second base and walked once during the first game after my father's offer. Instead of heading to the road, Ron cut through left field and crossed the edge of the corn field that bordered the outfield from the right field line to left center field, careful to stay in tone of the rows between the ankle high plants. Just beyond the field there was a service road that ran along the edge of the county forest. "My mom said she'd drive me to the video store if I got home early. Let's cut through the woods to get home."

"It's not that much shorter."

"It's way shorter."

A couple of minutes, I thought, maybe not even that. I said, "I don't think so."

Ron jogged down the service road and found an opening that looked like it was the start of a path. "What?" he said. "You're not allowed to do this either?"

He stepped into the woods. I looked around and saw two cars parked farther down the road, but nobody was around. We'd have wasted a couple of minutes if we turned around now, so, as he disappeared, I had to follow him or double back and look like a pussy.

I'd been in the woods dozens of times, but always below the waterfall that marked a sort of boundary. Below the falls families had picnics. There were swing sets and a slide and a couple of grills. Starting from a paved parking lot a mile or more farther down, the paths along both sides of the creek were wide and smoothed over with mulch. But above the falls was wilder, no tables or mulch or swing sets, just regular woods with nothing special for families to do, even if they were able to climb the slippery rocks beside the falls in order to get there, or even harder, scramble up the steep hills on either side. I'd only been above the falls a couple of times when I'd climbed up as my mother watched nervously and my father said, "Let him, he won't fall," while he fussed with getting charcoal started in the grill closest to the base of the falls.

Both times my mother had shouted, "Don't you wander off now. You stay where I can see you up there."

"You're right," I said, catching up to where Ron had turned to see how far behind I was. "There's a skinny path here and see, there's another skinny one. If there's paths, there's lots of people who walk through here."

Ron laughed in a way that made me wish I hadn't said a word. "You're so out of it sometimes, Futhey," he said. "Somebody could be watching us right now."

"Why would anybody watch two boys?" I said, but Ron was already walking, his back to me, and I had to hurry to catch up, saying "Why?" again as I heard the sound of rushing water.

"Jesus, you don't know anything, do you?" he said without turning around or slowing down. "It's like you're a little kid. Men come here to do things."

"That's what I said."

"For sex things," he said. "You know what I'm talking about?"

"Sure," I lied. "How do you know?"

"It's been in the paper."

"We don't get the paper."

"So you never even see our baseball scores? And when our names are printed because we had more than one hit or a home run? You were even in there once that time you had two singles in a game. My Mom cuts them out and saves them."

"I guess not," I said, but just then we came to the creek, and though it was late June, it was still running high and Ron seemed to be searching for a spot where we could cross without getting soaked. We drifted down to the falls where the creek widened and went shallow before tumbling over the edge, and I followed as Ron hopped across on a series of stones. Ron stopped then, as if he'd decided there was plenty of time to get to the video store, and I looked down over the edge to where the water pooled and the picnic table we used once each summer sat beside the empty grill.

"Futhey," Ron said, and I turned, but Ron was looking back across the creek. "See what I mean?" he said. "There's two guys over there right now."

I squinted, but I didn't see anything but trees and shadows. "Where?"

"You don't see those two guys? They think we're little kids spoiling their fun. I bet they wish we weren't standing around here."

I thought he was going to say "Grow up," but when I didn't answer, not even trying to lie, he said, "Those guys are early. Jesus, I bet they had to stop what they were doing when they heard us coming. Let's get out of here and let them do their thing."

I didn't budge. I couldn't see anybody, and just then I thought maybe Ron was testing me, seeing how much of a pussy I could be. I picked up a small stone and sailed it over the falls, and it splashed in the pool of water. "Now they're staring at us for sure," Ron said. "Next you'll stick out your tongue or something."

I hoisted a larger, round dry stone from the edge of the creek. I flipped it in the air, caught it in my glove, and tossed it as if I was in left field and a runner had tagged up and was trying to score. A big splash this time, one that those men I couldn't make out would hear.

"We're wasting time," Ron said. "I'll miss my ride."

I tried squinting again; the woods still looked empty. I thought about yanking up another round stone and tossing it toward where Ron had said the men were, but he was grabbing branches and exposed roots to pull himself up the slope to where the ground leveled off, and I followed.

"You need glasses if you couldn't see those guys," Ron said, but he kept moving.

"I saw them."

Which was true. I could tell that by the way Ron was acting. How he kept walking, not looking back until we were in the open field that swept up for a hundred yards to where our street was. "No wonder your old man offered twenty dollars for a home run," he said. "You should get glasses. Maybe you'd be good at baseball if you could see."

WHEN I GOT to the house, Beverly and my mother were sitting on the porch, an empty ginger ale bottle on the table. "Dad out back?" I said, acting normal, and my mother said, "He's off to the grocery store for something or other."

"What? More ginger ale and peanuts?" I started in, but Beverly said, "Where've you been?" before I could get my question up to a full-scale complaint.

"What's it look like?" I said. I thought she was warming up, for the eighth game in a row, to make fun of my uniform with the Dairy Queen ad, but she pointed to my legs.

"You're all covered with those burr-things. It looks like you sat in the weeds out behind your field. Or were you playing in the woods with your best buddy Benko?"

"That forest? You stay out of there," my mother said. "You never know what you'll run into over there."

Beverly blew a bubble and popped it. "Yes, you do," she said.

My mother shook her head like a dog drying itself off. "You're no help."

"It's a county forest," I said. "There's probably a park ranger or somebody like that around."

"It just means nobody can hunt there."

"Same thing. Somebody has to be checking up."

"Not according to what I hear."

"I know about the men," I said.

"Do you now?"

"They don't come until it's dark." Beverly said.

"It's never dark enough for what they're up to," my mother said. "And now there's that sickness everybody's talking about. You'd think they'd control themselves. You and your movies should tell you there's enough disasters to go around without looking for more."

My mother knew I was in love with disasters, the ones that looked so cool to survive in the movies, and because of Mrs. Benko owning a VCR, I was watching two or three every week that summer at Ron's house. The only ones I'd seen on our tv were old ones like *Airport* and *Earthquake* with all kinds of commercials, or else the disasters made for television like *The Day After*, the one my mother thought was so scary she'd told me to turn it off right after the nuclear bombs started exploding over Kansas City. I'd only learned how it turned out when I heard two boys in my class talking about how everybody in Kansas died, even the stars, while I nodded like I'd been allowed to stay up until the end.

Besides the one at the mall, there were two video stores in our town, both of them added on to other stores that sold books and carpets. We watched *The Towering Inferno* and *The Poseidon Adventure*, *The Hindenburg* and *The Cassandra Crossing*. There was a disaster for every place you could possibly be. "It's 1984," Ron said every time one of those movies was about to start in his living room. "How come you don't have a VCR?"

The next day I always told my mother about the movies we watched. "I don't need movies like that to scare me," she'd say. "Sylvia Benko should have you boys rent something happy."

"They're all happy in the end," I'd say. "There's always survivors."

"Just because you survive doesn't make you happy," she'd say, and then she'd give that dog-drying shake of her head.

AFTER OUR NEXT home game Ron didn't cross the road like we needed to in order to face traffic while we walked. "Don't even tell me you're afraid," Ron said as if he knew I was already hesitating.

"It doesn't make any sense to have the cars coming up behind us without being able to see them."

"Turn around then," Ron said, and when I did, he laughed and said,

"You look like you're a hitchhiker."

"Nobody hitchhikes except bums and psychos," I said.

"Where do you hear these things? No, don't tell me. I know."

I could have said, "Why doesn't your Mom ever say anything," but instead I stuck out my thumb. The first car that passed didn't even slow down. Neither did the second. Both times Ron said, "Cool."

I felt my heart racing. I walked backward on the narrow, rutted shoulder, stumbling a couple of times. Behind me, Ron walked backwards too. Two or three minutes went by before another car approached, slowing down, the driver staring like he was measuring us, before he accelerated and passed. I hoped another car wouldn't appear, and when I thought another two minutes had passed, the road staying empty, I turned and said, "We're getting too close to our street to be asking for a ride," and Ron didn't argue even when a moment later two cars came up from behind us and shot by as we walked.

THE NIGHT RON disappeared I hit my only home run of the season, a line drive to right center field that should have been cut off, but because the right fielder was a slow, fat kid who had been stuck out there to play his one inning, the ball rolled all the way to the corn field that served as a natural fence. Twenty dollars, that's what my father owed me now.

Ron, who had seven home runs by then, two of them reaching the corn field in the air, punched my shoulder and called me Hank Aaron. "754 to go," he said. There were three more games in the season, maybe four if we held on to second place and got to play for the league championship and a free sundae.

We won the game, too, but not until the eighth inning—our first extra inning game of the year—right after the umpire announced we only had time for one more inning before he'd call it a tie because it was getting dark. Ron was anxious to leave. "I'm getting *Rollercoaster*. There's a bomb in an amusement park. It sounds cool." I told him I needed to wait for our manager to clean up the bats and balls and catcher's equipment because I needed to ask him something.

"Hurry up," Ron said. He looked at the sky as if he was estimating how long he had before the video store closed by gauging the light. I didn't tell him I thought my father would say, "Was it a real home run or a bunch of errors?" before he'd hand over twenty dollars.

"Futhey," Ron said, drifting toward where the shortstop played, "Come on." Another minute went by before the manager had his car loaded. I walked into the parking lot and asked him to write on a piece of paper that

I'd hit a real home run so my father would have to pay. Frank Hertwick, the manager, smiled in a way I couldn't read. "So Jack Futhey promised to ante up?" he said. "You don't have to worry. It'll be in the paper tomorrow."

"We don't get the paper."

Frank Hertwick looked puzzled. I heard Ron shout, "See you later, Futhey, if you get home before midnight."

"Please," I said as Ron ran off toward the outfield, and Frank Hertwick found a scrap of paper in his car and wrote it down and signed it.

By the time I was halfway home, some cars had their headlights on. I walked fast, but *Rollercoaster* could wait until I handed the paper to my father. I wanted that twenty dollars in my hand when I went to Ron's.

Beverly was sharing an orange with my mother in the kitchen, taking turns pulling segments instead of splitting it in half and eating at their own pace. The first thing my mother said when she had her slice swallowed was, "Why are you're so late? Sylvia Benko already called to ask if Ron was sitting on our porch instead of reporting in."

"We played extra innings, "I said. "Ron took off while I was talking with Mr. Hertwick."

"Without you? What's the rush and why isn't he home long ago then?"

"I don't know," I said. I held out the paper Mr. Hertwick had signed. "Where's Dad? This is for him."

"He was called in to work." She glanced at the paper. "A home run? You stayed behind to have him sign this paper? You don't need a notary for a home run."

"Dad will say he needs proof."

Beverly licked her fingers and lifted the paper from my mother's hand. She turned it over, and I saw it was the coupon for 10% off at the Dairy Queen all of the players had been given after our first game. *Good until June 30th*, it said, and I grabbed it from her. "You're a week late, ice cream boy," she said.

My mother reached for the last orange slice, but she held it in her hand instead of putting it into her mouth. "At least we know he wasn't hit by a car because then you would have seen him laying there with people all around," she said.

I turned the paper over and said, "I bet he's home by now."

"Not unless Sylvia Benko calls to tell me that, he isn't."

I sat on the couch in the living room, the paper lying beside my glove, while she called Mrs. Benko to give her my news. "He's nowhere," my mother said. When I didn't answer, she added, "I know he cut through the woods without you telling me. I could tell Sylvia that much."

A half hour later my mother was fidgeting in a chair across from me, and I was still sitting there in my uniform when a police car drove past. Five seconds later, Beverly came down from her room. "There's cops," she said, as if I'd been sleeping. She was wearing an oversized t-shirt that stopped half way down her bare thighs.

"Put some clothes on or leave," my mother said.

Beverly curled up in a chair. She pulled the shirt down over her knees, stretching it, but she didn't leave. "You and your home run," she said.

"If he's honest-to-God missing, the police will have suspects," my mother said. "Around here, everybody knows who they are."

"You know their names?" Beverly said.

"They're filthy perverts, that's all you need to know. I wish I'd never heard of them and you will, too, if people don't know when to shut up."

WHEN I GOT up the next morning, there was a twenty dollar bill lying inside my glove. "Your father is working a double shift," my mother said. "He wanted you to see that first thing."

She and Beverly and I watched the news on television. They showed a photograph of Ron that looked like his school picture. The police were searching the woods and what the newscaster called "the surrounding area." Mr. Hertwick, the announcer said, had told the police he'd seen Ron jogging through the outfield toward the county forest, and he'd wished he'd paid more attention what with it being so late because of the eight innings we'd played.

There was footage of the police on the service road. The announcer stood beside second base. The camera angle showed the knee-high corn behind him. "Such a big place to look in," my mother said. "There's miles of trees in there."

"I bet that freak was parked along that dirt road," Beverly said. "Just waiting."

My mother kept looking at the screen as if she hadn't heard. "Let's hope they don't find anything. At least let's hope for that," she said.

"If freak-man was in a car, they won't," Beverly said, and my mother turned off the television and left the room.

THE NEXT AFTERNOON, when there was still no sign of Ron, every team in the league sent their players to help make the search party bigger. Nearly 150 boys plus managers and coaches who could get off work. There had been dogs the day before, but now the police were scattered among us, each of them explaining how we were to walk close together, our arms out to the side and our fingers touching. I was between our catcher and our third baseman. We entered the woods close to where the path Ron and I had taken began, but there wasn't any path. After a minute, with all the trees to walk around, our fingers stopped touching, but I could see both of them every time I looked, even when one of us had to climb over a rotting log or dodge a clump of younger trees. If Ron was where we were walking, we couldn't miss him.

For two hours we hunted, up and back, eventually going below the falls where the walking was easier, the adults and the police scrambling on the steep hillsides above us as we swept along both sides of the creek. Afterward, when nothing was found, the police thanked us, and all of our team's families formed a chain of cars and drove to the Dairy Queen. The players got free sundaes; everybody else got the 10% discount that had expired more than a week before. My father and mother sat with me in our car as we ate ice cream, but nobody talked. Finally, I said, "We didn't find his glove," which seemed to me to be a good thing.

"A man like that would keep it," my father said.

My mother said, "Hush up about that."

I didn't tell my mother I'd listened while our third baseman had told me his father had said Ron had probably been raped and murdered, that now he wasn't allowed to go anywhere by himself until school started and there were always other kids around no matter what he was doing. I didn't tell him that I thought only girls got raped, though sometime during the trip to the Dairy Queen it dawned on me exactly how that would happen to a boy.

TWO DAYS AFTER that we played our next game. "The boys need to keep busy," Mr. Hertwick told our parents, but we had exactly nine players show up, so everybody played the whole game and we lost by four. I didn't ask whether my slow roller to second base was called a single or an error, but after the game, as I walked through the parking lot on my way to the road, I heard our assistant manager, who was our third baseman's older brother, say, "Some piece of shit" to Mr. Hertwick. I didn't slow down to hear anything else. I wanted plenty of light to follow me all the way home.

We played the next two games as well, losing both of them and missing the playoffs. By then we only had eight players show up, and we played without a right fielder so any ground ball past second base was at least a double.

My father started bringing the newspaper home. About once a week, for the rest of the summer, that class picture of Ron was there beside stories about searches, leads, and mystery. Right before school began, the police made a sweep of the forest just after dark. Four men were arrested by undercover cops for exposing themselves or for lewd behavior. "That's for show," my father said. "They know they're looking in the wrong place. A man who would do something to a boy is always alone. He can't even stand himself."

BY THE NEXT summer my father had stopped talking about my growing up. As if I was all done with that. He was on permanent day shift now. "It doesn't matter if he gets paid a few pennies less," my mother said. "He's home nights, and you have a sister, too, remember."

Beverly was thirteen now. She had breasts and friends who were always whispering to each other. When the anniversary of the day Ron disappeared came around in July, she saw me sitting on the porch by myself and said, "What would you do if ten years from now you saw Ron Benko somewhere?" She was holding a *Seventeen* magazine full of pictures of girls she hoped she would look like in a couple of years.

"What are you talking about?"

"You wouldn't even recognize him. Think about that. Way out in the future you'd walk right by him in the street and never know he was alive."

"That's stupid," I said. "He'd come home. His Mom would have a party. He'd walk right up to me and say hello."

"Not if he was ashamed. Not if he didn't want anybody to know what happened to him."

I told her to shut up, but it got me to thinking about Ron. What would he tell me now if he returned? For sure, he'd say, "What's wrong with you? You don't even play baseball." I'd planned on playing, but when practice started in May and I didn't have anybody to walk with, I didn't go. Nobody called to ask where I was. Nobody at school said a word about it.

But even worse, if Ron asked what I was doing instead, I'd have to keep quiet about how there were fewer things that I wanted to do, let alone baseball.

And then I could hear him saying, "You need to grow up before it's too late," because he would see that I was timid and dreamy, how my new glasses made it obvious to everybody. He wouldn't be imitating my father. He'd say it straight ahead like he was telling me something I needed to remember for a test. Like I needed three examples to put in my essay so I'd get full credit for knowing what I was talking about, the disasters that could find me like being weak and submissive or being so inept around girls that I'd end up alone and miserable.

Every morning the paper was delivered to our house, full of news about AIDs because Rock Hudson was dying. My mother talked about how bad he looked and who would have thought, especially after she saw him with Doris Day, but we still didn't have a VCR. Even so, sometimes there were disaster movies on television. I could still watch one or two a week with volcanoes and meteors, avalanches and swarms of bees. I had to watch commercials and most of them came on after midnight, but nobody came downstairs to tell me to turn the television off

What frightened me more than those disasters was when I turned off the television after the movies ended. Past one a.m., it was so quiet I could hear tiny chattering and scratching outside. The house made noises. It was like a nuclear war or a deadly plague had already happened, like all the people were gone and only the things that made those sounds were left. Them and me. I could walk through the county forest and nobody would be there, but I'd still be terrified.

Mrs. Benko saw me one day in August and invited me into her house. She served me Coca-Cola and rippled potato chips, the ones that were Ron's favorites. "I can almost see him grabbing for those chips," she said, "because you reach for them just like Ron."

I sipped my Coke and didn't touch another chip. "You'll be with the big kids now—7th grade," she finally said. "Right there where Ron would be walking the halls."

It felt like Mrs. Benko was trying to conjure Ron. Like this was a séance she wanted me to witness so I could believe whatever success she had was true.

Which made me sure that she believed he was dead, that her only hope was with his spirit. That he'd been killed before the last Dairy Queen score had appeared in the paper, maybe even before I showed my mother the stupid note from Mr. Hertwick. "You're such a level-headed boy," she said, and in that moment I thought she wished Ron had been a pussy like me.

When she could see I'd finished my Coke, she asked me to go with her to Ron's old room. It looked the same except there was a new bookshelf filled with thick binders labeled, year by year, from 1972 to 1985, enough of them that I thought of the old encyclopedias that I shared with Beverly.

She pulled out 1984 and opened it. In early June, the scores of our games began to appear. She hadn't written anything beside those clippings, so there were no stories about the games. Nobody from a large newspaper would ever attend a Little League game, but Mr. Hertwick must have called all these details in, spelling the names of the players who had hit home runs or had multiple hits. I saw my name twice in June, and then once on July 8th. "He had three hits that night," she said. My name was first, the only home run, but she didn't mention it.

There were games missing, so I knew which ones Ron hadn't had two hits or a home run in. Like without those hits the game hadn't been played. Like our last three games, the ones we lost so we missed the playoffs. I had two hits the last night, what had turned out to be my final baseball game.

The rest of July was a series of articles about Ron's disappearance. On the next page was August, just two articles and then September, a blank.

She replaced the binder on the shelf and brought out 1985. "This is for when the news comes," she said. The binder was so skinny anybody could see it was empty, but she showed me one article in July when the paper decided to publish something because it was the anniversary date. She turned to September, looked like she was reading something written in a color in some spectrum her glasses allowed her to see.

"I know," she said, like I'd told her it was crazy to hope, but she pressed the covers together and laid the binder on Ron's bed, propping it against the pillow like a doll or a stuffed animal.

"Well," she said. "Thanks for stopping by," and she left me in the room as if Ron was there and we were going to play *Donkey Kong* or *Pac-Man*.

I waited for what I thought was a minute, then counted to ten to be sure before I walked down the hall. Mrs. Benko was sitting at the kitchen table working on a crossword puzzle in the morning paper. She had a candle burning even though it was so sunny I wouldn't have noticed except it was scented like peaches. She didn't look up, and I didn't say anything on my way out, guiding the screen door back into place so slowly it barely clicked when the latch caught.

What I did then was walk the mile to the service road, going straight down it as if I were retracing how whoever had taken Ron must have driven. There was plenty of sunshine. I didn't see any cars parked as far as I could see ahead of me.

Because I was wearing glasses now, the leaves on the trees were something other than blurs. It felt like I could see so deep into the woods I'd know if anyone was there while they were so far away that I would have time to hide.I stepped into the forest on the same path I knew Ron had taken, and everything quickly turned shadowed. I needed not to be a pussy even if nobody was watching, but all I managed was fifty steps, counting each one, my head swiveling as I scanned ahead of me and to the sides. I stopped, listening to my breath, and then, because I was ashamed, I made myself do fifty more before I turned around and hurried back, staying to the side of the service road away from the woods until I'd worked my way to the highway.

THAT NIGHT, WHEN I walked into my room after watching *When Time Ran Out*, Paul Newman and Ernest Borgnine and William Holden in danger from a deadly volcano, I felt the large, heavy body of a man follow me inside. I waited in the darkness and thought it would be some stranger who had seen me on the service road, and then, as I listened for his breathing, I thought it could be one of my mother's unnamed suspects before I thought it could be a neighbor, or even my father, and I flipped on the light and looked at the window to make sure it didn't frame a face.

I propped myself up in bed, opened a book, held it as if I was reading, and thought of Ron's glove sitting on a table beside a man's bed, something he would pull onto his hand in the dark. I held that book open to the page with all the stuff about copyrights and ISBN numbers and the author's name and age—Matthew Worthington, 1935-___, so he was alive in 1984 when the book was published, a man older than my father and probably alive now unless some disaster had found him.

I stayed awake like that for an hour, time to decide I was as guilty as Ron's abductor because I'd tried to act like a mother and failed, someone who couldn't make Ron walk home with me, facing traffic, single file. But if I'd just been eleven, a boy, I would have sprinted after Ron, catching up before he reached the woods. I would have shouted "Wait up" and followed Ron into the woods, something normal for a boy to do, disobeying and taking a chance when nobody was around.

I told myself that filthy pervert wouldn't have tried anything with two of us together. That freak would have been alone, somebody who was afraid of two boys almost grown up. That piece of shit would have gone home by himself.

THE DOORBELL RINGS, and it's Howard Bogan, the man who lives across the street. I figure he's locked himself out again. "Could you do me a favor?" he says.

"Sure," I say, and wait for a request with the word "phone" in it somewhere.

"Could you come over and help me look for some cats?"

"In your house?"

"Four white cats."

"In your house?" I say again and think about paying more attention to Howard Bogan who lives so close to my family.

"The police were here before. You might have seen them. They found two and put them out, but there are more."

I follow Bogan's hitch-steps up his sidewalk, remember that he explained to me once the misery of his arthritis. When the wind kicks up a little, I notice how he's combed his hair up from the side, letting it grow long enough to cover his bald spot. He pulls it away from in front of his eyes, and I look away while he lays it back on top of his head.

We go inside through his kitchen. Breakfast dishes are on one side of the table; the leftovers from lunch are on the other. Bogan goes right into a bedroom and gestures me in. "Here," he says. "One of them is in here, and I can't find it."

I see two pair of underpants beside the bed, and I'm sure, at once, that Bogan will ask me to look beneath it. "Does it mew?" I ask.

"No."

I wait for the explanation. Bogan opens a closet and peers inside. "Maybe it's not in here," I try.

"It's here. My daughter, Sherrill, saw it before she went to work. She said it ran under the bed, but I don't think a stray cat would stay in one place for long. Not if it was hiding."

I kneel down beside the underpants and look. A white cat is crouched inches from my face. It doesn't hiss or slash, so I pull it out and hold it.

"Right here where she saw it," I say.

"I didn't look there," Bogan says, "because I thought Sherrill would tell me the wrong place." He gives his head an odd twist to set the hair patch in place again. I wait for him to choose our direction, and he opens the closet again, closes it, stares at the door.

"Well," I say, "let's rid your house of this one and get on with finding the other." The cat is pure white. I can't imagine it being a stray. After I open the front door, I stroke its fur a couple of times, then drop it. As soon as it touches down, it runs into the shrubbery. When I turn, Bogan is right behind me. "Okay, where's the last one?"

"I don't know. The police got two; my daughter saw that one." He stands beside the table, framed by the crumbs and smears of the two meals he's had today.

"Well," I say, "we'll just close off rooms one by one and eliminate possibilities."

We search for fifteen minutes. The house shrinks until we have only the basement to investigate. "Has to be down there," I say.

Downstairs there is nothing but books, shelf after shelf. Two tables are covered with full boxes of them; what floor space there is stutters with more boxes. There is a smell of damp, rotting paper that makes me want to hurry this operation along.

"I collect books," Bogan says.

"Cat could be anywhere behind these."

"I buy at garage sales, whatever they have. I don't mind having a couple of the same kind."

I start to think of the quickest way to end this. "How many do you have?" I ask.

Bogan waves at the room from left to right. "All of these," he says.

I figure maybe a hundred thousand, though I've never won any of those beans in a jar contests. There is no way across the basement except sideways. The dampness, now that I'm resigned to it, seems like the only thing that keeps the place from igniting.

"You want to read some?"

I glance at the titles and authors on the nearest shelf. I've never heard of any of them. They look like the pulp fiction of fifty years ago. My aunt, I remember, has a collection. Grace Livingston Hill is the only name that comes to me, but I don't see any of her books here. "Maybe I'll look around sometime," I say.

"You're welcome. The books need reading maybe. I don't read much."

I call "Here, kitty" a few times and feel foolish. "Tell you what," I say, "I'll get some of the cat food my daughter has for Smoke and bring it over. It has to be hungry if it's been trapped down here for a while."

"Sure," Bogan says. "If your cat eats it, so will this one."

I come back with a dish full of pellets, telling myself I will leave as soon as this fails. I put the bowl on the cellar steps and try one more "Here, kitty, kitty." A white cat darts out from behind one of the shelves and races up the steps as if it had been waiting to be fed.

"There it is, the fourth one. We did it," Bogan says.

I let this one nibble at the food, and then I pick it up and toss it outside. The cat dashes to the curb before it turns to stare back at me.

"You want to look at the books now?"

"Another time."

"Sure. I'll get them arranged."

I look puzzled, probably, because Bogan says, "People need to gather something together. Arrange it. I do it by year. Did you notice? It's a chronological library. You want 1948? Maybe that's the year you were born. I have it. 1952? It's there. Soon as I get a bunch of new boxes, I spend a day down there rearranging. Keeps the dust off, all that handling."

I want to say something but just twist my lips a little.

"The boxes you saw down below are full of the 1980s. I might not have room to finish the 70s downstairs, but as soon as Sherrill gets married, I'm going to put what's left over, plus the 80s, in her room. It's big enough for more than a decade. By 1990, Stacey, she's in high school already, will be out having babies, too, and I'll run her room right up to the end of the century."

I try to unscrew my lips.

"And then I'll stop," Bogan says.

"Wow," I say, imagining fifteen more years of scouring regional garage sales.

"The twentieth-century of books," Bogan says.

"Yeah."

"So thanks. Who would believe it—four white cats in the house."

"It's rare."

"Hey, your cat food. You have a cat for real that can use this."

I open the cellar door to retrieve it. A white cat looks up from its eating. "Five white cats," Bogan says. "I thought there were only four."

"Look," I say. "I don't think there's even four. How many white cats you see in a day?"

"What d'you mean?"

I look from the cat to Bogan and back to the cat, giving him time to work things out, but he seems stumped, and I say, "It's one cat coming back."

"The police found two. We found two, maybe three."

"What did the police do with the cats?"

"Tossed them outside, just like you."

"How about your basement windows? They all closed?"

"Sure. It's still winter."

I walk down the steps to check. One of the windows is taped cardboard. "Here's your four cats," I say.

"I oughta get some glass," Bogan says, not giving up on his theory of the white cat family.

"That's where the cat gets in."

"It's not glass, but it's taped shut. The corner there is a little loose, maybe, but that's no place where a full grown cat can get in."

"Cats surprise you."

"That little spot?"

Bogan, at last, allows for doubt, and I reach up and tug. On one side the tape is not stuck to the wall. "See?" I say. "It just looks taped up. You have one cat over and over."

"The police didn't know that?"

"Guess not."

On the stairs the white cat works on the food. I pick it up and automatically stroke it. "I'll take this down the street a ways and you put some new tape on. Maybe it'll hold until you get the glass."

"Sure," Bogan says. "I've been meaning to get that glass for a while now."

I start to head down the sidewalk when Bogan calls after me. "It's a pretty name," he shouts. I stop and wait. "Smoke," he says. "It's a pretty name for a cat." I nod and figure a half dozen blocks might buy him enough time.

I WAKE UP for everything—the furnace switching on, my daughter's cough—but this time the noise justifies sitting up and concentrating on the first sounds of invasion or the reality of spirits.

"Karen," I say to my wife who is sleeping as if sealed inside lead. The squalling skids up a notch, like some alien octave leap. I shake her shoulder. "Karen, don't you hear that?"

She makes a noise into the pillow, and I shake her again. "Listen," I say.

She lifts just her head so the blankets stay wrapped around her. The next squall nearly shatters the window, and I am satisfied that her sleep will not return.

"It's a cat," she says and drops back down.

I shake her once more. "Wait a minute," I say.

"Haven't you ever heard cats when they want to make love?"

"Cats don't make love."

"Sure they do. Everything does."

"Cats hump," I say. "Cats screw. Cats fuck. Cats don't make love."

"Okay," she says, "these cats are about to fuck. Now go to sleep."

I go to the window and lift the blind. There is still some snow in all the shadowed places, but the sidewalk is clear except for three cats.

One of them is Smoke. She is sitting on the cement watching two others who are trying to stare each other down. I think I recognize Bogan's white cat; the other one is orange with stripes that nearly glow under the streetlight.

Both of them are wailing. Smoke is doing nothing but somehow driving the two males into a public frenzy. The orange cat is so ugly I immediately root for the white. Every time the orange cat squalls, I see my daughter hating me forever; nobody, when the time came, would take an orange and gray kitten, and I would have to listen to each of them howling inside the weighted sack I'd drop off the bridge in the dark.

When the orange one looks as if it will succeed, I pull on my shoes, go to the kitchen, and fill a pan with cold water. I open the front door and run right at the orange cat, heaving the water on it as it and the others bolt. It is cold enough that I imagine the water freezing on the orange cat's fur, bringing on some fatal chill.

"You're crazy," Karen says the next morning. "In a couple of minutes they just came back."

"I didn't hear them."

"You were asleep."

"I'd have heard them if they came back."

"So you think."

"Who'd want an orange cat?"

"Lots of people have orange cats," Karen says, a touch of impatience amplifying her words.

"What's wrong with them?" I say, which makes her go back to the morning paper as if something important needs to be read.

JUST BEFORE DINNER, my daughter, Lee, comes back from selling magazines. She is crying, and I think at once of the blue van that has been in the newspaper for weeks because its driver solicits children. Heart-shaped windows, a gold stripe—the police have not spotted it. The driver queries both boys and girls, seems to have no preference.

"The mean lady's moved in at the Bogans'," Lee says.

"What mean lady?" I am happy. I see that Karen is happy.

"She yelled at me. She told me to go away."

"Who?"

"The mean lady. The witch. She even has a black dress on, and she slammed the door while I was still standing there so close I could feel the wind it made."

"Bogan's wife," Karen says.

"Bogan has a wife? Where's she been?"

"She lives in New York City. She visits a couple of times a year. We just haven't lived here long enough to know."

"Bogan has a biannual wife?" I start to make connections with the books, the cats, even the hair helplessly flopping against his eyes.

"She stopped over after lunch. She told me she's an actress—character parts, off-Broadway mostly."

"So Bogan lives here for how long and she lives there in New York, and who just stops over anyway?"

"Well," Karen says. "I'd already listened in on a fight she was having with Howard Bogan, and she must have seen me standing there listening, so she stopped over, maybe to make things better."

Lee, by now, is just whimpering, so I let Karen go on, hearing the story of how somebody's wife chooses twice-a-year visits, this time stepping out of an old green Buick like it was a cab. And it was, I find out, because Karen says the woman who turned out to be Bogan's wife told the driver to "wait right here," shouting it back a couple of times as she sidestepped up the sidewalk across from where Karen was standing with a grocery bag.

"Howard," the woman yelled at the door. "Howard, I'm here," and when Bogan opened the door, she barely turned her voice down. "I need fifty dollars to pay George over there for the ride he gave me from the city."

Karen pauses. She is thinking, I'm sure, of what part of this Lee will understand, but I'm ready for the rest of it and say, "Go ahead."

Karen tells me she rested the bag on our car roof and heard Bogan say, "I'm not paying any George. You promised him, you pay him."

Karen glances once at Lee and lets out a breath. "Okay," she says, "Bogan's wife shouted, 'Look, Howard, you've got fifty dollars doing nothing right now. Pay George and he'll leave,' and Howard Bogan hollers, 'You go back to New York. Go back to where you came from. Go back with George there and pay him a hundred dollars for the round trip,' and right about then George started honking the Buick's horn and revving the engine, which made me miss a few lines just before the woman walked away and stopped by the car door. 'Ok, Howard,' she yelled. 'I'm getting back in here with George so I can give him fifty dollars worth. You know what I mean, Howard? You know?'"

This time I glance at Lee to see how she's taking this in, but by now Karen must think stopping would produce more curiosity than finishing it, and she carries on. "The woman waited for a couple of seconds, but Bogan didn't even shrug, and then the horn went off again. 'See?' she shouted. 'See what I'm doing?' and all Bogan said was, 'Do me a favor and don't come back,' which it looked like she did, but the Buick returned a few hours later. The woman waved it away and disappeared into the house. A half hour after that she showed up at our door. An hour after that, it looks like Lee tried to sell her magazines."

Lee perks up at the sound of her name. "She said 'Come in' from way inside the house," Lee says. "I went in because it was the Bogans'."

"We live here six months," I say, "and still we don't even know our neighbors."

"Let Lee finish now," Karen says.

"She asked me the names of the magazines I was selling. She was sitting there in her black dress, so I said a couple of names like *Jack 'n Jill* and *TV Guide,* but she said she wanted me to name them all so she could decide, and I couldn't. Could anybody? And then she said I shouldn't be out selling magazines if I didn't know all the names, that nobody should go around with things they didn't know, trying to sell them."

"It's an arrangement," Bogan says when I see him the next day. I give him a second or two to go on. "You're wondering about my wife. Your daughter is afraid of her."

"At first," I say.

"I hate New York," Bogan says. "I didn't want the girls growing up there, so we have this arrangement. Claire doesn't mind. She's like an aunt. She gives them souvenir posters from her plays. They visit her once a year, and she takes them to the theater. Now Sherrill's nineteen and getting married, and Stacey refuses to go by herself."

"That makes it awkward."

"So now it's over, the going to New York, and here's Claire saying she's staying for a week to make up for it. Her name's way down at the bottom of the poster this time. The girls noticed it right away, and already the fighting starts."

"Maybe they should spend more time together," I say.

"Maybe they should spend never," Bogan says, and he smiles. "Cat's gone. Knows that Claire is here."

"It's the glass."

"Still cardboard down there."

"It's the new tape."

"Claire's the tape. Claire's the glass."

WHEN I MEET Bogan's wife, it's because Stacey is in our yard fooling around with Smoke. She is helping Lee tie a red ribbon with a bell on it around the cat's throat, an excuse for Claire to cross the street when she sees me step outside.

What I pay attention to is her electric hair, the kind Art Garfunkel had in the "Sounds of Silence" days. It is circular and orange, and I say a couple of things about the weather and New York after we name ourselves. Stacey doesn't look up from the cat, but says, "My mother watches TV all day" to Lee as if nobody else is there, and Claire goes on about how warm it is for March, finishes with "Well, look at that cute thing," and bends down toward Smoke, who is already trying to work the ribbon off her neck.

"Do you want to come live in an apartment with me?" she says to Smoke. "Do you want to ride the train with me to New York?"

Lee looks up at me. "It's an outdoor cat," I say. "It really belongs on a farm."

"Oh," Claire says, "you look too sweet to be a dirty old farm cat."

Stacey says, "My mother hitchhikes."

Claire glances down at her and back at me. "You get resourceful when you don't drive," she says. The bell has not stopped tinkling since the ribbon has been tied.

"Bell like that'll drive you crazy in a day," I say.

"But such a sweet thing."

"She wouldn't really like the city," I say and feel stupid, relieved when Lee clutches Smoke and walks away with Stacey. I watch her until I can't hear the bell. "With luck, she'll have the thing worked off in an hour," I say, and then, "Nice meeting you."

A few hours later, I'm standing in the street tossing a Nerf football with my son. David has been watching the USFL for a few Sundays and getting confused about seasons. "Doug Flutie goes back to pass," he yells before he heaves another flutterball. "Doug Flutie scrambles for daylight," he shouts and flings one sidearm that hooks into the yard.

While I'm trotting to retrieve an overthrow, I notice Bogan's wife at the end of the block. I'm sure right away I'll keep an eye on her until she's nowhere near our game because she's watching the collection box, staring into the mail slot as if something important has gotten away from her, stamped and sent when she wasn't herself.

Or maybe this isn't herself, since I'm stuck looking down the street for maybe a minute while she holds her purse and guards the blue box until I have to turn and throw the Nerf ball to David again, trying not to be so obvious.

David fires back a spiral for once, saying nothing before he passes, so I know he's watching too, and by the time I let an underthrow bounce away, turning to pick it up, she's stopped in front of the white shed we have out back, what substitutes for garage space on a street like ours. I see that the doors are open, that she could be counting bicycles or tools if there were any reason at all to be taking a census.

I lob some long passes, the kind that give me time to watch a woman standing twenty feet into my lawn where nobody would think she was anything but far enough drunk to forget there were eyes or a reason to stop staring at rakes and saws. David fumbles the ball toward the curb, and maybe he catches her eye, but she starts walking again, right at him as he bends to get the ball, me noting she's wearing black high heels, what no one would want to wear more than a few blocks. David says "Hi."

She nods and crosses the street, stops at the base of the three steps up to Bogan's door as if her legs had finally gathered so much weight there is no completing the trip. When David flips the ball to me, she sits down on the bottom step and stares at the sidewalk or else has her eyes closed, but either way I have to give up our game, walking inside with David and trying to figure what you can do with two hours of an afternoon to end up a zombie.

Karen is standing near the window. "My God," she says, "I can't take my eyes off her."

David laughs, flipping the ball up to the ceiling and catching it. "Now everybody who lives here knows she's crazy," he says.

THE NEXT NIGHT, I have to drive home through the end of the warm front's rain. Every station on the radio says something about how the temperature is still rising after dark, and when the windshield clears with thirty miles to go, I roll down the windows like a teenager and stick my hand out to remember what sixty degrees after dark feels like.

In the last small town there are a half dozen cars in the Dairy Queen lot, families coming out for cones or maybe the off-season, half-price sundae sale. Kids stand under the yellow lights that don't yet draw any bugs, their jackets open while the last of the black snow sinks into puddles around the picnic tables.

When I park, finally finished with a hundred miles of night driving, I lean against the car for a minute, making up reasons to stay outside. I find the two dippers in the sky. I pick out Orion's belt, and that is the end of every star formation I know. I think about walking for a while, giving up the evening more slowly. Instead, I step up onto the porch and hear voices.

Somebody else is outside, I figure, the key in my right hand. I fix on the tone, surprised anyone would be arguing if they were out on the street tonight. And then I stand there for a few more seconds because I realize the voices are coming from Bogan's house, that the door and a front window are open to welcome early spring.

I get to hear whoever's facing the window, words swelling and fading as if somebody is running along a row of spaced microphones. What I make out from the fragments is that it's all four of the neighbors in this argument, Bogan and his wife and his daughters.

"The witch, here, is going," Bogan says twice, and neither time can I hear what's answered.

"The books," Sherrill yells. "The books are already in my room and she's in there with them like some old orange Goldilocks." For now, she seems to be standing still right in front of the window. "You want me to move in with Jerry right now? You want me sleeping with Jerry because there's no bed here?"

"So, you're a virgin now?" Bogan says, so clear that I know he's standing close to her.

In my left hand I'm holding the light jacket I'd taken on the trip with me, sure that the warm front would pass before I made it home, but by now I can feel my shirt sticking to my back and chest from sweat. Ten seconds are lost among the four of them, and I'm about ready to go inside when Bogan says, "You wonder what brings it on." This time it sounds like he's speaking directly to the street, like he knows I'm standing there listening, because every word comes clear. "You do something with yourself and then you wonder how to account for it."

"Jesus Christ, Dad," Sherrill yells.

"I don't look for God's hand in anything," Bogan says, not turning from the window. "It's just a choice that could have been another choice."

"Listen to the philosopher," Claire says, audible for the first time.

"Shut up," Bogan says, his voice so steady and full I give myself up to listening closely.

"The philosophy of 'shut up.'"

"If you like."

"What's to like? What's anything that deserves to be liked?"

"Your truck drivers?" Bogan says. "Your chauffers? Your—"

The rest of his snarling list is cut off as Claire says, "The fathers of both your girls."

I expect Bogan to curse, but it's Sherrill who yells, "Fucking good one, Claire. Now Stacey knows."

I hear Stacey yell something that sounds like it comes from way back in the room, maybe even from the kitchen, the words keening up into a wail, the pitch wavering before the sound cuts off as if she's being choked, that possibility strong enough to start me back down the stairs.

I even take a few tentative steps into the street before I see Bogan standing in the doorway, the wail swelling up again from somewhere behind him. And though I can't make out Bogan's expression, I know I'm being watched, so I open my car door, the interior light flashing on as I fumble on the driver's side seat as if I've forgotten something.

I don't look back after I shut the car door. I climb to the porch and lift the key toward the lock. Somebody thumps on a window, and I have to look back at both of the dark ones, trying to work out which of them is giving me a last chance before they lift a rifle. I think about ducking as I shove the key into the lock and figure myself for such a fool listening to someone's humiliation.

Bogan shouts then. "Go out there and get run over." It's not him knocking on the closed window, standing right in front of the open door, every word reaching across the street as he keeps it up about truck drivers and how many wheels would smear his wife into a highway stain until Claire says she'll go right outside and wait for him, if that's what he wants, to get the balls to run her down.

"But first you put those goddamned books in the car for extra weight," she yells. "You dump them in there for ballast so nothing tips you over when you get those headlights on me." She walks outside like she's ready to lay herself down in the street, but then she heads straight past my house in a direction that makes me think of the blue mailbox, how she might spend some time giving it a second look. And then somebody raps on the glass again, and I think maybe this time a fist will burst through and whatever I'm going to do will happen then.

But that's the end of it—the shouting, the thumping—and I know, at least, it's Sherrill or Stacey standing behind that closed window in the near dark, and because whoever it is has moved a little to allow the light from the hallway to make more of a difference or because I'm concentrating, I can see she's holding up a stack of books, enough of them that she's steadying the pile with the hand that's been pounding.

So I wait a few more seconds, stand there with the key resting in the lock while Smoke hops over the edge of the porch and rubs against my leg, the ribbon and bell gone. Across the street, a light comes on in the window-thumper's room, and I see it's Stacey holding the books, and now Sherrill, who must have turned on the light, is beside her and opening the window. A moment later, Stacey dumps the books, every one of them, I'm certain, published in the 1980s, most of them falling into the shrubbery, a few of them scattered onto the lawn.

Bogan opens the screen door, not looking my way at all. He hurries to the books, reaching into the shrubbery to retrieve them, restacking them on the lawn. Smoke looks up at the key and then at the bottom of the door, back and forth like that with her eyes until I see Bogan's hands fluttering as the next stack of books tumble, those sisters maybe just starting a job that will keep them busy for an awfully long time.

THE SORROWS

1

ONCE A MONTH, on Sunday evening after church, the sorrows kept the women in my grandmother's kitchen. My mother's cousins. My grandmother. My aunt and my mother, all of them foraging through the nerves for pain.

My sister and I knew to have books or board games to keep us busy. In that house, television was three years away. Those women sighed and rustled until one of them would name her sorrows, a cue for sympathy's murmurs and the first offering of possible cures: three eggs for chills and fever, the benefits of mint and pepper, boneset, sage, and crocus tea. Nothing any of those women needed came over-the-counter or through prescriptions because those remedies didn't bear a promise from the God who blessed the recipes handed down from the lost villages of my great-grandmother's Germany. For the great aunt with dizzy spells. For the second cousin with the steady pain of private swelling. For passed blood, for discharge and the sweet streak from the shoulder.

In the pantry, among pickled beets and stewed tomatoes, there were jars of dark, honeyed liquids, vinegar and molasses sipped from tablespoons for sorrows so regular the women spoke of them as if each pain were laundry to be smoothed by some enormous iron of faith that set creases worthy of paradise.

From across the shadowed room and through the doorway, they might have been speaking from clouds like the dead. What mattered when the room went dark was the voices reaching into the lamp-lit living room of men who listened, then, looking past each other and nodding at the nostrums offered by the tongues of the barely seen.

2

ONE SATURDAY, EACH month, while my father and his brothers argued about whether or not to drop atom bombs on Moscow, my mother and my aunts would hush them with pig's feet and liverwurst, olive loaf and summer sausage, three-bean salad, pickled eggs, and a brief prayer that blessed our food and the wisdom of God "that passes all understanding."

The summer before I turned five, my father's sister insisted the crow that lit on her clothes post stared sickness through her son's west window, that she knew the exact same one had returned, this week, with death. The men stopped their talk of atomic war and waited while my mother and my aunts comforted her, nodding their heads as if the evil power of crows was a threat to all of them.

My father's sister, at last, said, "So be it," the crow's ominous luck past all understanding, and passed a plate of blind robins, those fish so heavily salted I thought I was swallowing the ocean while the table started in on the Rosenbergs and what they deserved for treason.

Later that night, when my father scattered twenty of his years-old records on the carpet of our living room, I became the four-year-old who could read all the big words because I could correctly choose each requested 78. My relatives must have known I was performing so well because I'd attached the color of labels to the shape of titles, selecting, by memory, the tunes he thought they wanted to hear, but they did nothing but marvel and applaud as I handed up one and then another like the world's youngest DJ. For that night, at least, I was so perfect I could have possessed the wisdom of God, passing all understanding in one of the three upstairs rooms we rented just outside of Pittsburgh.

The dead boy, twice my age, had been buried with books in each hand for his lessons, taking his third-grade homework to heaven, according to his mother, who clapped when I finished. As if it took brilliance to remember the shape and color of "Tennessee Waltz" and "Slow Boat to China." As if I could sort and choose among an eternity of records if someone would supply them.

3

OUR FAMILY DOCTOR declared measles the most contagious of any disease, saying nothing about jealousy, greed, and the rest of the seven deadly sins whose figures I colored in Sunday school. The fat face of sloth, the mole-plagued mirrored face for envy, and the face of lust covered by a thousand pock marks as if desire caused a terrible rash, all of them handed out by an old woman who encouraged second graders to stay within the lines.

My mother, for my first twelve years, trusted that doctor who, twenty-five years earlier, had scarred her thigh with a silver-dollar-sized vaccination. He made house calls; he'd delivered her at home and kept her from diphtheria and smallpox and the complications of infections. She stored his medicines until I caught what my sister had suffered months or even years before. Ear drops. Penicillin. Antibiotic creams. They aged like the interest on money saved, and more where that came from if we scrubbed our hands with hot water before we prayed one after the other and sat up straight to clean our plates.

"God's medicine," she said, meaning obedience, and she was right or as lucky as that doctor who thought he understood the simplest cure of childhood, taking out my tonsils to ease my earaches so frequent I thought their pain a common curse, and they disappeared like baby teeth, bringing me the good fairy's overnight reward because I'd put my faith in the anesthesia of what I didn't know.

4

MY FATHER INSISTED the name of God was work, half or more of each day but Sunday. But there was time for food, God's bounty, endorsed by Betty Crocker, who explained "The New Design for Happiness," meals which showed love for the families in America's homes by working the convenience of canned soup and cake mixes into picturesque miracles of ready-to-eat.

In her cookbook, in full color, she demonstrated the pictorial charm of food by stuffing pie shells and sweet green peppers, by filling tomato halves and sculpted pastry, creating, on my father's favorite page, mock steak from ground beef and Wheaties, a strip of carrot for the bone.

So pretty those meals were, yet economical, and on our table, the Sundays we didn't spend at my grandmother's, were decorative dinners prepared the night before: the shimmering, shaped Jello, the rank and file of peeled and slivered peaches.

At Christmas, my mother baked anise cookies from which, if I chose carefully, I could recreate the manger scene, complete with Magi. For Easter, she browned crosses into sweet rolls. Four times per year, May, June, July, and November, she showed allegiance of another kind by making the flag with celery and carrots, the field of coconut holding forty-eight walnut stars.

And once, as a favor to our pastor, my parents hosted a visiting minister who was traveling around Pittsburgh to declaim the death of

God. He sat, so heavy, at our table, the pinwheels of sweet peppers seemed to churn on their cucumber cogs. While we passed bread, he unrolled four slices of ham and beef. And he unfolded, while we poured milk, three cheeses, and formed the stack of a child's simple sandwich.

My father waited for him to swallow one bite, and then he bowed his head to give thanks for the care with which our food was prepared, directing his message to the living God and his resurrected son while the minister who had lost his faith held his sandwich in both hands halfway between his mouth and his plate.

We all raised our heads together without looking at our guest. We decorated our bread with arrangements of tomatoes and onions and lettuce before we added the roll-ups of meat and cheese, each of them shaped like the pipes of the church organ I listened to, this morning, for the first time in thirty-five years, my mother dead fifteen of them, my father driving the two of us to her grave near the unmarked site where exactly one-tenth of the ashes of the God-is-Dead minister, according to my father, were scattered five years ago like a tithe for the damned.

5

ALL MORNING, MY father wove pine boughs while I read, and then he called out the passing of each mile to thirteen, the right turn through the open gates to the plot in the Garden of Dreams. He laid those evergreen crosses by the headstone of my mother, her sisters, and her parents in a symmetry of remembrance, and then he removed what he'd left for last month's anniversary, adding those branches to the full plot's border of woven designs so they could extend the decorative work of God.

"To look at you," he said as we walked back to his car, "nobody would know you have a problem."

6

WHEN MY MOTHER talked about sickness, she named the foreign diseases she was certain we would not get: Elephantiasis, Yellow Fever, Cholera, Yaws. "Such places," she said, meaning their sources, though she had never traveled to one of those countries where the world's worst maladies seem to begin, slaughtering thousands before experts arrive to track the index case. I've never entered a jungle where men bleed from their pores or women swell into monstrous clouds. I've stayed at home and seen no one die but my mother, everyone else succumbing in another car or house or hospital.

When I talk about sickness, I mention my mother and her sister and the rest of my family who slipped silently to death. I mean their shattered hearts or the sudden lightning of massive stroke. My wife used to name the hidden tumors of her family, and I would think of the threats to brain, kidney, and bone for which both of us had been scanned, the symptoms that drove our bodies, once each, to be wired for walking the treadmill for the EKG before we listened anxiously to our pleasant doctors.

For years, at forty and near fifty, we would worry but learn we were fine each time, left to talk about the worst diseases we'd really had, pneumonia and rheumatic fever, continuing to set odds for our bodies in the outbacks of self-treatments, the ones we offered ourselves because we expected to recover from symptoms originating in alcohol and fat, stress and lost sleep.

And then, four years ago, our son returned home from college to visit, and he described AIDS at the health club where he worked part time, the lesioned intruder he had to ask to leave. Because he was naked, Rick explained. Because he was drunk and broke the rules, not because, that evening, he was as skinny as the anorexic member who did sit ups in the sauna, weighing herself six times per hour.

"Why can't people control themselves?" my wife asked, and I managed to last three days before I drove back to the park where men who were sensible nearly every moment of their lives gave themselves up to risk.

That night, after I slipped out of a man's parked car, through with giving and receiving pleasure, I thought of the ancient index cases to be excavated from distant digs. So many ways our bodies can be entered, so many exotic names: Ebola, Lassa, Marburg, Machupo. They sound like a roster of devils. They sound like the angels of faithlessness who manifest themselves to the healthy.

7

THE SUMMER AFTER the fat minister visited, I failed the buddy system of the church camp pool because I followed the wall to fourteen feet to pretend I could push off into a beautiful backstroke. Reach and pull, I said to myself as I posed. Reach and pull, I repeated, strokes so simple the animals used them, though suddenly jostled free of my handhold, I reached back and sank in silence.

I touched bottom and rose. I said nothing and reached, sinking again and floundering up a second time to the white inner tube of the lifeguard as if I'd been swimming for hours and cramped, dragged ashore like an exhausted channel crosser.

That morning and the remainder of that week, I was learning the rewards for faith—health, hope, salvation, and the Bible's great promise that the Balm of Gilead would heal the faithful. Nothing was said by the camp counselors about the way a door-to-door boot polish salesman named Samuel Solomon, over a hundred years earlier, had lifted that name from Christianity's public domain and claimed its second coming a cure for drunkeness, debauchery, the horrors of the mind, and most impressively, a yellow fever epidemic in New York. How that entrepreneur had suspended "God's gold" in solution and completed the other 90% of that popular potion with the distraction of brandy, something like the sugar content of "Salvation's Candy," ten cents for Life-Savior Jesus, "scripture message included," what I bought at the church camp's store an hour after I was saved by the O-ring of the lifeguard.

8

"MILKTOAST," MY FATHER said, when I whined about the home remedy of diluted boric acid for athlete's foot, poison ivy, or hives, calling up a name for timidity I'd never heard.

When I asked him what that meant, he muttered "Fairy" and stared at me. "You know what that means, don't you?" he said. "Fruit. Queer. Homo. You know what to look for?"

For each of the five years I cruised the park, I thought about encountering a man who recognized me, but that apprehension stayed as vague as the one I carried to the doctor's office on the day of my annual physical. Chance, I knew, lurked in a parked car or in the shadow of trees, but I exercised three days a week and even, in my lust, seldom swallowed a stranger's semen.

Who I didn't think of meeting was an undercover policeman. That night, a priest was arrested, too. Among others, a doctor. It was as if that park attracted the educated. "Since when?" my wife asked, and when I didn't answer at once, she said, "A year? Two years? More?"

"It's the twenty-first century now," she went on. "You're fifty-three years old. You have to be crazy to do what you've been doing."

"I know."

"And I know there's no living with that kind of secrecy," she said. "I can't have you touch me now."

There is a difference between desire and love, I thought, but didn't say.

"Well then," she finally said, like someone reading about bad news happening to strangers. It sounded like relief, like she'd just heard from a long-sought corroborating witness.

And when I didn't elaborate, she said she'd make arrangements for a blood test for herself and asked how long it would take me to find another place to live.

9

HOW LITTLE DID I know of the history of the diet mania, dismissing, all through high school, the lard ass, the porker, the big belly of the slow and sloppy? At Slaney High School, in the mid-1960s, the overweight did the dance of pills and chalk-flavored shakes, or else they sat it out with sugar-substitutes.

Fat was ruin. Fat forced the side effects of chemistry. Fat was the first question when one teacher assigned Kafka's "A Hunger Artist" and cited its main character as part of his campaign for denial.

That teacher lived so close to my house, one son my age, I knew he ran his three children like dogs and used the leash of his leather belt on their softest parts to free them from sloth. I knew he took no sick days from teaching, missed none of his nights securing the mall.

That teacher adhered to the diet of coffee and cigarettes; he stuffed himself until cancer opened the secrets of his throat while I matched, during my senior year, the story of my pulse rate to the published numbers of the thin and fit.

I did calisthenics and ran for miles because I wanted to achieve the slow breath and pulse rhythms of world record holders, even the professional fasters like Ann Moore, who claimed six foodless years and beat the witness tests with milk wrung from the towels she washed with. Or Sarah Jacobs, who lasted through unverified months, according to her parents, without food and water. Both of them heard applause until they were watched by experts on deceit. Ann Moore confessed, on the ninth day, by turning so weak and thin she asked to eat. Sarah Jacobs, however, recanted nothing, rapt with belief in herself until she died.

10

FOR HEALTH, ONCE, some people drank wine or warm water to loosen the scum in the sinks of their stomachs before they swallowed something called the stomach brush, inch by inch, using liquor to relax the gag reflex.

With something as intrusive as a brush, they kept it down or else so that the doctor could scrub before he withdrew that brush and flushed their deep-cleaned organ with water. They were fine for a week or more, the walls of the stomach invisibly sparkling, its drains opened and cleaned, primitive plumbing for the simple simile of medicine, nothing I laughed at, all through college, bent over sinks to vomit the dregs of fast food and beer.

I watched that poison swirl dozens of times toward the pause of the elbow joint, tucked my rotten mouth under a strange faucet for a makeshift rinse, and believed I was cleansing myself with a medicinal dose of education, the old prescription of a doctorate, the twenty-five years of book-a-day.

These days, I have the natural brush of my hiatal hernia to swirl up the acids of every hour-old bite, recalling the thick fat of bargain meat, the sulfites and dyes that invite the scrub of surgery. Just in case, I paint with antacids, double-coat everything I swallow. Like the smiling ministers of television, those who understand the close-up; like the famous singer, last night, who lip-synched, brought his own audience to applaud, and, in case they didn't scream and punch the air, had recorded screams prepared.

11

"You're careful, aren't you?" my father said when we were nearly back to his house.

What do you mean careful? I thought of answering. I wanted to explain the difference between falling and jumping, but my father understood only how close to the edge I was standing. "Usually," I said.

My father looked above my head as if he noticed a spider lowering itself toward me from the ceiling of his car. I knew he was calculating my odds, guessing how many men and where I'd met them, maybe even, because I'd moved only eight miles after my wife had turned me loose, some place he'd recognize.

"There's help for this," he said.

"I'm okay," I said.

"In the church."

"Dad," I began, and what we both meant hissed out the badly sealed side window behind him. "I'm fine," I said then, though of course I didn't know that for certain since my last test had been a year ago, just after I'd moved out.

Two weeks after being arrested, I went back to the park. *Just to see*, I told myself, driving up the narrow road, but counting eight cars, wondering if each of them was driven by a man who had never been there before or didn't read the local newspaper.

I left without stopping, but returned the following night, counting eleven cars before I parked and walked down a path, thinking how impossible it was to police need. In others. In yourself. Everything that pleased me had come from learning a language built on characters other than an alphabet. Eye contact. Head movement, hand gesture, the pace of approach—until a sentence with the phrase "I want" was constructed. The rest was the short story of the body intensified by risk. The one I cannot tell my father. Or my wife or my son.

What else I knew was I wanted to recognize the parked car of some other married man I have known for years. I wanted to open the door and say, "Hello, _____."

12

TOMORROW I WILL wait for my turn to be tested, believing the odds are still with me because I live where AIDS cases are few. A week of flu is almost always a week of flu. The three months of good health that have followed are what's expected by everyone who recovers. And if I hear the results in the hushed urgency of positive, there are remedies.

Invirase, Norvin, Crixivan. The names come as readily to me as Penicillin. How they prevent the infection of new cells. How T-cell counts rebound from 300 to 500 to 700 to the normal life.

There are fusion inhibitors now. New miracles, early in the century, for the sorrows, the combinations as complicated and perfectly-timed as the herbs and menus of my grandmother. If you want to live, you count the pills. If you want to live, you measure the hours and spend the money.

Risk is such an easy thing. It surrounds us. All we have to do is call out a name for the one we're willing to barter with for pleasure even though afterward, nearly always, the trade seemed badly made. Regret, disappointment, chagrin, humiliation, depression—there is a thesaurus full of perfect or near rhymes for the necessary sorrow of desire.

13

MORE THAN TWENTY-FIVE years ago now, I read about the coincidence of swine flu shots and sudden death yet still thought it sensible to volunteer for a dose. I had high school and college diplomas from the protest years, an advanced degree that backdated me to the disco era. I lived in Pittsburgh, where two people had died, perhaps, from inoculation, but I signed the forms that waived my rights, scrawling my name in the crowded ward of drafted doctors where I took my dose, managed two steps, and smiled my regret at the nurse before I slumped to the floor of the government clinic.

"Should've known better," a doctor declared after I came to, and I agreed with him as he gave me orange juice to drink and ordered me a cheeseburger. He returned three times in half an hour to where I sat behind a curtain, making sure I was recovering, filling me with advice about the consequences of skipping lunch that day, how prudence protects us, the shot I'd received the right thing despite the strange, miserable luck of those dead strangers in another part of the city.

And that same autumn, in Africa, doctors were recording sudden aches and fevers, bleeding gums, nausea, and odd vomit filled with black, digested blood. There were nuns and nurses dying. There were physicians fleeing like the Yambuku villagers who thought this virus began in the wrath of terrible demons.

And when specialists arrived, when they landed near the Ebola, where the living washed the dead, wiping blood by hand, they worked back to bodies scrubbed by the hands of the dead who had bathed those who had already died, purifying them for the afterlife.

Three years from a common cancer, my mother recited, when she watched the news, the fresh names for horror. She fretted over my infant son and reminded me of the good medical fortune of where we lived.

Those disease experts, before long, were flying to Tanzania where men and women died like infants, thin and small and wracked by diarrhea until they were similes for "the slim," dying from what had yet to be called AIDS far from the terrible anger of the God of Sodom.

Panicked, they bought pesticides to swallow, so many, so fast, the village stores ran out, restocked, and ran out again, leaving them to lesions and tumors.

Those experts retraced, from Tanzania to Uganda, the history of a bolt of material which became known as the Juliana Cloth because that name was so wondrously woven through it that women, with nothing else to barter for fashion, paid the trader with their bodies. All of them had died, the women who loved that cloth, Juliana's stitched name spooling back with those dead, leading science to the dark country of resignation where even the unborn drifted toward the loving hands of the unknowing who wove their inevitable names.

What's Next?

His mother's obituary, the one Harry Joyce had spent an hour preparing, had seemed foolproof. Just like he'd figured, the newspaper, at deadline, had taken the obituary on faith, nobody checking with a funeral home more than a hundred miles away in Los Angeles. He'd called in at work, leaving a message the night before, and packed up his car with gear for camping and fly fishing. The three bereavement days he was allowed would run right into the weekend like a well-earned vacation.

He'd set the tone in the very first sentence, using the phrase "entered into heavenly rest" and following it with a list of reasons for readers to believe that assumption: His mother's fifty years attending Emmanuel Lutheran church, meaning from before he'd been born. Her years of volunteering with Habitat for Humanity and neighborhood recycling projects. Her late afternoons delivering for Meals on Wheels. In fact, Harry was even considerate enough not to mention his deadbeat father's name, knowing his mother would appreciate that respect for her privacy about being deserted for thirty years and running.

Unfortunately, he'd hit a snag that began with his decision to celebrate with two six packs, a pepperoni pizza, and three hours of 80s and 90s rock songs, all of which led to sleeping in and discovering that he had made a bad double-down on temporary joy when the police rapped on his door at nine a.m. because they'd been informed his mother was alive and reasonably well.

He'd been happy to discover that prison wasn't at the end of this scenario, but the shame was worse than the fine. The smirks of the police. The story in the local paper. The stares of his neighbors in the townhouse development. His immediate unemployment.

And his mother leaving a message on his answering machine that began with "Heaven isn't very much different than Southern California, so drive down here, park your fool behind in my living room, and explain why you didn't just kill off your father."

His mother, when Harry arrived after eating dinner by himself half way to Los Angeles, was wearing shorts, something unusual, and he noticed her legs were tanned but spider-webbed blue with patches of veins. "They're not varicose," she said. "That's a blessing. You start pushing seventy and there's a limit to what you ask for."

"There's no need for that," Harry said.

"I know when you come here you look at me and evaluate. Maybe that's what gave you your brilliant idea."

"You know what I'm really thinking? It's hot as hell in here, and I wish I was wearing shorts."

His mother sat down, and Harry dropped into a chair, his suitcase in front of him as if he were waiting to board at the airport. "If I'd known what you were up to, I could have locked my door and stayed inside for a few days before the notice ran, let the newspapers pile up on the sidewalk and give Sue Ellen Briggs and anyone else who cared to look a good scare."

"I was fired," Harry said.

"Well, maybe that's what you wanted all along wanting to quit all these years. You'll be fine. You're not like that homeless guy with his shopping carts moving in on the vacant lot last year."

"I remember."

"Who could forget what with his raggedy clothes flapping from the tree branches like a bunch of ugly flags?"

"The newspaper I sent it to is over a hundred miles from here." Harry thought of explaining how he knew the paper wasn't the *LA Times*, that it had a skeleton staff and reprinted wire service reports for everything that happened more than twenty miles away, but he settled for the short version: "I didn't think anybody would read that paper more than thirty miles from my house."

"Well," his mother said, "the word got around, that's for sure. Sue Ellen comes knocking and then she's texting and tweeting and Facebooking my survival to people she's never even met and pretty soon the news boomerangs right back to where it started."

"Sue Ellen has a Twitter account?"

"That's what she calls it, but she's right next door so she just opens her mouth to let me know all her news. I could have told you she reads all the newspapers from here to San Francisco on her computer. She lived up that way for more than thirty years so she checks the death notices because there's so many her age, she says, that's dropping like flies."

"Incredible."

"Not when you're pushing eighty, it isn't."

"It's a good thing she didn't move more often or she'd never find the time to read all the roll calls." His mother seemed to be looking past him, and he shifted in his chair toward her gaze, feeling his damp shirt cling to the vinyl back.

"She told me she saw me on the patio putzing around the day before and thought to herself nobody dies and gets a notice that fast except the president."

"So what possessed her to drop a dime on me?"

"You and that crime show talk. *Law and Order* this, *Law and Order* that. Sue Ellen just thought she'd put the paper straight and save them from a prank. One thing led to another. You want to hear my real news?"

"Sure," Harry said, happy to move on.

"We have a peacock."

"We?" Harry said, and for a moment he glanced around the room for evidence his mother had taken in a boarder.

"Me and Sue Ellen and whatever neighbors care to come out and take a peek. Best guess is it was blown here by the big wind storm a few nights ago. I thought the roof would come off, but all that happened was a tree or two down and the peacock on Sue Ellen's roof the next day. She's about sure that big bird blew in from Griffith Park. It's only a mile or two, and there's more than a few strutting around up there. The thing would get caught up in that storm and come flying like all get out, and now here you are keeping me company, too. You and your fishing the start of all this. What kind of fun is that anyway standing in the water all day and all by yourself in the middle of nowhere?"

"I like being by myself."

"I sure hope so. All these years I've been worrying for you liking nobody but your own self, and now here you are out of work so you can be happy and go fishing any time you want." She threw her right hand in an arc that Harry followed as if he'd asked to be hypnotized. "But first you need to lay low like those outlaws you talk like. Enjoy the peacock. It's more fun than a fish. Wait until you hear it. You'll get chills right down your spine."

Harry stood and carried his suitcase toward his old room where the drapes were pulled shut, the space so dark he walked straight to the draw cord. "Be careful there," he heard his mother say from behind him. The drapes skidded apart, but the room stayed nearly as gloomy because the thick branches of a large pine tree were pressed against the window.

"Jesus, Mom. You said there were a few trees down, but you left out the detail of one right up against the back of the house. It looks like you just missed having a big problem. Can you even get outside through the back door?"

"It had to be God getting the distance just right. There's no other way to explain something like that."

"I can think of some."

"I know how you think. But here it is just sitting there with a peacock blown into the neighborhood. It makes you wonder how there's no accounting for what's next, doesn't it?"

Harry brushed past her to the kitchen and tried the back door, but it didn't open. With all the branches folded against the windows, he felt like he was visiting a terrarium. "It's that hunchbacked one that fell?" he said. "Right?"

"That big old pine was leaning when you were born. After a while you think it's not going to take a tumble."

"It was the only pine above the house. Maybe it was about fire protection or something. Maybe somebody once upon a time thinned out the trees most likely to spread flames down to the houses. Like somebody took them all out years ago and didn't have the heart to kill the cripple."

His mother rapped on the table with the knuckles of her right hand and slowly shook her head. "I've come to hate that word."

"You want me to say that the tree was vertically challenged?"

"For all its life, by the looks of it."

Harry tried to wind the window open, but it was jammed as tight as the door. He yanked hard on the handle and felt the sweat that had formed in his armpits begin to trickle down his sides. His mother had no air conditioning, and now she had no cross ventilation. "Have you called anybody about it?"

"It's not hurting anything lying there. It was fifty years getting to where it is. I can give it a few days rest."

"There used to be a saw in the basement. I can take off the branches, at least give you enough space to use the back door again."

"A wind like the one we had comes once every twenty years. That tree could have outlasted me if it had made it through the other night in one piece."

"God's plan, right?"

"When the next one falls right on top of me, you won't think that's God either, but I'll surely know."

From outside there was a loud squawk that sounded close. "Mmwaah-ah." The peacock, Harry thought, and turned to the window, but all he could see was a spray of pine needles. "Mmwaah-ah" sounded a second time, the call lifting at the end like a question, louder and more foreign than he'd imagined it would be. Tropical, he thought, vowing not to admit it, and nearly threatening, what he was sure he'd keep to himself. "Listen to that, Harry," his mother said. "Sue Ellen named it Dorothy."

"It's female?"

"We don't know for sure. I was going to look it up but haven't gotten around to it. Anyway, it's more fun to believe it's a girl swept here like little Judy Garland."

"Mmwaah-ah." The third call resonated so close Harry expected the bird to fan its feathers while it perched on the downed tree. "Let's go outside and take a look."

"Oh, but that's not Dorothy," his mother said. "That's Sue Ellen. She's gotten really good at imitating the call, but I can still tell the difference. She must be trying to attract it or else she saw your car and is showing off."

When the call came again, this time from near the front door, it seemed to Harry to be a sound check for lunacy, but he caught himself holding his breath and listening for the echo of an answer. "How often does she do this?" he finally said, whispering in spite of himself, but his mother was already turning away, hurrying so quickly to the front door that Harry followed her, imagining that he was about to see the peacock strutting toward his mother's squawking neighbor.

Sue Ellen was wrapped in so much olive-shaded loose cloth Harry thought she might be wearing a makeshift sari to camouflage the folds of fat she'd displayed since she'd moved in a decade ago after she'd retired. "I may be big," she'd announced back then, "but I have the heart of a bull. My mother lived to be ninety-five, and she carried more weight than me."

Now, though, she looked at Harry and said, "The prodigal son. Aren't you the lucky one to be welcomed back."

"I'm not making him any feast," his mother said. "This was just my second day of fasting, so there's plenty in the refrigerator he can help finish for me if he has to have a snack."

"Fasting?" Harry said, the word suddenly sounding more peculiar than a peacock's call.

"Three days every month. There's proof it makes you live longer."

Sue Ellen patted her stomach. "I'm seventy-seven without ever missing a meal. Like that place on Sunset Strip way back when."

"I've seen that," Harry said.

"Now that's where you're wrong," Sue Ellen said. "You weren't even in your mother's wishful thinking way back then."

"There's reruns of everything."

"So tell me, how much more handsome can a man be than that

Efram Zimbalist was?"

Harry hesitated, not ready to admit he hadn't watched for more than five minutes before he'd settled for a movie made since he'd been born, but his mother broke in. "Kookie was the cool one."

"Ed Byrnes and all that hair combing. See what a difference ten years makes?" Sue Ellen said. "Your mother was a teenager and I was already thinking about my first divorce."

For a moment, Harry was afraid they'd make him choose the sexier actor from his prehistory, but his mother turned and vanished into her bedroom. He remembered that Sue Ellen had run through three husbands, making him reconsider her size, the sort of men who would have married her and wanted to unwrap her. "Grace has told you about Dorothy, right? That beauty was right up on my roof this morning. She's too smart for coyotes. You'll see her for yourself soon enough. She loves being up there on the red tiles with that great view. If she could work a camera, she could take pictures of Los Angeles from up there."

"The peacock was in yesterday's paper," his mother said, coming back from her bedroom with the paper folded to a photograph. "See there? That's Sue Ellen's roof and there's Dorothy."

"They didn't bother to write anything about her," Sue Ellen said. "All they put in was a caption as if something like this happened every day. Like it's not a story, just a peacock on a house."

"They should have printed it in color, too," Harry said.

Sue Ellen gathered her light green drapery around her as if she felt Harry tugging on it. "Peacocks don't need a color photograph. Everybody who knows anything knows how beautiful they are. Wait until you see how deep the blue is on Dorothy's neck."

An hour later, Sue Ellen finally gone, twilight giving him a chance to beg fatigue for an early shower and bed time, Harry logged on to the ancient computer his mother had kept in his old room for ten years. Even on the sluggish machine, it didn't take him long to confirm that a deep blue neck signaled the bird was male, that females had green feathers on their necks. There was more, how the females were mostly drab gray and brown except for that green, but he decided to leave it to chance whether or not his mother would ever fact check.

When he inspected the shelf underneath the computer to see if there was anything to read until he fell asleep, he found nothing but a copy of his mother's obituary printed out from his local paper's web site. Sue Ellen, he thought, must have made the copy because his mother didn't have a printer. "Grace Anne Joyce went to be with her Lord. . ." it began. Harry was careful about replacing it exactly in the spot where it had been lying.

BY THE TIME Harry made his way to the kitchen in the morning, his mother had coffee ready. He finished half a cup before he rummaged in a cupboard and found what he feared was the same box of Honey Nut Cheerios he'd eaten the last time he'd visited four months ago. His mother sipped water. "Day three," she said as he opened the refrigerator and saw a scattering of leftovers, all in the small black plastic trays that signaled Lean Cuisine meals. He opened the milk and sniffed, relieved it smelled fresh enough to pour on the stale cereal.

"Now that we're all settled," his mother said, "what's next for you?"

"First thing is clearing up that tree before it gets too hot out, Mom. You need to get some windows open at least."

"Then what?"

"One thing at a time."

"Don't we all wish," she said, but she was already opening the front door like a tour guide, expecting him to follow.

On the patio, all three outdoor chairs lay under the trunk of the tree, the cheap aluminum arms and legs collapsed in a way that reminded Harry of how Wile E. Coyote always ended up splattered in the Roadrunner cartoons. "It was like God aimed them at those three your father brought home pleased as punch from K-Mart one day. Like the good Lord was tired of seeing that junk lined up there all these years."

"The heavenly perp," Harry said, and she frowned in a way that said *stop the silly talk*. The chairs had padded seats, but they were cheap and never comfortable way back when Harry lived here. "Look at that thing. When it first came down Sue Ellen started in talking about the difference between white pines and grey pines and all that, but I didn't listen long enough to know which one I had here besides real big and awful crooked."

"You should make yourself some breakfast, Mom. This fasting thing can wait another month. I'll find the saw and at least get this started."

HARRY STARTED WITH the thinnest branches that were splayed against the back of the house. The saw, despite its rust, seemed sharp enough, but soon he was sweating and his right hand ached, blisters beginning to form. He found a pair of his mother's old gardening gloves and forced them on, tugging at them until his fingers were enclosed, the floral pattern on the palms stopping an inch short of his wrists. Already, though, his arms had begun to itch.

When they brushed against his bare arms, the pine needles produced tiny welts, reminding him how, as a boy, his allergies had forced his mother to buy an artificial tree for Christmas because his eyes swelled shut and his breath shortened to a thin pant from sitting near a real one. He knew he needed to go inside and run hot water over his arms, but his mother, if she noticed, would tell him to stop and the whole day would open in front of him with nothing to do but answer questions about his future and wait for a peacock sighting. Soon enough he'd have to give in. The thick trunk would be impossible. Somebody with a chain saw needed to do the work. And finally, half way down the trunk, the branches thickened and slowed him until he took a break, sitting on the patio wall, the saw dangling from one gloved hand.

As if his mother had been waiting for him to stop, she came around the corner of the house and started gathering the scattered branches. "That can wait, Mom," Harry said, but she dragged them like makeshift brooms, beginning to clear a space along the back of the house. He watched her for a minute, noticing, in spite of himself, how the backs of her thighs and the space behind her knees looked even bluer than what he'd seen the day before. And then, as she bent to drag another severed branch, she fell forward onto the limb and another caught beneath it without throwing her arms out, and he thought, as he dropped the saw and scrambled toward her, that she'd been right all along about God's design and justice.

"Mom?" he said, turning her over, and her eyes snapped opened.

"What just happened?" she said.

"It looks like you fainted." He heard rustling and heavy breathing and knew Sue Ellen was hovering behind him.

"I told you a thousand times this would happen," she said. "Didn't I?"

His mother slowly sat up, brushing pine needles off her legs and arms as Harry tried not to scratch his reddening skin. "It's nothing but low sugar," she said. "All I need is a pick me up, some orange juice or whatnot."

Harry looked up at Sue Ellen's looming pastel blue-swathed body and waited while she stared at him and his mother looked up the hill as if she expected to see a coyote with a rainbow of plumage jutting from its mouth. He took one more breath before saying, "You still think not eating is good for you?"

"I bet I flopped just like that old clock up your way fell down during your earthquake last winter."

His mother paused, but he wasn't going to prompt her now even with Sue Ellen making circles in the air with one finger like an umpire calling a home run. Maybe his mother talking like she enjoyed collapsing would make the peacock curious, draw it to the patio wall to perch.

"I'd bring something over myself if I thought Grace would take a bite," Sue Ellen said. She pointed a finger at Harry. "Don't you dare let me come back and find out your mother hasn't eaten."

As she crossed the yard between the houses, Harry's mother said, "Look at you now, you're covered with the zizzits. From that tree, right?"

Harry opened the refrigerator and pulled out one of the half-eaten Lean Cuisines—he thought he recognized Pasta Primavera, the portion so skimpy to begin with, but half of it still tucked under Saran Wrap. "How can half a Lean Cuisine fill anybody up?" he said, setting the microwave. He lifted a corner of the Saran Wrap and sniffed. "This hasn't been sitting in here for weeks, has it?"

"Not eating much doesn't make you crazy."

"Agreed," Harry said, but two minutes later, when she reached for the fork he'd set beside the tray, his mother's head turned to the side like a bird's making Harry afraid she'd begun rehearsing the mannerisms of a peacock in order to keep up with Sue Ellen's vocals. He began to reheat the other three leftover meals, all of them tiny, half-eaten pizzas with a few vegetables scattered on a thin crust of cheese.

"Sue Ellen doesn't care about that old clock, but I remember I was visiting the very day before the earthquake, and we went Christmas shopping and stopped for ice cream right there in Paso Robles and walked right past that old landmark clock twice. It was around three o'clock. The hand was straight up by the twelve. Less than twenty-four hours that clock had before it took a tumble."

"You wanted to watch the elephant seals before you left. We went back down to the ocean."

"What do you think those seals do during an earthquake?"

"They have other things to worry about."

He noticed she was still picking at the pasta even though he'd devoured all the skimpy pizzas, but she let the fork rest in the tray and said, "You'd think by now that bird must feel like Robinson Crusoe."

"Or Tom Hanks with his volleyball on that deserted island. Wilson—they made it sad when he fell overboard."

"Tom Hanks drowned?"

"Wilson the volleyball drowned. Nobody would let Tom Hanks drown."

"Maybe so, but that bird won't last. It needs company like the rest of us."

Mmwaah-ah—the sound came like an argument with his mother's reasoning. "It's uncanny how good she is, isn't it?" his mother said. "They say peacocks talk more when they're mating."

Mmwaah-ah. Nearly a honk, Harry thought. "Maybe so," he said, "but she just makes it sound lonely."

His mother went quiet then, and Harry knew she was listening for the real voice, but all he heard was the traffic from the highway two streets below, a furious surge that told him the light had changed. Mmwaah-ah. He had to admit that Sue Ellen emitted the same sound each time, but either the peacock wasn't fooled or else it sensed the need for silence.

DURING THE AFTERNOON, Harry worked on and off until all the branches were severed, even the thick ones near the base of the trunk. His mother, sipping orange juice, insisted on dragging all but the heaviest to what proved to be an enormous pile. After a shower, absolutely starving, he opened the freezer to find something for dinner and discovered only a dozen boxes of Lean Cuisine.

He sensed his mother watching him, anxious, he was sure, that he was holding the freezer open too long. "Is this all you ever eat?" he said.

"I can't be making things that leave leftovers."

"We could go out."

"I'm happy using some of them up. I promise to eat a whole one."

"And I promise to eat three." He pulled out four that had the word "chicken" on the package and set them on the counter to open. "Chicken Makhani," he announced. "Chicken Marsala. Chicken Parmesan. Chicken Pecan."

"If you're wondering, I always buy only one of a kind in alphabetical order. They have a lot of different chickens. I'll take the one I never heard of before, that Makhani one. Maybe it's good."

When the Makhani was ready, Harry spooned it onto a plate and poured her an ice water, serving it like a waiter. He started with the Pecan on his plate, avoiding alphabetical order. He was halfway through it when he noticed her tap her fork on the plate twice instead of lifting up another mouthful. "You look like a little kid toying with a plate of spinach and broccoli."

"I always leave these dinners in their little trays. They get lost on a big plate like this." She slid her fork into the small portion of pasta. "It takes time to get back to eating after the fast." She took two bites and laid the fork across the soggy chicken while Harry microwaved the Marsala.

By the time he sat down again, she seemed to have forgotten she was eating. "Remember when you had a liking for that girl who lived beside the vacant lots down the street?" she said.

"Cassandra Burke?"

"You called her Cassie when you walked to school together."

"That was middle school. We were like thirteen or something."

"What if she was down there at the house right this minute. Wouldn't that be something?"

"We're both forty now, Mom. We wouldn't even recognize each other."

"With a little more hair on top you'd be the same as you ever were. And anyway, you don't forget the ones you were stuck on."

"She has her own life, Mom. The last thing she needs is a stranger saying 'remember me?'"

"Lucky you, then," she said, bitterness in her tone. "Now you have an excuse. But I bet she visits her mother more than you'd think. That homeless man probably got more of an eyeful while he lived next door than you ever do. All he had to do was crawl up that bank and look inside from where all those trees give him a good hiding place."

Harry nodded as if he agreed. His mother was right, at least about the hill, which was steep enough to prevent anyone from building behind the houses on his mother's side of the street. The trees there were mostly palms that towered up and littered the ground with dead fronds that always looked as if they were ready to ignite, setting the high grass that was never green on fire.

But three houses down, that steep hillside slid in between two houses like a double lot-sized tongue and there was a scattering of pines that could have suggested a park if it had been maintained. A year ago, the homeless guy living there had parked two shopping carts, one loaded with cans and bottles, the other with clothes, an old quilt strung over a line between two trees that seemed set on creating privacy. Cassie's mother still lived on the far side of that open space, and neither she nor the two women who rented on the other side had been willing to wander in there to clean up even when the litter must have been visible from their decks.

"You know what bothers me?" his mother had said. "I never see him, just his stuff. He must be there when I go by, some of the time at least. I walk past there two or three times a day and all those ratty clothes and those shopping carts give me the willies. And just think of the stink up in there."

Harry, finally, had called the police during each of the three visits he'd made over six months, yet each time he returned the homeless man was still there. "The police have better things to do than evict bums," his mother said each time, but when he arrived for a fourth visit, three months after the last, the lot was vacant, and his mother didn't know whether the police had rousted him or he'd left on his own or maybe even died, but whichever way, the makeshift closet had been emptied as if invaded by burglars.

"You'll clean me out," his mother said after Harry polished off the Parmesan, her voice softened again. "You know I love remembering my high school boy friends. Dave Morrow, Sam Dressler, Jack Smith. Imagine being Jack Smith, so many of you in the world there must be ten thousand of them just in the United States. If your name was Smith, wouldn't you want to name your son Rumplestilskin or something like that?"

"Nebuchadnezzar."

"The King of the Jews from that old song? That's no name for a Smith, but I remember every word of that song and I can see Jack Smith and the others like it was yesterday."

"What are you now? Worried about Alzheimer's?"

"Why do you say that? Don't I sound like I'm talking straight?"

"You sound fine."

"Well then, I'm putting on a good show because I love my *LA Times*, and I'm having trouble with reading any of it these days." She pointed to the newspaper that was lying beside the coffee maker. "Take a look. I haven't even opened it and here the day is practically over."

Harry dumped his empty trays in the garbage and ran water over his plate before he carried the paper to the table. "Maybe newspapers will start printing in large type for all the baby boomers who still read what they print."

"It's not that simple."

Harry unfolded the paper, then folded it again. "What's that mean?" he said.

"For a while the words were blurry and wavy, like they were on a boat, but now I have this empty spot that gets in the way."

"That sounds like migraines? I've had those off and on."

"I wish. You know when I first noticed that spot? A couple of weeks ago Sue Ellen was all in a dither about the coyote she could see so close it was like somebody's pet. She pointed up the hill like she was showing me Jesus standing among the palms, but there was this smudge right where her finger was leading, and when I turned my head to try and see around it, she touched my arm like I was a little girl so I looked right at the smudge and nodded like I was seeing that coyote plain as day. You'd be surprised how being agreeable keeps people from asking questions."

"It doesn't show, Mom."

"You don't have to lie to please me. It's been going on for almost two years. I haven't ignored this, Harry. I'm doing what they tell me, but if I'm going to ever see the ocean again, you'll have to come get me. And those seals will have to get along without me saying hello. Right this minute if I want to see your face, I have to look over your shoulder. Sometimes I have to tell myself not to bob my head around to see past the spot."

Harry blinked twice as if the room had filled with smoke, his eyes so dry they felt gritty. Everything his mother was saying sounded like a version of what he'd been anticipating. "I didn't notice," he said.

"That's because you don't look me in the eye." His mother's voice hardened again. "You look at every part of me but my face. It's no wonder you don't have a girlfriend."

"That's not why."

"Good then. But it's a nasty habit and this thing has been creeping up on me. Macular degeneration. You know what's next? It will go from bad to worse. I'll lose my driver's license as soon as I let on. I won't be able to get around."

"It won't kill you."

"That's where you're wrong. Blind is the same as dead. I'd rather have the Alzheimer's, then you could just put something in my juice and use that death notice that's ready and waiting."

Harry tried to think of what he could say that wouldn't cost him anything more than a few extra minutes of listening, but he hesitated so long his mother stopped talking, her expression turning sullen. "When you stay clammed up like that, you look just like your father."

"I'm still here," he said, so immediate and certain she squeezed his arm and held on as if she was about to faint again.

"Whatever did you do at that job anyway? You never told me."

"You want me to confess? Rat myself out?"

"I want you to use plain English that good people use."

"I worked with computers."

"See there? You're still not telling me."

"It's complicated."

"Well then, not anymore, it's not. Now you'll have to start over with something you can tell me about without being ashamed."

"It might be a while."

"Take your time. Pick something you like this time, not something I have to die to save you from."

"You want me to finish that chicken?" Harry said, and when she nodded, he was happy to let the conversation die before he admitted that as much as he'd hated his job, now he was terrified that he wouldn't be able to make himself apply for a new one. Updating his resume felt like writing a novel.

And he couldn't tell her that it had been a year since he'd talked to anyone at work. That he'd been surprised how easy it was to say nothing except "Hi," eventually settling for a nod. That the others called him

"Harry the Hermit."

"I'm going for a walk," he said. "A fast one," he added, eager to be alone.

THE FIRST THING he noticed was an empty shopping cart parked among the pines in the empty lot. It shimmered like a chrome-slathered antique car, but nothing was draped from any of the branches, and he saw no one in the shadows. But sitting there, the early evening sun reflecting off the latticed metal, it seemed like the first rogue cell in the vacant lot, one that would divide and then divide again, the thin small forest filling with the lost.

A few seconds later, when he saw Cassie's mother trimming shrubbery, she looked even older than Sue Ellen, and it reminded him that Cassie had been the youngest of three, her brothers older by nearly ten years. He waved, and she looked his way without speaking, her hair the same shade of rust-red he remembered from more than twenty years ago. Between that color and her heavy makeup, she looked like a doll who'd been cursed.

He took a few steps closer and waved again. "Nobody's home," she said.

"It's Harry Joyce," he called, and she made a visor with one hand and squinted.

"Harry Joyce," she said. "I thought you were here wanting to sell me something."

"I'm visiting my mother and needed some exercise."

"Me too," she said, clipping two more thin branches, and her answer stuck in his throat until he coughed, but nothing shook loose. "Well," he said, "I'll see you maybe on the way back."

"Let's hope we both feel better by then," she said.

When Cassie's mother wasn't in the yard an hour later, Harry turned into the vacant lot and walked past the empty cart, but there wasn't a sign that anyone had moved in among the trees. As if he'd planned on climbing, he started to work his way up the steep slope, but after he reached the height of the roofs, he stalled because he needed to grab branches and tree trunks just to keep from skidding back down. He was sweating hard by now, and all he could do was glance around as if the peacock might be spotted or he could detect the cart's owner in the shadows below him before working his way back down.

He paused by the cart, steadying himself, checking to be sure Cassie's mother was still absent before nudging the handle with the heel of his right hand. It rolled a few inches and caught on a clump of thick weeds he couldn't identify.

Keeping his eye on the Burkes' yard, he slipped into the shadow of the nearest tree and sat against the trunk, positioning himself so he could see if anyone stepped onto the deck. He felt exhausted, as if he'd walked more than all the way to Griffith Park before circling back. He let his eyes fall shut, but when something rustled in the tall grass to his left, he bolted to his feet, shuddering. The grass was still, but he stared, counting slowly to twenty to settle his fear before backing away, suddenly sure that he was being watched as he scrambled to the street.

"Well?" his mother said five minutes later.

"Well what?"

"You know what."

"She wasn't there, Mom. I said 'hi' to her mother. Cassie's been married for years. She has three kids."

"Sally Burke told you all this?"

"Cassie and I still keep in touch from time to time. She emailed me a picture once."

 "Has she taken care of herself?"

"She has three kids."

"That's no excuse for letting yourself go and looking like those seals of yours. They're so fat they look like something that shouldn't be."

"Elephant seals are supposed to be big and fat," he said. "And Cassie's just fine."

"And you missed hearing Dorothy while you were out gallivanting. She did her Mmwaah-ah four times in a row. Like this—Mmwaah-ah." Her bleat didn't sound anything like a peacock, but Harry smiled. "Aren't you excited? It was for real. Dorothy is still here, alive and calling. I don't need eyes to know it's her."

She walked to the bedroom window and waved him to stand beside her. "You can count yourself lucky you didn't end up with Cassie Burke."

"I haven't ended up with anybody."

"There's enough pine boughs out there for a hundred Christmas wreaths."

"Or a garbage truck full."

"There's your father talking again. Just stick yourself here and look for a minute. We have a porthole now."

Harry felt exhausted, but standing at the window seemed important, and it quieted his mother into something fragile, the silence opening a space for the sound of traffic, his mother's wind chimes, and a door slamming at Sue Ellen's.

"You know you need to find somebody while I can still see her with my own two eyes."

"I'll call somebody before I leave in the morning," Harry said, and when she didn't answer, he added, "about finishing the tree."

"I can pay. Don't you go wasting your money. You'll be needing every penny."

"I'll find a job, Mom. Computers aren't going anywhere."

"In that dinky town?"

"I can move. I don't have much to deal with."

"But you won't have seals."

"There's always something no matter where you live."

"I guess that's true. Now I have a peacock to watch before I go blind."

"You'll be fine, Mom. You have years yet before this thing gets you down."

A year or two, Harry thought, five if she's lucky. She'll be seventy and helpless.

"You'll be right if I'm dead by then."

He thought he saw color and movement over her shoulder, but he was afraid to take his eyes off her face. "You'll outlive Sue Ellen. Short skinny women live practically forever."

"And if I don't, you'll have me ready for the newspaper all wrapped up with a bow."

"I'd start over and get it right."

She turned her head slightly and reached out to lay a hand on his cheek. "You already did good," she said. "You made me a saint."

THE COMPLETE STATS

THROUGH THE KITCHEN window, Joan Edgerton watched her son Bryson play basketball by himself, standing three steps back so he wouldn't see her if he glanced toward the house. Bryson called out the names of players as he passed the ball among them by lofting it into the air several feet away and chasing it down on the first bounce. He brought the ball to his shoulders, snapping his head up and hesitating an instant before leaping off the ground, all the while maintaining an announcer's descriptive chatter. "Iverson shoots. It's off iron. Coleman rebounds. He takes it to the hole and scores," her son shouted. "And one," he added, and because Joan had watched him play like this since he turned eleven, she knew he had just tacked on an imaginary foul.

Joan followed Bryson through the next sequence as he called a foul on a player named Pierce, giving what she'd learned was a referee's signal for holding. It would be cute, she thought, if only her son didn't have a whistle around his neck and blow it before each call. Traveling, three seconds, illegal screen—she recognized them all by now, even the mysterious technical foul for imaginary bad behavior, Bryson blowing that whistle before he said, "Shut up, now" to a fantasy player who apparently had not only complained too loudly, but also gotten too close from the way her son backed up a step while he made a T-sign with his hands.

Because they lived fifty miles from Philadelphia, her son favored the 76ers, calling fewer fouls on them, giving them more rebounds, repeating their names so often they were more familiar than the names of the boys who played for the local high school. She opened the oven door and peered at the casserole dish to see if the cheese on top of the vegetable lasagna was turning brown. The clock above the burners read 4:38. By 4:40 her husband would be home and ready for their 4:45 dinner.

Her husband was training for a marathon. Bart was up to fifteen miles at a time, which took him two hours. It was remarkable in itself, Joan thought, his running time outlasting those of most movies. A few weeks ago, she'd slipped in a DVD as he left to run. She watched the whole movie and had time to make coffee before he returned. Bart has driven her over the distance, a loop that nearly doubled back on itself, passing through two nearby small towns. She wondered if anyone who saw her husband would think he was running fifteen miles. All summer he returned at 8:30 when it began to get dark and her son came inside from the driveway basketball court where he went after dinner to play more fantasy games. Now that school had begun, the light was gone by 7:30, and Bryson played under the flood light that shone from above the garage door until Bart reappeared and shut it off.

The race Bart has entered will be in the city in November. One Sunday afternoon in mid-September he'd driven her and Bryson over the course. In the car, because of all the stoplights, it took forty-five minutes to complete, nearly as long as it did to make the return trip home.

Monday morning, she looked up the history of marathons on her computer. "Marathon deaths" she typed into Google, trying to learn how risky it was to run such a ridiculous distance. More than 28,000 people had entered a marathon in Beijing the year before, and two of them had died. 6,000 runners from one Chinese college had entered in order to receive phys. ed. credit. One of them had died, a photograph of his prone body illustrating the site. On another site, the fatality rate was given as one per two million miles of cumulative running. It sounded like the way NASA might calculate the fatality rate for astronauts.

When she brought up the deaths, Bart shrugged. "If I was going to die doing this, I'd already be dead," he said.

"It's another ten miles past what you're doing."

"Eleven," he said, "and 385 yards."

"You're only doing a little more than half then."

"If you run like I do, you know. Your body tells you what's up. It doesn't lie."

It sounded like something she used to hear in church.

BRYSON FILLED NOTEBOOKS full of statistics from his one-on-none basketball games. During his games, he scribbled marks on a tablet that sat on a chair under the porch roof overhang. Afterwards, he made a neat, clean copy in his room and entered the numbers in one of the notebooks. While Bryson was in school, Joan flipped through the pages of the newest notebook. The numbers and letters were printed with care—G MPG FGA FG FTA FT R PPG AST 3PA 3P. Each of the elaborate box scores was dated, an attendance figure listed.

"I saw Iverson scored thirty-seven against the Celtics," she said at dinner.

"Yes," Bryson said, but when she looked for the notebooks a few days later, he'd moved them. She found the newest one hidden between two thick winter sweaters. Two others were pressed against the wall at the bottom of his closet behind three pairs of shoes. She was afraid to look in any of them for fear he'd memorized the exact angles at which they had been stored.

After school Bryson asked her to look through the door to his room. "What do you see?" he said, extending his arm toward the floor, the palm of his hand open and up like a tap dancer finishing a routine.

"What am I supposed to see?" she said.

"Look at my carpet." Each morning Bryson vacuumed his carpet, always ending by the door so the room looked unlived in, and now, because the rest of the carpet was smooth, she saw her footprints going from his desk to his closet to his chest of drawers.

"I get it," she said. "Okay."

Bryson did his own laundry as well. On Saturdays, he even stripped his bed and washed the sheets and the pillowcase. "I don't want my stuff mixed with anybody else's," he'd told her, and until this moment she'd believed it was because he was embarrassed to have her see his underwear.

"You should be thankful," Bart said when she mentioned it. "He could be the opposite like every other boy his age."

"It's like he's compulsive."

"He's just finicky. He's super neat. You keep looking things up on the Internet, you'll sure enough find something to worry about. He's not washing his hands twenty times a day. There's no harm in vacuuming the carpet every morning."

She didn't tell Bart that she was afraid all the business with the laundry and the carpet meant her son was hiding something among his clothes. Pornography, she thought. She'd smell cigarettes on him, and what else would a thirteen year-old need to hide?

HER HUSBAND WORKED in an office at one of the two banks in their town. All Joan knew about his job was that he was well paid. Unlike the tellers, the people she talked to each time she had business there.

Bart had explained there were ways to manage their money that would eliminate all of her trips to the bank, but she ignored them because she enjoyed her short conversations with Amy and Shirley and Karen, the names on the plates that remind her of Scrabble troughs. Each of those women had pictures of her children in small frames on the shelf above her window. Shirley's was a sort of mosaic of her two sons, both of them aging from infants to boys who looked, at their oldest, to be a year or two younger than Bryson. Their names were Alex and Ronald, and when she asked how they were doing, Shirley always smiled and said, "Just dandy, thanks" or "growing like weeds."

She didn't see her husband when she used the bank. His door was always closed. Sometimes, though, he came home and reminded her that it wasn't 1965, the year she was born, anymore.

ONE SATURDAY, WHILE Bryson was playing in the morning, she came out on the porch to water her potted flowers. Bryson called a time out, touching both shoulders to indicate, she remembered, a thirty-second one. "You don't have a ticket," he said.

"Pardon me?"

"You have to leave."

"I'm busy here."

"These seats are all taken." He put the ball beside his feet and stood with his arms crossed until she finished and went inside. "A near melee," she heard him say. "A disgraceful display." The whistle blew and the ball thunked against the pavement.

He uses bully's words, she thought, with the voice of a child. If he was in third grade, he would frighten his classmates. In eighth grade he must make them laugh, but at open house, six teachers tell her Bryson seldom speaks, that his voice barely carries to them when he is asked to answer. "He's not like that at home," she said to each of them, but by the time she left, she realized she should have said, "He's not like that when he fantasizes."

BART AND BRYSON were both gone by 8:15 every weekday, leaving Joan with seven hours to herself. It seemed like such a long time that Joan wondered, sometimes, what she'd done before she had a computer. Bryson had started kindergarten one month before Bart set up their first computer in the spare room, sticking a desk among the discarded furniture and boxes of old toys that lined the walls, but she seldom touched it. She watched television and humored Bart when he asked her to watch a picture inch down the screen. "I'll be back when it's ready," she'd say as if it were a pie baking. After a while he stopped calling her back, but four years ago he'd bought a new one and said, "Watch." The pictures opened like the power windows in her van. He flicked from site to site, and she sat beside him, listening to his instructions. A week later she had stopped watching television.

NINETY MILES A week Bart runs, skipping Sunday because he read somewhere that six days on, one day off, is how to train. On Sundays he cut grass and trimmed bushes and painted fences. By dinner he claimed to be "absolutely exhausted" and went to bed by nine. None of the dozen training regimens Joan found online suggested ninety miles in six days with one day off.

What most interested Joan was the Rosie Ruiz scandal, how she was crowned women's champion of the Boston Marathon after jumping into the race a mile from the finish line. The other runners knew right away that Rosie Ruiz had cheated because she didn't look like anyone who'd completed a marathon. Her mistake was jumping in and winning, other runners explain. If she had jumped in five minutes later, she would be in the record books. Nobody thoroughly investigated a ninth place finisher.

Joan began to evaluate her husband's exhaustion and sweat when he finished his workouts. How far down his shirt was stained. How drawn and strained his face looked. He never looked like a first-place finisher. Sometimes he looked like someone way in the back of the pack, someone could be unfaithful. Once or twice a week he'd look as fresh as Rosie Ruiz. When she said, "You look like you could run another fifteen miles. You're hardly sweating," Bart had the look of someone caught off guard.

"I didn't know you paid so much attention," he said.

"I have eyes."

"I felt sick half way out. I walked for half a mile, and then when I tried again, the feeling came right back and I turned around, walking and jogging to get here in two hours."

It seemed so plausible she was certain he'd had it prepared for weeks. "I've done it before, you know, but maybe you weren't watching on those days."

"I'm watching now," she said.

He raised his eyebrows. "It's okay," he said. "It's not heart trouble or anything like that. It's what I eat or when I'm eating it. I cut corners. I'm not serious enough." Rosie Ruiz had run less than a mile. Joan decided the woman he was meeting must live nearby. Or maybe, she thought, she picks him up in her car and lives miles away.

"IF YOU COULD, what else would you like to do in your spare time?" she asked Bryson one afternoon when it was raining so hard he was in the house at four o'clock.

"I don't know," he said. "Nothing."

He was already backing away, but Joan was afraid to grasp his arm for fear he'd wrench free, spin her off balance with the violence of his escape. "It doesn't have to be a big thing," she said. "Nothing special."

He smiled and she felt herself turn light with hope. "Be a scorekeeper," he said. "Somebody who writes down all of the numbers for basketball."

"There," she said, but he shook his head.

"I want to do it for my games. There's nobody else who would get it right."

Joan thought of the tablet with all of the hurried marks. "I could do that. It doesn't sound hard."

"That's why everybody gets everything wrong. They think stuff is easy."

"Like schoolwork," she said, trying to keep him talking.

"No," he said. "That stuff is easy for real. I mean hard stuff like keeping track of everybody's performance, the complete stats. You wouldn't know the substitution rotations. You wouldn't know the minutes played for everybody on both rosters."

Joan didn't argue, but as soon as Bryson closed the door to his room, she thought of December, January, and February, the mostly unplayable driveway months. Basketball tryouts began on November 1st. It was marked on the school calendar just like auditions for the senior class play and the dates for the SATs.

Bryson was tall and thin. A basketball player's body. A coach could evaluate his future by the size and shape of him. Big boys were enticed to football, tall ones to basketball. He might be invited to try out even though he had never played for any of the school teams, not even in fifth or sixth grade. His shots went through the hoop as often as not. When he dribbled, the ball came back to his hand. Bart had played with him twice a week until last year, but of course Bart was much better, stronger and quicker. Bryson was twelve then, but he argued about fouls and the score so often and so long Bart soured on playing, threatening to quit five times before finally doing it.

"He's impossible," he'd said.

"You're his father."

"I'll play again the day he grows up."

JOAN WAS RELIEVED when she saw Bryson playing with a boy who lived at the end of the street. The other boy was quiet and awkward, someone who would give up basketball soon, but for now he was a better opponent for her son than empty air. Now there were real fouls to signal with the whistle and the rehearsed gestures. And though the boy didn't handle the ball as well as her son's imagination, within minutes she heard them arguing.

"Charging," Bryson shouted. "I had position."

The other boy sounded calm when he said, "Settle down. We're not in the NBA."

"Time out," Bryson yelled, and when she looked outside, he was crouched in the grass as if he was in a team huddle while the other boy bounced the ball by what she knew was the chalked three-point line that ran off the end of the asphalt at two places.

"You'll be taking that weak shit home to your momma," Bryson said as he stalked back out on the court. "You bringing nothing but lameness to this party."

"Whatever, ghetto boy," the other boy said, but he pulled up near the foul line and shot an off-balance jump shot that barely caught the front rim, and Bryson dribbled back to the three-point line. "Air mail, special delivery," he shouted as he faked right, then left, and lowered his shoulder into the boy before he picked up his dribble and leaned forward as he launched a flat jump shot that rattled back to front and back again before dropping through the hoop. "And one," he yelled.

The other boy gathered the ball and began to dribble. "No way," he said, and he drove to the hoop, laying the ball up too hard but chasing it down while Bryson stumbled backward and shouted "Charging" again.

"Weak shit," the other boy laughed. "Lameness." He drove again, this time scoring.

Bryson kicked the ball into the garage and disappeared after it, and Joan's heart sank as she listened for the door to the kitchen to open. Instead, he reappeared with a length of chain, swinging it around his head like a lasso. "Where did he find that?" Joan asked herself, but there was no time to answer because Bryson was swinging that chain at the other boy, who backed up into the street to avoid being struck before turning to run.

Joan watched Bryson replace the chain and go back to basketball, calling an immediate foul on the air near the three-point line. He made both free throws before he marked the tablet and tossed the ball into the air, saying, "Hardaway sets a screen for Marbury," raising up for a jump shot that missed badly to the right. Bryson blew the whistle. "Hacking," he yelled, pointing at the air. "Two shots."

"HE'S ACTING OUT or something," Bart said when she told him just before he was ready to run.

"You're not worried?"

"Boys get angry about stupid things. They fight and forget about it. If they didn't, they'd all be dead."

Bart stretched as he talked, one leg and then the other extended, his shorts pulling high up his thighs. "Normal boys don't swing chains like lunatics," Joan said. "You have to be a father now."

"I've been a father for thirteen years. Each and every day."

"You need to face up to things."

Bart stood up straight, flexing his knees as if he meant to begin jogging in place like runners Joan had seen waiting to cross an intersection. "You're with him a lot more than I am," he said. "You know much better than I do what's troubling him."

"He's going to hurt somebody," she said. "I want you to know these things. I want somebody else to learn them."

That night and the next day, after no one called or showed up at the front door, Joan imagined the boy not telling his mother about the swinging chain. When that sounded impossible, she imagined the mother listening and instructing the boy not to go near her son again. She saw the father listening to the story, shaking his head and saying, "Sometimes boys are just assholes." Nothing, Joan thought, will happen except that boy repeating the story to everyone in the eighth grade who will listen.

Two days later, when the mother of the boy her son has chased with a chain walked by with her dog and said nothing to her as she crossed the yard toward her mailbox, Joan was certain she had been labeled unfit and talked about over dinner in a hundred houses.

As SEPTEMBER ENDED, Joan left the shopping to Bart, whose method was to pick up everything that claimed high carbs in three-day cycles. "Shopping makes me late," he said. "This minimizes it because I know where everything is before I get there."

He didn't buy anything else, so Joan rose early on Sundays, entering the store so close to its seven a.m. opening that for three Sundays she was first through the check out line. The fourth Sunday, when she came through the line second, the clerk, a woman who repeated the names of each item as she scanned them, said, "You're running late."

Throughout October, Joan investigated child psychology on the Internet. No one in their immediate family had died since her son was born. No one was sick. They hadn't moved. She found a list of twenty common traumas that precipitate depression and anger, but only parental behavior seemed viable. Of course, it said at the end of the items, this list cannot account for every pronounced change. Perhaps no one is to blame.

When her attention flagged, she learned that it was illegal to drive a car in Alaska while blindfolded. In Kentucky, it was illegal to carry an ice cream cone in your pocket.

There was time to learn that Subway's double meat meatball sub had 1560 calories, a sort of champion of potential weight gain despite the commercials with the skinny guy who used to be fat. Hardee's two-third pound bacon cheese Thickburger was a close second with 1,340 calories, but she couldn't remember Hardee's doing anything but claiming that sandwich was perfect for people who want to make a pig of themselves.

She was afraid she'd start spouting these things aloud, that she'd become one of those people who announced they know the up-to-date number of the people who have died from AIDS as if whoever is listening might give a damn.

When did Bart and Bryson stop using the computer? It was in a room where Joan hadn't seen the door closed in weeks. She stayed awake at least until midnight. From ten o'clock on her husband and son lay motionless in their beds.

When she shut off the computer at 3:30, she poured a glass of wine and set out whatever pasta Bart had stocked in the cupboard. Bryson came home at 3:35, walking up the hill from the school by himself. The weather was more chancy now. Joan imagined the shooting percentages dropping because of the wind and cold.

ONE NIGHT AT eleven o'clock she found an old game on ESPN classic. The Boston Celtics were playing against the Los Angeles Lakers. *The 1986 Championship Series*, it said on the screen. She put the television on mute and watched the way the players moved when they had the ball. What their feet did. Their shoulders and arms. None of the players looked like her son when they were in motion.

They're professionals, she told herself, but there were things she expected her son to have in common with them. The boy who had played for half an hour wasn't in the pictures of any team in the two yearbooks her son owned. She imagined those boys in the pictures, even in 7th and 8th grade, moving in a way that anticipated the men on television. Even in their awkwardness, they would promise to grow into basketball.

SHE ENTERED BRYSON'S room and opened the closet as soon as he left the house. The old notebooks were exactly where they were a month ago, and she lifted one out and read. The Celtics were listed, and the 76ers, the Knicks and the Nets, but the Lakers weren't in the league her son had created. There were two full seasons in the notebook—eighty-two games followed by playoffs. She replaced the notebook carefully and slipped one finger between the pages of the new notebook in the sweater drawer, trying to turn them without moving anything. The current season had barely begun. The 76ers were 11-4, but the Knicks were 3-12, headed, it looked like, for a terrible season even though there were dozens of games left to play. Poor Stephon Marbury, Joan thought. All of those points he scores, yet his team loses almost every time.

She searched Bryson's room then, drawer by drawer, carefully lifting underwear and sweaters. For a while she was afraid of what she'd find, but by the time she was on her knees in the closet, looking underneath two folded blankets, she was afraid she'd find only those notebooks. At last she lifted the mattress and ran her hand over emptiness. She lay on the floor and examined the underside of the box spring, but there was nothing.

As she backed out the door, running the vacuum over the carpet, she thought of the garage. She rummaged through tools and discarded paint. She ran her fingertips over the length of chain hanging from a peg on the back wall and found herself breathing heavily. It took her twenty minutes to settle down.

THE NEXT MORNING, Joan shut off the computer at 10:08. She walked from room to room as if they might contain work to be done. The only thing out of place was a book that lay beside the living room chair Bart sat in for hours before he went to bed.

The pages fanned open to 384 and 385, what looked to be the middle. She closed the book and stared at the back cover where a photograph of a man who looked impossibly young to have written so many pages filled one corner. All of the sentences above and beside him began and ended in quotation marks and were attributed to other people, three of whom she recognized from watching television.

She wondered why anyone would buy a book because someone famous recommended it. She couldn't remember buying one thing because of an advertisement, but when she replaced the book exactly where she found it, she knew that couldn't possibly be true.

By 10:25, she was so restless she took her son's basketball outside, bouncing it with one hand like she knew it was supposed to be done. Her first shot, taken from the foul line, hit high on the backboard, and the ball ricocheted almost directly to her.

Her second shot, aimed lower, hit the left side of the rim and caromed toward the street where it rolled, taking the slope that ran for a hundred yards to the highway. She walked after it, but then, as it gathered speed, she started to jog, imagining the thing rolling under the wheels of a truck, crushed like a careless child.

Joan was half way to the main road when she caught up to it, and she carried it back with two hands, holding it in front of her so the grime that coated it didn't smudge her clothes. When she reached the driveway, she stood close to the hoop and shot three times until the ball dropped through the net. "There," she said aloud and, after wiping it off, returned the ball to its spot just inside the door to her son's room.

The clock read 10:44 when she entered the living room again. She returned to the kitchen and opened the refrigerator. Tucked near the back of one compartment were two plastic cartons half filled with mold-covered meat. She sealed the lids tight and dropped them in the wastebasket. She folded the oldest newspaper her husband had bagged for recycling and covered the cartons before she closed the lid.

She turned on the television and ran through the channels to a station that showed nothing but movies. The volume was still set at mute from the night before, and she stared at the figures on the screen who were dressed in a manner that suggested the future. They walked in a stilted way, and they didn't touch each other. She turned on the sound to hear what sort of music was playing behind the action. An instrumental, nothing she recognized, and she shut the television off.

When she went back to her bedroom, she opened the top drawer of her husband's dresser and ran her hands beneath his underwear. Nothing was there either, and she left the room without opening another drawer. At 11:02 she logged on again. Two of the news headlines on yahoo.com had changed.

On November 1st, Joan sipped from her glass of wine and watched out the back window, hoping her son would not appear. When Bryson plodded up the hill as always, she walked into the living room and sat, holding her wine without drinking until he changed his clothes and went outside with his basketball.

At dinner, she said, "So you're not trying out for the team?"

"What team?" Bryson said.

"Eighth grade basketball."

"No."

Bart laid his fork on his plate and sat up. "You could go tomorrow and tell the coach you had a doctor's appointment," he said, putting both elbows on the table and leaning forward. "It's not too late."

"Charging," Bryson said, suddenly standing up to make a referee's signal.

"Sit down," Bart said. "That's enough of that for one day." Bryson made the T-sign with his hands, and Bart gritted his teeth. "Sit, goddammit."

Bryson T'd him up a second time and said, "You're outta here."

Bart reached across the corner of the table and grabbed Bryson's arm. Joan waited for Bryson to make another call, but he lifted a fork from beside his plate, and she stared as if a whistle would blow and someone would separate them even as Bryson swung the fork and Bart let go, rising from his chair.

"Bryson," she screamed, but he swung again. Bryson looked like someone else's son, a boy in a movie or a newspaper story. Bart stepped around the table and gripped both of Bryson's arms, twisting until Bryson dropped the fork and sat back down in the chair. "Now you sit and keep your hands to yourself and think about who you are," Bart said, and for the next ten minutes the table was as quiet as a basketball court two hours after the game has ended.

THE NEXT NIGHT, no one saying a word about basketball or forks at dinner, Joan drove to one of the roads her husband ran on and parked along a side street. She climbed a path through a vacant lot and stood among a sparse group of trees. Bart had been gone nearly an hour and this, she remembered, was almost exactly half way.

She waited, rechecking her watch to make sure she had the time correct. There was one bird chirping, running what sounded like ten notes in succession every time. She tried to count them, but the sequence was so fast she couldn't be sure. Nine. Ten. Maybe even eleven or twelve. It was so distinctive, she felt ignorant for not recognizing what kind of bird it was. For two minutes there was no other sound but cars traveling along the main highway a hundred yards away.

When a motorcycle came down the side street and parked in front of her car, she tensed, judging, in spite of herself, the distance to the nearest house, but the man who dismounted walked directly onto the porch and through the door of the house beside her car.

She slowed her breathing. The bird seemed to have flown off. Another minute went by, and she couldn't help checking behind her, peering into the thickening trees before she saw her husband approaching. He was running more quickly than she imagined. Like somebody doing a few laps around the high school track. Long, relaxed strides. From where she was standing, she couldn't hear him breathe or see his sweat. She watched him run around a shallow curve and disappear before she walked to her car. She waited exactly six minutes and then she turned and followed his route. A mile later she saw her husband half way up a gradual rise in the road. His stride was shorter now, his arms swinging. He looked so much like a man who wouldn't make it to the top that she was elated.

Four straight days of rain kept Bryson in his room before and after dinner. On each of those days, Bart strode to the table in the warm-up suit he wore now that the weather had cooled. Joan felt like she was looking down the bench where the players who never got in the game sat, but he left at six o'clock now, running for two and a half hours. None of the marathon sites encouraged running so shortly after eating. All of them suggested tapering off as race day approached. The marathon was a week away.

The morning of the fifth day was clear, and as soon as Bart and Bryson were gone, Joan started to walk Bart's training route. Three miles an hour would be easy. She had seven hours, plenty of time to finish before Bryson came home.

She had the odometer Bart used with her. It took her eighteen minutes and fifteen seconds to finish the first mile, but after two miles, she'd used thirty-nine minutes and fifty seconds and sweating inside her jacket. She could feel blisters forming on her feet.

Joan turned back at fifty minutes, two and a half miles exactly, and retraced her steps. When it looked as if she wouldn't get back by the two hour mark, she jogged the last two hundred yards to reach her street before the time was up.

A dog rushed out at her, barking, and she braced herself. "Mystery," she heard a woman's voice call, and she realized it was the mother of the boy her son had chased with a chain. "Sit," the woman said, and the dog, a black lab, did, though it stared at her as if someone had told him Joan was the mother of a boy who swung chains and forks.

"Sorry," the woman said, crossing the lawn. "He knows better."

"It's all right."

"You look like you've had a good workout."

"Five miles," she said.

"Really? That's a long run. You trying to catch up to that husband of yours? I see him take off, and he doesn't come back for hours."

"He's going to run a marathon next Sunday," she said.

"Whoever thinks of these things?" the woman said. "Isn't it like twenty-five miles or something?"

"Twenty-six," Joan said, "and 385 yards."

"Yeah, right, as if another few yards makes a difference."

The dog quivered, but it stayed sitting. The woman looked at him a moment. "Okay, Mystery," she said, and snapped her fingers. The dog rose but didn't move.

"Our boys are in the same grade," Joan said.

"Is that right?"

"Yes."

Mystery growled. The woman looked down and then up again. "I think this dog's an eighth grader, too, sometimes." When the dog growled again, she clapped her hands and it sat. "Well," she said, "take a long shower. You've earned it." She snapped her fingers, and the dog walked alongside her to the porch

Joan was so tired now she sat on the bed to undress, dropping her clothes on the floor. I need to get up and into the shower, she thought, but she didn't move, and then she lay back on the bed. What is it about vigilance? she thought. There is such a necessity in it, though she couldn't name what sort of harm she would bring to those she loved if she stopped.

She worried that she might fall asleep naked, but it was only 10:35, and even if she did, she would wake long before Bryson came home. She closed her eyes and opened them at once, propping herself on her elbows. In the mirror, she could see her shirt and shorts, her scattered shoes and socks and underwear. They looked like they'd been lying there a long time. They looked like they belonged to someone else.

The Habits of Insects

"WE KNOW YOU'RE a Commie spy," George Mueller said, speaking as softly as Johnny Staccato, our favorite television detective, talked to the evil women he seemed to meet nearly every week. George was wrapping a length of clothes line around both his little sister and the tree I was holding her against in the state preserve that started on the other side of the field behind his house.

When she wasn't sobbing, Stacey kept saying she hated the Communists. She said the pledge of allegiance, including the "under God" their father said was one of Eisenhower's worst ideas. It was enough to convince me. As soon as I let go of Stacey and took a couple of steps back so she couldn't kick me, I knew this was an idea way more stupid than anything Eisenhower had ever cooked up.

"We don't believe you," George said, and he pulled out a cigarette and lit it. I was a patrol boy now, but he'd been taken off duty in February because he'd been caught smoking. "Who cares?" he'd said. "I'll be in the high school next year, and you'll still be stuck down here with the babies." Now, he leaned against the tree next to hers and let the cigarette droop from between his lips like a private eye. She was a Commie, all right, he said, and she needed to be left there for the animals because anything she said now would be a lie.

I didn't say a word about my deciding George was an idiot. It wasn't me tying her up instead of hiking with her to the pond where we'd gone swimming together since public school had ended. My father had decided it was okay for me to have a summer vacation because I'd been back at Truman for a year since my mother's dying had ended home schooling forever. Stacey wasn't my sister, so it would be George's choice about what happened to her, whether or not he thought she'd run home and tell on him or just let the game play out. When we started to hike out of the woods, I was busy keeping branches from my eyes because George was bending them forward and letting them go as he passed. When I stepped off the narrow path so they stopped smacking me, there were jagged leaves that opened my ankles, thorns on the brush that smothered everything right up to where the main trail to the service road began.

And then we heard Stacey scream like I thought no Soviet Union lover ever would, tangling us where the path confused itself for a knotted moment. George stopped, but he didn't look back, standing there as if he were sniffing the air. And then he kept going forward, not saying anything when I told him I was going back to check.

I listened for him to start following, but I didn't hear anything but Stacey's second scream just before I stopped where she couldn't see me, standing behind a thicket off to the side. I told myself if she screamed again I'd step out and untie her. I told myself I needed to wait for George to end this, and I crouched down until numbness edged up my legs.

Neither one happened, but during those three minutes of watching, I heard myself swallow and thought I'd surely catch leukemia or whatever other cancer boys got for having anything to do with this. And then I scuffled in place like I was just scrambling back to save her, pushed aside the branches, and untied her.

"I was counting on you," she said. "I knew George wasn't coming back."

Once she was loose, she started to sob. I walked in front of her, holding branches as she ducked, her shoulders quivering, her arms tucked around her waist. When we reached the field, she ran past me without speaking, and I watched her until she disappeared through the Mueller's back door.

"Hey, numb nuts," I heard from behind me, and I spun around so quickly I threw my arms out to the side for balance. "Look at you," George said, stepping out of the woods. "Who did you expect with that scared face? The boogeyman?"

"I thought you went home."

George moved up beside me, put his hands on my shoulders, and turned me so I was facing his house again before he spoke, his voice lowered as if he was telling me a secret. "You know what I did? I doubled back just like you and watched Corey Gillis sitting in the bushes staring at my sister all tied up. I thought you were going to jack off right there on the ground."

With his hands on my shoulders, I felt dizzy. His house looked like it had moved farther away. "I set her free," I said.

"After you got done playing with yourself." He shoved me away, and I kept walking. "Go home before you do that, Gillis. Remember how sexy she looked when you unzip."

That night I watched the story of a scientist turned mute by secret pain. For twenty-five minutes, nothing helped because the doctors believed he'd been driven to madness by noise. The torturers on this show, *Science Fiction Theater*, were always Communists, but the scientist, a free world hero, hadn't cracked, and neither did the doctor who solved the case, deciding total silence was what had made the man a lunatic for sound.

During the last minutes of the show, the doctor mentioned things that prevent such unbearable silence like crickets, raindrops, and even distant traffic. He said the quietest place you know has a comfort of sounds. And after he shocked the patient back to sense by overloading him with decibels, I sat in my room, my father asleep, my sister out somewhere getting drunk, and heard all the sound-effects of midnight, the creaks and groans of stealth. I went to the window like the soon-to-be-murdered, looking for the blade of the crazed, somebody like George Mueller sneaking up on me, and thought that the only way I could be rescued was if I did nothing but pay attention, listening and looking until even evil fell asleep for the night.

"YOU KNOW GEORGE, but I don't know the Muellers," my father said, when I told him my birthday was the same day as Mrs. Mueller's. "They're just our neighbors with a boy your age."

It was true. George had been in our house a hundred times, and I'd been in his a lot, but even when my mother was still alive, our parents had never visited each other. Mr. Mueller worked for the Pennsylvania Liquor Control Board, "a patronage job" according to my father, his way of saying it didn't matter what Mr. Mueller did because he hadn't earned it. "That boy acts older than you," he said. "Like he's more than thirteen."

"He's not much older, Dad," I said. "I'm catching up to him tomorrow." My father glanced at me as if he was surprised to hear my birthday was July 8th. He was working the graveyard shift at the mill now, because being home at night wasn't so important without my mother to be looked after. He was never home for dinner except on weekends and during the summer.

"He'll stay thirteen," I said, "until October."

My sister shook her head. "Mrs. Mueller is going to be thirty, Dad," she said. "Thirty."

"How do you know these things?" he said, but I could see my father was subtracting George's fourteen-to-be like Susan wanted him to and figuring that Mrs. Mueller had gotten pregnant when she was sixteen, that my sister, seventeen since May, was months past that point of no return.

My father nodded, and for a moment I wondered if he was as excited as I was imagining Mrs. Mueller as a sixteen-year-old getting pregnant. And then I thought about Mr. Mueller, how lucky he must have felt to be having sex with a girl as beautiful as Mrs. Mueller must have been.

I didn't care if my father disapproved of the Muellers and would never set foot inside their front door. I went over to their house at least three nights a week because George, since he'd moved in two years ago, was the only boy near my age on our street, which had the state forest on one side and a farm that had been sold to developers on the other. "You'll have plenty of new friends when those houses start going up," my father said from time to time, but right now there was a model home that nobody lived in and three bulldozed piles of dirt.

At night, Mr. Mueller read newspapers. The television was in the game room downstairs, but he stopped us every night I was there to tell us, like my mother had done for nearly two years, one news item he said we needed to know. On the day after my and his wife's birthday, he was more excited than usual when he called us toward him. "Listen to this," he said. "Two Americans were killed at Bien Hoa in Vietnam." Neither of us said anything, and he rattled the newspaper. "Soldiers," he said. "We had soldiers killed."

George said, "Where's that?"

"Vietnam?" Mr. Mueller said. "It's beside Cambodia." And when George shrugged, he added, "Near China."

"Why are there soldiers from the United States in some place I never heard of?" George said, and Mr. Mueller sat up and folded his paper in his lap.

"We're meddling," he said. "We stick our noses in everywhere we're not wanted."

"Okay," George said, and he backed up to the stairs, turned, and disappeared, leaving me with his father.

"For a minute there, I thought George might want to know something," Mr. Mueller said. He poured a splash of Four Roses onto the melting ice cubes in his glass and unfolded the *Pittsburgh Press*, the paper he read even though we lived twenty-five miles from the city, and everybody else on our street had a box that said *Beaver County Times*. I wondered if it was true what my father said, that he got a discount on whiskey because he worked at the Control Board.

"It's time for *Peter Gunn*," I said. "He's just in a hurry."

"You keep him company then," Mr. Mueller said. "His time will come soon enough. It's just a question of where."

That was the way Mr. Mueller always talked, sounding like he was getting ready to say something mysterious and important, and then dribbling off into something that made you want to say "Huh?"

Since school had ended, Mr. Mueller had made George and me follow him through the woods every Saturday while he named things like the trees we passed, calling out hickory, hemlock, beech, and ash like I was still being homeschooled. He was hard of hearing, deaf in one ear from something that happened in the Korean War, so when we wanted him to move on, we had to stand to his left and say *sure* or *okay* after he repeated elderberry, sassafras, blue spruce, birch.

Stacey, who was going to be eleven in a few weeks, was never asked to come along, and I wondered, for a while, whether she didn't have to do anything with George anymore, that she'd told the Commie spy story or how George pulled her top down when we were swimming, and all of these nature hikes were part of a plan to make George see the woods was something more than a place to hurt people. What I knew for sure was she'd never gone swimming with us again, and George didn't want to do anything in the woods but get our hikes overwith and make fun of his father.

George would say *bitch* and *bastard*, words he'd started using regularly in the spring, while he walked on his father's right, looking over at me and smirking. "Mountain laurel," Mr. Mueller would say, and George would mumble "motherfucker," his father nodding. "Skunk cabbage," his father said, and George would murmur "Shit-for-brains."

After a month of Saturdays, Mr. Mueller looked at me more than he did at George when he named things. By then, he'd told us that he wanted us to learn how to take care of ourselves because we'd need to when the next war started, the big one. "The grand finale," he called it. and that's why he was teaching us the forest as if he was teaching the times tables, automatic with shape and size, spouting the habits of insects as if we could memorize them like the products of one-digit numbers.

He gave George and me our own canteens that were always filled with ice cold water. He had us each carry a banana and a bag of peanuts still in the shell. "None of those grease and salt things your mother feeds you," he said to George, and we always had to carry the peels and the shells back to their house, his hands staying free because he just sipped from his canteen and never ate anything during any hike.

"You know what my old man has in his canteen?" George said on the way back one Saturday. "Seven and seven."

I nodded like I knew what he was talking about, but George snickered. "Seagram's Seven and Seven-Up," he said. "In case you want to stop pretending you know from shit about mixed drinks."

I nodded again, but Mr. Mueller started talking about crickets then, how we could know the temperature if we counted their chirps for thirteen seconds and added forty. "It's not any harder than converting Celsius to Fahrenheit," he said.

I expected him to tell us to listen to crickets for him, that somewhere in the background of noises around us was a natural thermometer as long as we carried a stopwatch and could distinguish the difference between forty or fifty rapid chirps while we were following a sweep hand.

"You have to listen at night, though," Mr. Mueller said, "because that's when the snowy tree cricket starts up. They're the most accurate of all the crickets, and they synchronize their chirps so you don't get confused."

Maybe it was possible. There wouldn't be many nights when those crickets would be chirping more than twice per second; there might be a reason why you'd want to know whether it was sixty-two instead of sixty-four degrees. "We'll camp out some night," he said then. "We'll see if you remember."

George motioned me to stand beside him on his father's right. "Wait until we catch some of those crickets and set them on fire. They'll chirp a mile a minute and tell us how hot it is when a bug fries."

"YOU NEVER KNOW what Mueller might be doing out there," my father said after he came home from church the next day. "Him with his ideas and such."

He was facing Susan as if even though she came home after midnight every Saturday, she was the expert on Mr. Mueller in our house. She looked up from where she was half asleep on the couch. "It's the middle of the day, Dad," she said. "They're in a place they know. Anyway, Mueller is some kind of Boy Scout. He won't forget which way is up even if he gets loaded."

"How about you?" my father said, but he didn't raise his voice like he did when they talked about the boys who picked her up every Saturday and Sunday. He'd taken to drinking himself, at least on weekends. Susan rolled over and put her head on a throw pillow, but she'd said enough to keep my father from forbidding me to go into the woods with Mr. Mueller.

I was glad he didn't want me around on Saturdays when he spent all of his time fixing things and taking care of the yard while he drank gin over ice. My father didn't watch television or read a newspaper, so he didn't talk about anything at all. "I have to believe Tony Mueller likes his drink more than others, that's all," my father said. "I have to believe if he was a Communist, he wouldn't get a job from the Republicans like he did."

The rest of what I learned about the Muellers that summer drifted toward me from my sister when she was sneaking drinks after our father went to work. "Mrs. Mueller can't get enough from her husband," she said. "You keep an eye out and you'll see she's always ready for strange."

"Okay," I said.

Susan took a sip of her drink and laughed. "Strange, Corey. Men besides her husband fucking her when he's not around. She's really pretty, right? You can see that right away, can't you?"

She lounged back in her chair in a way that meant to tell me she'd had some "strange" herself. "You know that Dad's driven Tony Mueller home a few times from the Plank Road Tavern." I didn't say anything, but as I turned to leave, she added, "Dad's getting to be a regular, too."

On Friday nights Mrs. Mueller watched television with us because she liked *77 Sunset Strip*. Stacey would watch that show with us because having her mother there shut George up from repeating things during commercials like how he wanted to be a private eye so he could screw a woman with different-colored hair every night of the week. Mrs. Mueller served all three of us root beer in frosted mugs and put a bowl of mixed nuts on the coffee table. "Nuts are quiet," she said. "You can't have potato chips when you need to hear things." And then to show us what she meant, she always picked out two Brazil nuts and bit into them. "See?" she'd say, smiling, "even these big ones don't make noise," and then she'd settle back with her gin and tonic to watch.

After Kookie, the cool parking-lot attendant, combed his hair and the case was closed, Mrs. Mueller told jokes. "Here's a good one," Mrs. Mueller would say. "The little moron was playing with matches and burned the house down. 'Your daddy's going to kill you when he gets home,' his mother said, but the little moron laughed and laughed because he knew his daddy was asleep on the couch."

George laughed so root beer shot out of his nose, but his sister looked so disgusted I kept myself from even smiling. It wasn't that hard to do. I'd heard that joke in fourth grade. Even Ed Benson, the dumbest boy in the room, rattled them off at recess. "Why did the little moron take his ruler to bed?" he'd ask, and when nobody answered, he'd shout, "He wanted to see how long he slept."

Mrs. Mueller finally asked about my straight face. "What do you think is funny?" she said.

"I don't know," I said. "I guess whatever I laugh at."

She looked at me as if she'd just noticed I was thirteen years old. Stacey nodded. "George thinks everything's funny. He laughs all day like a little moron," she said.

Mrs. Mueller took a sip of her drink and smiled. "You don't laugh all day, do you, Corey? You look like you're full of seriousness."

I glanced out the window behind her and hoped something would happen in their back yard, but everything was at ground level, what rabbits and squirrels saw. At the moment I was thinking about whether Stacey would end up having breasts like her mother, and whether or not Stacey, just two years younger than I was, thought about that, too, what would happen to her body during the next couple of years. Already, I was worrying about going bald early like my father, something, I was sure, that would keep girls like Stacey from seeing me as secretive and moody, somebody who'd grown up to be like Johnny Staccato.

When I was leaving, Mrs. Mueller followed me outside. I waited on the grass in the twilight because it seemed like she had something to say. "The world's full of weaknesses," she said. "You have to laugh at all of it. It's not cruel."

"Okay," I said.

"There's a million drunk jokes."

"Okay."

"There's a million religion jokes. A million sex jokes."

I stood there in the half-light and stared at her, watched her breasts rise and fall, and I didn't look away. Suddenly I thought I knew the secret of having my way with girls was mystery, that keeping things to myself would make me irresistible. She laughed a little, the ice cubes jiggling in her nearly empty glass.

And as soon as I turned away, walking toward home, I was convinced that was wrong, that Mrs. Mueller had been warning me to lighten up or I'd turn into somebody like her husband, a man to be cheated on.

"I'M GOING OUT," Mrs. Mueller said to George and me when we came back from our walk in the woods late the next afternoon. She was wearing the kind of dress my mother had worn twice a year on her birthday and her anniversary, and she was telling us because Mr. Mueller had walked upstairs without speaking.

She was holding a drink and keeping an eye on the front window. "God," she said, "what did you do, run out of things early to talk about with nature boy?"

"It's going to rain," George said.

"Really? Did the chipmunks tell you that?"

I kept my mouth shut. I was sure Mr. Mueller was standing at the window in George's bedroom that looked out over the driveway. "You'll see," George said.

Mrs. Mueller looked away from the window and poked at the newspapers on the dining room table. "Two of them every day," she said. "Who has time to read two newspapers except somebody who doesn't do anything else?" She glanced up again at the window, her free hand turning the papers so their headlines faced her. "And this one, the *New York Times*. We don't live anywhere near New York. We don't know anybody in this newspaper."

I heard a car pull up, but it didn't turn into the driveway and the engine didn't shut off. I listened for Mr. Mueller's footsteps, but if he was above me, I didn't hear anything. "Well, see you later," Mrs. Mueller said, and then, just before she closed the front door behind her, she turned and said, "It's just a movie. Tony has his papers to keep him busy, and I have Rock Hudson." George didn't move, but I watched out the window, and when she opened the door of the car, the light came on inside, and I could see the man who was driving was wearing a coat and tie.

"He's not Rock Hudson, but she doesn't care," George said. He turned and smacked my shoulder with his fist. "Your sister doesn't care either, does she?"

"What's that supposed to mean?"

George hit me again, but only a tap this time. "You know. I heard she does everything we're always dreaming about."

"I never heard that."

"You're her brother," George said. "You're the guy nobody tells the stories to. If you didn't live in the same house with her, you'd know she was something else."

EARLY THE NEXT week, Mr. Mueller stopped us by waving the *New York Times* like a fan. "Here's one for the history books," he said. "Nixon and Khrushchev had an argument about appliances in Russia."

"Who's Khrushchev?" George said, but I thought he was just acting like he didn't recognize the name to make his father angry.

"A man who could start World War III some day."

"So could Nixon," George said.

"Well, it looks like Nixon might have won this argument because the United States has better household goods than the Soviets."

"Good," George said. "Let's get a new television."

"And Khrushchev almost got hit by a remote-controlled dishwasher that lost its bearings. I'd like to have seen that."

"Watch television," George said. "Maybe the news will have pictures."

"If there were good pictures, they'd be in the *Times*," Mr. Mueller said, but George had drifted to the top of the stairs, and Mr. Mueller didn't shout, "Stop," when he turned away.

Downstairs, even though it wasn't Friday, Mrs. Mueller and Stacey were sitting on the couch without the television on. "I'm telling Stacey about the model home I walked through today," she said. "You should see what's coming for whoever moves into the new plan."

Stacey looked uncomfortable, like she thought because *77 Sunset Strip* wasn't on that George would start in about the breast sizes of her girlfriends. Mrs. Mueller laughed then, the ice cubes in her drink rattling off the oversized plastic cup she was holding. "You know what your sister said just now?" she said, and George grinned because Stacey swiveled and looked over the back of the couch as Mrs. Mueller kept going. "She said, 'Are there people living in that house?'"

George snorted. "Can you imagine her, twelve years old this January, saying something like that?" Mrs. Mueller said. "I couldn't either. How could it stay a model house if people lived there. Things would get used."

Stacey turned back toward us, her face suddenly defiant as the Communists on *Science Fiction Theater*. "I just wondered," she said. "I wondered what the people would look like."

"Well, I couldn't imagine," Mrs. Mueller said, her voice going soft. "That would be something, though, wouldn't it?"

THE NEXT SATURDAY, Mr. Mueller told us he had a surprise. "I marked off a kind of maze in the woods this morning," he said. "I'll show you a sample of trail signs, and then you get to see if you can find the way to the end of the maze. I'll just follow along behind."

For once, George looked interested. He paid attention while Mr. Mueller explained the intentions of stones and twigs and slash marks. "You go to the left when there's a stone on stone and one smaller one to its left side," Mr. Mueller said, and George didn't say, "Check my stones," like I thought he would for something so obvious even the little moron would understand. "This is detective work," he said. "Everything's a clue."

Once we started, Mr. Mueller stayed about ten feet behind us, but he kept talking. "You're going to need to know everything sooner than you think," he said. "Nixon will be president before you know it, and then we're in for it."

George was a whiz. He turned right and left and straight through knee-high weeds I didn't recognize. Sure enough, on the other side sat two stones to tell us we were still on the trail, but all I could think of was

Who else would mark the woods like this if we needed to find our way?

George got us to a sign that said YOU WIN in less than an hour. Two Mounds bars were taped to the sign, and Mr. Mueller said, "Help yourself, boys. Just carry the wrappings out of the woods."

We retraced our steps, but even though we'd only been gone an hour, Mr. Mueller didn't seem to have any more lessons for us. "I bought Coca-Cola, too," he said as we crossed the field toward his house. "You might as well enjoy these things before they stop being made."

"Coca-cock," George said, walking to his father's right. "Coca-cunt."

Mr. Mueller was smiling. "The Soviets are sending rockets toward the moon. Pretty soon they'll land one, and then we'll see what Nixon has to say about the power of dishwashers."

I waited for George to come up with one more obscenity before we reached the front door, but just as we stepped onto the porch, the door opened and a man I didn't recognize stepped out. He had a cigarette in his right hand, the ash so long it broke off and fluttered onto the cement. "Hi there," he said, bringing the cigarette to his lips before Mrs. Mueller spoke from behind the screen door.

"This is Stan," she said. "He's thinking of building a house in the new development."

Stan took a long drag and exhaled. "Nice neighborhood," he said, but Mr. Mueller stepped past him without answering, pushed the screen door hard enough to make Mrs. Mueller lurch back for balance, and began to climb the stairs. "Well," Stan said, "you boys have a good day," and then he walked down the driveway and started down the street to where I could see a car parked three houses away.

"That guy looks like Johnny Staccato," George said. "I bet he's a private eye."

"Corey," Mrs. Mueller said. "Could you run along?"

She held the screen door open, and George stepped inside. "Sure," I said, already turning to cut across the grass.

MONDAY NIGHT, WHEN I came through the living room with George, Mrs. Mueller was sitting in a chair holding the *Pittsburgh Press*. "Surprise," she said, but Mr. Mueller didn't look at her when she spoke.

George and I waited until Mrs. Mueller spoke again. "We've been taking pictures of the earth from space," she said. "It's like a big blue marble when you see us from up there."

"I thought everybody knew that," George said.

Mrs. Mueller smiled. "But now there's proof."

Mr. Mueller stood up then, folding the *Times* and tapping it against the palm of his free hand. "You know what the Soviets are going to be able to do next?" he said. "They'll be able to take pictures of the dark side of the moon. Now that will be something."

Mrs. Mueller looked up. "Why?" she said, sounding genuinely surprised. "It'll just look like the side we see all the time. It's like seeing the other side of a rubber ball. You know what's there before you roll it over."

Mr. Mueller slapped the newspaper harder against his palm. "There's always a chance until you know for sure. The earth is for sure."

"We're not on the moon, Tony. This is where we are."

Mr. Mueller held the newspaper steady. "The Soviets will be on the moon," he said. "That's where they'll be."

Mrs. Mueller laid the *Pittsburgh Press* on the floor and stood up. "What are you boys watching?" she said. "Who's solving crimes in half an hour tonight? Peter Gunn? Mr. Lucky? Johnny Staccato?" She disappeared down the stairs, George close behind her.

Mr. Mueller tapped me on the shoulder with the newspaper. "It's not about her pleasure," he said. "It's about when it comes through my door like some sort of repairman."

I kept my eyes on the *Press*, but it was too far away to read even the headlines. "You understand?" I heard Mr. Mueller say, but he didn't tap me again, and I started toward the basement stairs. My father was right. Mr. Mueller wasn't any more a Communist than Nixon. "You know what the most important thing you should learn in high school is?" he said as I reached the doorway, and I paused to let him finish. "There's more to life than fucking."

"Okay," I said. Just like that. As if he'd asked me to bring the newspaper from across the room. I heard the television come on, and I was afraid to turn around and look at him, because I believed, in that moment, Tony Mueller would have been right to hit me if I did.

"Why did the little moron take his ladder to church?" Mrs. Mueller said. She'd followed me onto the porch after I'd made an excuse and told her I had to leave instead of watching television.

"For High Mass," I answered right away, and she pursed her lips.

Mrs. Mueller turned her back to me and curled her fingers around the screen door handle before she spoke. "My husband wants to tell you to be careful with yourself," she said. "To make sure you know where you are in this world, but all those names he tells you, they're all for things you don't have to worry about, so you need to pay attention to what's left over to learn after he's finished with you."

She talked toward the screen door, but I thought she understood that I would hear her better if I didn't see her face as she spoke. She opened the screen door without turning, and the porch, lit by the floodlight that beamed toward it from the side of the garage, seemed like all the white space at the end of the first paragraph of a term paper, something to fill in to keep the idea going after you found out you only had three sentences worth of things to say.

THE NEXT SATURDAY, I was surprised when Susan said it was a bad idea for me to camp out overnight with George and Mr. Mueller. "There's only another two weeks until school starts," Dad said, looking more surprised than I was by Susan suggesting caution. "Tony's able to get up and go to work every day. And there hasn't been a problem on a Saturday all summer."

"Night is different than day," Susan said.

I thought my father might say something bitter and nasty to Susan, but he didn't change expression when he said, "There are worse things than a few drinks."

"If it was a sleepover, you'd say no," Susan said.

"You bet I would."

"We'll see who's right when he gets back, then, I guess," she said, one of those things that made me reconsider Susan, even when she sounded as if she was wrong.

CAMPING TURNED OUT to be mostly work—pitching a tent, digging a pit for a fire, carrying wood. Mr. Mueller said, "Pay attention," and, "Do it right," so many times, I wished he was drinking instead of giving us orders without his canteen in his hands.

George and I fell asleep early, but Mr. Mueller shook us awake even though it was still dark, and as soon as we stirred, he started striding toward the woods. "Walk over this way, boys," he said. George started to groan, but then he kept the sound in his throat and his father, on our left, twenty feet away, couldn't have heard it. "Over here."

Mr. Mueller made his way so easily I knew he'd been hiking in this direction while we were asleep. My watch said 4:15. Twice I caught myself, tripping over roots, the trees, mostly maples and locusts, close together here. If George stumbled, I didn't notice, and Mr. Mueller, even though he glanced back every ten steps, looked as if he was on a sidewalk. I started to shiver, but if the snowy tree crickets were telling me it was less than fifty degrees, I didn't hear them.

"I want you both to see something," Mr. Mueller finally said, and when we ducked under the branches of a weeping beech, it was like entering the hallway of a house and there, ten feet in front of us, was a drop-off so we could see over the undergrowth and the trees to where a cone of pale yellow light had formed near the horizon.

"Look," he said, and because there was no moon, I guessed that light was in the east. And then, because my watch read 4:22, I thought he meant us to know the H-Bomb had finally fallen, that our campground was fortunate to be fifty miles from Pittsburgh, more than 300 from New York, the city I guessed was first to explode.

George sat on the edge of the overlook, his feet dangling. I stared at the end of the world, thinking of Mr. Mueller watching the sky all night because the *New York Times* had foretold the beginning of World War III. I waited for him to explain what would follow, and when that glow faded, the first question I managed, thinking radiation, was "How far away was that?"

"How far away is the sun?" Mr. Mueller said, sounding so symbolic I expected to be dead that day until he added, "Now you can say you've seen a false dawn. Now you've seen something special."

George pitched a stone over the edge and pushed himself up. "See my sperm," he said into his father's right ear.

"You boys go back to sleep," Mr. Mueller said. "George, I bet you know the way."

I nodded as if he'd included me in that assessment, but as soon as I turned, I was lost. It seemed darker now, but George was like Daniel Boone, and he moved so quickly and quietly I was afraid he'd leave me behind.

I broke branches, fell once, and began to sweat, but I stayed close enough to keep him in sight. In the tent, a few minutes later, I pulled my sleeping bag up to my chin and said, "You think he's staying up all night?"

"Who cares?" George said, and when I didn't answer, trying to keep from shaking, he added, "It's always something nobody's ever heard of. It's all stupid shit you don't need to know."

WHEN WE WOKE up for real at eight o'clock, Mr. Mueller wasn't in his tent, but George began to circle the camp site, spiraling out until I saw him pause. "Jesus Christ," he said, pointing until I stood beside him. "He left us trail signs. If we don't follow, who knows when he'll come back."

"Maybe there's Cocoa Puffs for breakfast if we find him."

"Cocoa prick," George said, though his father wasn't walking beside him.

I knew the first forked twig George pointed at, long to the far side of us, told us we had a big distance to go. I knew the stone on stone that followed ten paces later reminded us we were on the trail. But George was cursing to himself like somebody who wanted to find his father and yell, "Fuck you," into his good ear. And then George sped up, beginning to pull away from me, so it didn't matter what the twigs and stones said because all I had to do was jog after him, staying close enough that I didn't have to remember the significance of bark slashes and stone stacks until he stopped, ten minutes later, at three stones piled into a tower.

"Danger," George said, though I wasn't sure he was right. I thought it just meant *stop*, that we were to wait right there. For one stupid second, I thought Mr. Mueller had kept us from knowing the cone of light really was a bomb blast, and that he had dug us a bomb shelter, the door to it hidden somewhere near our feet. I looked down the trail to where it turned into a thicket of sumac. In front of those close-knit trees was a large stone with a smaller one on top.

And so I was two steps behind George when he pushed aside the sumac and said "Dad?" just before I heard the shot go off so close to George I expected him to grab his chest and collapse in a bloody heap until he pushed me aside and began to run.

I stood beside the stacked stones and counted to one hundred by fives with my eyes closed as if I was "it" in hide and seek. Every sound George was making as he sprinted through the woods disappeared, but now even I could find my way back. George had broken branches and snapped twigs. He might as well have ridden a motorcycle from the sumac thicket to the camp site.

"He could have waited," Susan said that afternoon. "If he wanted to teach somebody a lesson, he could have walked in on his wife and done it there. What kind of man shoots himself in front of boys?"

"I'm thankful he wasn't the man who could do worse," my father said. "You getting my drift?" and Susan raised a finger to her lips and held it there so long I knew exactly what my father meant.

I told them I was going for a walk, that I was all right, that it was George they needed to worry about. "Can you imagine the look on their faces?" I heard my father say after I left the room. "No matter what he says, I know Corey looked. Anybody would. I hope he never has to have that expression on his face again."

I waited in the hall, holding my breath. "You're thinking backwards," Susan said. "You're seeing those faces from the wrong direction. It's the look on Mueller's face that nobody should see."

And then they both shut up, listening, I was sure, for the front door to close behind me. I let it slam so they could keep talking. I didn't care about anything they would say if they thought I could hear. It looked to me that what people kept to themselves was most important to them, and that if I ever wanted to know anything, I'd have to listen when they didn't speak.

When I walked outside, I headed for the state forest, telling myself I was going to read about false dawns, study up so I understood what Mr. Mueller had shown us, but even then, it sounded like the promise I made to keep my room clean.

As soon as I took three steps along the main trail, I stopped and listened, trying to make out something I hadn't heard before. Bird calls, rustling among the bushes, something digging in the earth. Everything seemed amplified; I started to expect cricket chirps in the daylight, a girl screaming.

"It's space debris," Mr. Mueller had said from the dark at the edge of the overlook, and I imagined the small particles of an exploded Earth drifting toward somebody who knew, like George's father, what false dawn was, how dust could glow when aligned exactly right in the moonless night. In ten days, school would begin twenty-five miles from Pittsburgh, still there, and I was going back as an eighth grader whose friend's father had killed himself so close to where I stood I could make out his shattered face when I reached one hundred and opened my eyes.

Side Effects

My first night at Mineo's, Herman Rumbaugh, the owner, and him no more Italian than I am, handed me a shirt striped to match Italy's flag and pointed to the guy slipping insulators around boxes on the counter and told me, "That there is Sorry Bob, and you ought to ride a shift with him to see how things work."

"I get it," I started in, figuring to discover the delivery habits of Sorry Bob some other way besides firsthand, but he waved me off.

"You need to get Mineo's," he said. "There's more to delivery than driving a car."

Sorry Bob laughed as we walked to his car, him holding all the boxes and bags even though I had two hands and didn't use a cane. "No tips for you," he said. "It sucks for sure."

When he opened the door to the rusty Plymouth, I saw his backseat was gone. Sorry Bob laid the boxes on the floor where the seat should have been. "What the fuck, I don't need a back seat," he said as if I'd been thinking out loud. "And this way everything lays level so the cheese don't slide or some such shit as that. Customers remember. Some of them anyway. And them's the tippers whose doors you want to be knocking on."

It looked as if he'd laid a toddler's picture puzzle on the floor, one of those kind with big pieces that make a puppy if the kid gets everything lined up right.

"How long you been doing this?" I asked.

"Six years. Going on seven. I got this wife now, and she's been telling me she's with child."

It sounded like he was quoting from the Bible. *With child*—that was Mary or maybe Abraham's wife when she was so old nobody gave her a chance of getting pregnant. I couldn't help looking back at those six pizzas, four large and two medium, each of them supporting a bag of breadsticks or a foil-wrapped meatball sub.

"Yeah," he said. "I know. A kid means a backseat's important again."

"Maybe there's a way to strap one of those car seats to the wall in the back," I said, friendly as I could muster.

He lifted his hands off the wheel and punched the ceiling with both fists. "Maybe there's a way to have peace on Earth, good will toward men." He put one hand back on the wheel and thrust the other my way. "I'm Bobby Scheib," he said. "You?"

"Russ Yordy," I said, taking his hand. It felt so calloused I was embarrassed, but if he was evaluating how soft I was, he didn't let on.

"Welcome aboard."

"Thanks," I said, shifting my feet when something hard rolled against my heels.

Before I even identified the thing as a baseball bat, Bobby said, "Insurance," as if he was certain my changing posture couldn't be from any ordinary sort of discomfort. "Go ahead. Pick it up."

I lifted what I saw was a Louisville Slugger, Sammy Sosa model. "Old school," I said, but I was paying attention to how part of the handle was sawed off, the rest wrapped with double-sided tape that caught my right hand like flypaper.

"People know there's cash and such in here," Bobby said. "You ought to be getting yourself some."

I worked my hand off the tape and hefted the butt end of the bat. "You ever use this?"

"Not yet, but ain't that what insurance is? Something you have and hope to God you never use?"

What I wanted to ask him a minute later after he hadn't offered up another word of encouraging conversation was how he'd come by his nickname, but I felt the car slowing and decided to wait on that until we'd made a few deliveries. We passed six driveways in the dark, and I started to think about getting hit from behind while Sorry Bob was seeing if he could deliver a pizza without touching his brakes.

By the seventh driveway we were down to speed bump pace, and Sorry Bob eased the emergency brake back, jerking us to a stop. "The brakes is all shot to hell," he said. "Thank Christ I know the route so I can manage." I thought of curves and down slopes and just how little I was going to make on this job. It was hardly a menu to go over twice, looking for a favorable combo. "You just follow me on up and help wish for this fella here to have his beer buzz on and not slipping down yet into the time zone where the clock is set to piss and moan and near to exact change."

RUMBAUGH HAD A small load of orders stacked when we got back, Bobby coasting to where the lot sloped uphill a bit even though it left us six slots from the door, five of them empty. "It looks short," Bobby said.

"It don't look, it is," Rumbaugh said, "but they're quick hauls."

Bobby shrugged. "I can wait and see."

"I got new guy here to be doing that."

Bobby looked my way for a quick second before he picked up the pizzas and the address slips, but Rumbaugh was already guiding me to the phone. "It's always 'Mineo's, how can I help you?' Nothing else but the order, the address, the phone number, then 'Thirty minutes, thank you' at the end. Got it?"

"Sure," I said, watching Bobby head out.

"We'll see soon enough," Rumbaugh said, leaving me to feel useless for ten minutes watching him make two pizzas and three subs for the family that was sitting in one of the three booths and the couple parked at the small table in the corner. When the phone finally rang, I answered exactly on script. Two large, one mushroom, one pepperoni—Rumbaugh grunted when I passed him the order with an address and phone number.

Ten minutes later, when I'd handled two more phone calls, one for delivery and one for pick-up, he handed me a township map that was so detailed every street was named, even the ones in the two trailer courts. "Any place outside of this map is another planet as far as Mineo's is concerned," he said. "You study on that every chance you get. You think you know your way around, but there's a test every time you go out that door with boxes and bags in your hands."

"Okay," I said.

He rang up both sit-down customers and checked the oven. "It's Tuesday," he said. "A slow night, but it'll get you broke in."

His voice sounded softer, and with nobody around, I said, "How'd Bobby come by his nickname?"

Rumbaugh squinted at me a moment before he slapped a box down for the large veggie he had coming out. "Sorry Bob? Fuck, you'll see soon enough. He's been apologizing for fucking up so long everybody calls him that."

"He looked to be doing fine tonight."

"Well, even the blind squirrel..." Rumbaugh started, but then he seemed distracted, looking me over then looking at my order slips, back and forth like I'd given him a fake ID. "I never hired on an adult before," he said.

"Bobby's in his 20s."

"He was eighteen fresh out of school when he signed on. So was Chaz, you'll see him around. Kids, and still kids for that matter, not middle ages like you."

"Thirty-seven isn't middle aged."

"You better hope it isn't," Rumbaugh said, "but it makes me wonder what gets a man your age showing up for this kind of work when he's a citizen who can read and write English."

SEEING HOW RUMBAUGH thought I was maybe overqualified, there was some bit of pressure on me when I drove off on my own with pizzas and strombolis and toasted subs. Enough to make me conjure up synonyms for "sorry," what I might be called before too long. *Pitiful*, I thought, before I slipped into approximations like *worthless, useless,* and just plain old *shit-for-brains*.

My first customer took the pizza and gave me a ten for a $9.25 medium pie, but my second, a guy, regrettably, with no shirt, looked to be talkative. "You new?" he said. "Bobby quit?"

"No."

The man looked relieved. "Tyler, who brought cold half the time then," he said. He let his jelly-gut sag even farther. "Good. I was afraid Bobby'd been let go, him ready to be a Dad and all."

"You know Bobby besides delivery?"

"Not rightly. Just small talk at the door. He's excited as all get out about being Poppa Bobby."

"He mentioned it right off."

He put out fifteen dollars for the large, two-topping pie on special that ran $12.95. "You keep that change. You must have kids half grown, and that's a cost to bear."

"Thanks."

"You tell Bobby, 'Don't be no stranger.'"

It turned out half the customers were one dollar tippers, handing me the dollar or a hand full of coins after I'd made change, making a ceremony of it. Half the others were ten per centers. I could live with that, but when some went with fifteen or twenty per cent, I starred that address on the map.

Easy enough, the whole thing, though I caught a few checking their watches while they counted out bills and change. Mineo's was punctual. I got it.

BACK AT MY apartment around eleven, I heard Joplin, my cat, skitter down the hall. First thing I did was check the living room and my bedroom, sniffing. Since Janelle, after a four year stay, had moved out, Joplin had taken to pissing on my leather couch and chair. I thought she'd get over whatever anger a cat feels, but it had been three months, the last two with the furniture covered with aluminum foil. That stopped Joplin's nonsense except when I forgot to re-cover on the occasional night I drank too much to rental movies on the tv that was otherwise dark since I'd had the cable shut off.

It was hard seeing my furniture that way. The one time, since Janelle, a woman came home with me, that's the first thing she asked. "I'd have that cat put down," she said, and I waited for fifteen minutes and one drink before I told her I was feeling sick and would drive her home before I felt worse.

Right after that, the cat pissed on my bed, something I wouldn't spread foil over, so I'd taken to shutting the door, leaving her the slick, hard surface of the bathroom and kitchen as well as the spare room where her litter box was, nothing there but a beat up couch that housed a pull-out bed, what she'd never soiled even though I left it uncovered for her.

THURSDAY, WHEN OUR shifts ended, like every week day, at ten, Bobby called me over to his car where it sat six slots down. He popped the trunk, reached into a cooler, and pulled out two beers. "You're official now. Your cherry's busted."

"It's a job," I said, taking the beer. "It'll do until it doesn't."

"You part-time somewheres else?"

"No."

"There's hell to pay doing double." Bobby dropped his empty in the cooler and pulled out two more. "You got some catching up to do."

"I'm going slow these days."

"Right." Bobby snapped open one and held the other along his thigh, looking like he wanted to keep me standing there a few minutes longer. He took a long pull and laughed like there was a cartoon playing in his head. "I'm thinking about working part-time at the porn shop down to the highway, you know where."

"There's a job," I said, buying time.

"I got a better one for you to consider on," Bobby said. "I was what they call a human subject once. It pays good, and all you have to do is swallow what they give you and let them watch for a while. Most of the time you're doing nothing but watching television and getting paid."

"Nothing happened?"

"Oh, something happened, all right. I had myself some dizzy spells and such. Fell right there in front of them one time. Fainted. You know. Nothing serious. It's all gone away."

"What did you take?"

"Damned if I know, but when I see those ads on the tv, and it says side effects may be dizziness or fainting, I think maybe that's what I ate back then and they figured out it was worth it not matter the black outs."

Joplin stayed hid when I returned. I looked under the couch and in the empty closet in the spare room, closing the door before checking the bathroom and the kitchen where there were so few hiding places I knew she was in the living room with me as I sat in the dark waiting for her to decide to come out. I left the stove light on. I sat, aluminum foil beside the chair, until one a.m. I didn't move. It was like watching a late movie, I told myself, waiting to see what happened, but the cat never appeared. I walked into the kitchen to turn out the stove light, and when I returned, remembering the foil, I heard Joplin's paws land on the wooden floor, the piss on the chair warm when I laid my hand on the cushion for confirmation.

FRIDAY WAS CRAZY with deliveries, the table and two booths full. The whole crew was on, Chaz working orders and doing bus boy stuff while Bobby and I came and went.

Just after ten, the place shutting down, Rumbaugh pulled me aside. "There was a family in here tonight, you know, a husband and wife and three kids like regular people, and you know what the father said to me?"

"No idea."

"That when he saw you, it knocked his socks off seeing as how you worked here way back when he wasn't the father of nobody at all."

"I guess that's so, but it was temporary," I said, but when Rumbaugh's eyes narrowed, I added, "A summer job. Nothing to put on an application or anything like that."

"You worked here in the summer once?"

"Eighteen years ago. I was in college then."

"He didn't say anything about that."

"It didn't work out."

Rumbaugh looked curious for a second, his beefy arms folded up on the counter, his face tilted up from where his double chin usually folded right into his neck. I thought he might have been a powerful man once, maybe still, if he got you before he was winded. "But you went? You were smart?"

"Two years. I went and then I didn't."

When I got home I took the foil off the chair and sat on the carpet ten feet away. I waited in the near-dark for two hours, but Joplin didn't show. Some time after one a.m., I fell asleep and woke, what turned out to be minutes later, to the smell of piss. The next afternoon I called the vet and made an appointment. "For fixing you one way or the other," I said to Joplin as she drank water from her dish.

Sunday night, the place empty, Rumbaugh started telling a story about one of the regulars, a guy my age who picked up every other day, half plain, half pepperoni. "So he was either splitting a pie three days a week or alternating with himself. The guy 's telling me how his cat has these kittens, he doesn't know how, the dumb fuck, and nobody will take them and he doesn't have the heart to toss the sack of them off a bridge like you have to. Instead, he tells me he took them up to the state forest three weeks ago and dumped them, thinking maybe they'd do all right there. That dumb fuck. Those kittens would've been better off at the bottom of the river." Rumbaugh snorted once. "Can you imagine?" he added.

"He ought to know better than that," Bobby said, though I wished right away that he hadn't.

Rumbaugh stared at Bobby as if he'd fumbled his delivery boxes to the floor. "He sure as fuck should. A child would know better."

"It's not dumbness, it's ignorance let's a man do that."

"Sorry Bob, the philosopher."

"Cats don't hurt nobody."

"You go look up there where he said he tossed the lot of them. Maybe there's one you can save after these weeks have gone by."

Bobby shut up as if my wishing him quiet had finally made it so, but Rumbaugh was fixed on the clock. The shop was still empty, and I realized nobody had called for half an hour or more, a small pie pick up that had come and gone twenty minutes ago. I slid one of the hard green plastic chairs away from the table and sat down.

"Hey," Rumbaugh said. "That's not Mineo's you lollygagging there like some homeless fuck-up."

"There's nobody," I started, but Rumbaugh waved me up.

"Do something," he said. "I'm paying you to do something."

"What?" I said. "There's nothing to do unless somebody shows up or calls."

"Yeah," Bobby said, one more thing I wished he'd kept to himself.

"Both of you fucks need to do something. There's always a need somewhere."

"Okay," I said. "In a minute," and I walked to the employee's bathroom and opened the door. I was afraid Rumbaugh would follow me because everybody knew the lock was broken, but I closed the toilet lid and extended my leg to press my foot against the door. I needed to settle my pulse.

Less than a week, and I wanted to quit. I thought of the porn shop job. Bobby had brought it up again early in the shift while we waited for calls, telling me the old story about how a clerk had been murdered there six years ago, nobody sure whether it was a customer, a thief, or the mob. "I live around here, too," I'd said, but that didn't slow him down.

Bobby wanted it to be the mob. "They run porn," he said. "Even way out here sixty miles from Pittsburgh. I bet that guy crossed them somehow. There's no windows in those places, you ever notice that?"

"There's probably a law about that."

Bobby looked up. "Yeah, that sounds right. They're spooky places, but you walk right in anyways, right?"

"No."

"You don't have to lie to me. With the wife puffing up like she is, I'll be regular almost these next months."

"Maybe you were testing Viagra way back when," I'd said. "Maybe you never got over it," and Bobby had looked down at his crotch as if he was showing a side effect.

When I came out of the bathroom Rumbaugh told me to go home because there was no sense him paying me for nothing. "If I could do everything myself, I would," he said. "That would be Mineo's made perfect," he tacked on as I left, and I had to hold my arms at my side to keep from tearing down the poster of the Italian flag he had taped to the wall by the door.

I went home and canceled with the vet. I drank without the tv or the stereo until I had a case of beer piss, holding it for so long I thought I might just let it loose on the couch like Joplin. I put the foil back on when I went to the bathroom, but I didn't bother to take it off when I returned.

Janelle had worked with me at the Big Buy. If Rumbaugh wanted to know what makes somebody be a delivery boy, that's it in a nutshell. We both worked registers. It was steady money, but I couldn't stay knowing she'd moved in with Kenny, who did stock and found ten excuses a day to walk past and act the pussy-whipped fool with me right there two counters down. I didn't know which of them I most wanted to hurt. Though I cared for Janelle as much as any woman I'd ever lived with, that didn't make her some fucking angel I'd be afraid to break like one of those cheap plaster bullshit statues of Elvis or whoever we sold to people who couldn't get enough of idols.

I drank and pissed and sprawled on the foil and told myself I believed there was a life I deserved that I could enter if I kept myself free of terrible thoughts and acts. It was the same way a better diet worked. You can't see your arteries, but you trust that they're clearing. And just like there was no backsliding to chicken wings or custard doughnuts, there was no giving in to wishing Kenny a disease that crippled him to test whether Janelle would stay to nurse him. Which there was no way of happening, because if there was one thing I knew, wishing made nothing so.

Lying on that foil, I remembered how every day near the end Janelle had said she was tired of living with a child, and when I asked her what that meant she said "You're growing down, Russ. You're on your way to infancy."

"That's a movie," I said. "That's Brad Pitt in makeup."

"Him, too. I know that story without using up ten dollars on a ticket."

"And you can fuck yourself, too. It's just not as much fun." Saying those words made me look at her body like I'd never touched it, how she could still wear jeans that seemed stuck to her and took your eyes right up along her slim thighs.

"See, Russ? That's what I mean. Boy talk."

"Jesus fucking Christ," I heard myself say like some asshole who deserved to be hurt right there on the spot.

"Exactly. You're so angry. You need to hear yourself."

"I was angry when I met you."

"And then you weren't. You were so grateful when I moved in, you were adorable, you and the cat both."

"Fuck," I said. "Fuck," nothing coming to me but heartbeats, breathing, and obscenities. She was out the door and driving away before I broke out of it and kicked Joplin's water dish, wanting to call after her that I'd checked to see that it was empty, that I was in control in ways she wouldn't understand.

Being stupid like that, I didn't consider the next arrangement, how she and Kenny were right there in front of me every day. And, for sure, I knew what Joplin missed. Janelle's softness. How she calmed me with her body, not just the sex, but being in the apartment, sitting in a chair, anything. But Janelle wasn't coming back, already moved in with Kenny, leaving Joplin and me stuck with the worst kind of anger, one mixed with hope.

MONDAY AFTERNOON, NEAR the end of my hangover, Bobby called to invite me over for a few beers and burgers. "You got Rumbaugh's map?" he said. "Check it out on Old Rt. 42 up to Water Street. Left at the intersection and there our trailer sits plain as day."

Bobby's wife, when I saw her, was so small and thin I thought she'd lost the baby, but after she said, "Hello," she smoothed her blouse down and smiled when I saw where she was swollen just enough to verify his story. "More than half way there," she said, keeping her hand low on her stomach. "It won't be long now."

"Congratulations." For a moment I was sure she'd die in childbirth, but then I remembered there were caesarean sections, a way for somebody who had the body of a thirteen-year-old to have a baby without killing herself.

"Bobby says nice things about you."

"Then it can't all be true."

"You're not as old as I expected."

"Bobby's unreliable about most everything then."

Bobby handed me a beer and said, "Sit yourself down." The chair was some sort of plastic cross-hatched to make a checkerboard of the seat. I was careful sitting, afraid to lean back for fear of sinking right through. The other two chairs were from a different set, metal, both arms showing rust. I was glad Bobby didn't invite me inside the trailer where I might see how awful his real furniture could be.

Bobby held up his can as if he was reading the label. "This here Busch tastes bad, but it's cheap and once you get used to it, it's close enough to average for drinking."

"I have it in my refrigerator right this minute."

Bobby smiled. "Really? That's some coincidence."

"More like expected."

Bobby looked puzzled, but his wife smiled again. "It'd be even less expensive if it stayed in its place at the store."

"A man's got to give his own self an allowance."

Bobby's wife rested both her hands on her stomach and looked at me. "Bobby tells me you went to college some time a way back."

"Yeah. I even thought about going back after I quit, and then I stopped thinking about it."

"Did you ever think you'd end up being a pizza dude?" Bobby said.

"I'm not 'ended up' yet," I said, and I must have looked annoyed enough for Bobby's wife to get to her feet and gesture toward the door.

"My little boy," she said. "You ought to be starting the burgers right about now." She gestured again. "Come inside for a minute. Bobby's got no manners, but have a look at this thing he did."

The living room turned out to be spotless, but she opened the door to a small bedroom, and what I was seeing would have taken anyone's eyes away from inspecting for dirt and dust. A crib with a mobile, the ceiling covered with stars and planets and a moon. "We'll all get to watch the sky every night," she said. "There's just enough room for it. You wouldn't know it to look at him, but Bobby's handy."

"This baby will have it good," Bobby said, coming up behind us with a package of pre-formed burgers in his hand. "This is the real sky. I copied it right off the planetarium page from over to Wheeling. It's what you see if you just look up in October when the baby will be born." He looked up at that sky and said, "There was three moons once. You know that, Russ? We had three moons up there spinning around us?"

"No, I never heard that, Bobby."

He smiled. "I liked finding that out so much I wasn't going to mention it to anybody. Something like that gets spoiled if you talk about it. You can't count on others to respect it the way they should."

"Where'd the other two go?" I said.

"I heard they were sucked into the sun, something like that. You know, all burned to hell."

BOBBY WAS OFF Tuesday, and I was off Wednesday, so it was Thursday when I saw him again, and the news was bad. Rumbaugh had answered the phone twice while I waited to make a run, and both times it was somebody saying their pies were so late they thought something had happened to Bobby.

"Those people should be pissed, not worried," Rumbaugh said. "Something always happens to Sorry Bob."

A minute later Bobby walked in carrying three boxes that he laid on the counter as if Rumbaugh had ordered them. "These got wasted," he said. "I got broadsided up to where 16th crosses the highway."

"You and that fucking car," Rumbaugh said. He opened the top box. The pizza looked like it had been raped, all of the cheese and even most of the sauce plastered against one side so all that was left on the dough were a few red stains. "You drop these?"

"I told you. I got hit. The guy ran a stop sign. I only had four pies left, and I took one to the door and they bought it for half price. I told them they could straighten out the cheese and heat the thing up, but I couldn't face the other two customers, not with them being regulars who expect more than what's been ruined."

"This new guy doesn't know which way his ass is cut, but he's genius compared to you. Cars need brakes like people need brains."

"It wasn't the brakes. It was the other guy who ran the stop sign."

"What's the police report say about that?"

"We worked it out right there among our own selves. He was sorry."

"There's a lot of that going around," Rumbaugh said, but he followed Bobby and me outside.

The car was drivable. Bobby had proved that getting back to Mineo's, but the passenger side door and the panel behind it were crushed in a way that made me remember riding shotgun. "Who's going to believe your story knowing how long you've been driving without brakes?" Rumbaugh said.

"It's true," Sorry Bob said, the phrase somehow sounding effeminate.

"You want I should have it parked out front with a sign that says "Look here for proof?"

"I'll talk to both customers."

"The hell you will. What you'll do is make up the difference. Those three pies comes to $33.75, and the half price one puts you out another six because there's no way in hell you did the math. It's lucky you only had two deliveries left. I'll give them a song and dance and have Yordy deliver the new batch. You go home and decide if you're up to it for tomorrow. Call in or show up. Your choice, but next fuck up is the last fuck up. I've been thinking how two delivery boys might be one too many these last few nights."

Bobby turned left from the parking lot, so the car looked just fine as he drove away. "What a moron," Rumbaugh said. "Did you know he sold himself to some drug company a while back? Ate whatever for tests?"

"So he said."

Rumbaugh started working the dough for the new pizzas. "What kind of person respects himself so little he does that?"

I watched him slather sauce on the dough for a few seconds before I said, "Bobby might appreciate you slacking off with the criticism."

"Would he now?" Rumbaugh said without looking up. "You butt buddies already? You finding time on my clock for cocksucking and such?"

"I'm just saying."

"Sorry Bob knows where he is, but maybe you don't."

Rumbaugh laid a hand on my forearm and looked directly into my eyes. "Listen, whatever you did that ended you up here is nothing I give two shits about."

"Okay."

Rumbaugh's eyes seemed to circle my face. "It's not okay, but it's the way it is. All I need is for you to be the guy I thought I hired. I don't need you to be changing into somebody else, and I sure as hell don't need you putting ideas into his Sorry Bob's pin head."

"Ideas?"

"Negativity. Back talk." Rumbaugh pulled his hand away and turned toward the ovens. He didn't look back to see what I would do next.

I ADDED BOBBY'S orders to my next run, which started with a small half-mushroom, half-pepperoni for a girl who looked to be ten or eleven and her little brother she was babysitting. I was just back in the car when my cell phone rang. It was Bobby. "You on the move?" he said.

"Yeah."

"Fuck that Rumbaugh."

"Sure." It was easy to be agreeable as I scanned mailboxes for the next address.

"No," Bobby said. "Really fuck Rumbaugh."

I parked. "Gotta go," I said.

When she opened the door, the woman who'd ordered had an extra button open on her blouse, enough to let me see how her cleavage ran into her dark blue bra. "Bobby quit or something?" she said, lifting her hand to tug the blouse together before extending it for the pizza.

"He's behind, so I'm on some of his regulars."

She looked past me as if Bobby's car might be drifting on to the gravel patch where my car was idling. "That fucking car of his. I bet he finally fucked himself." Her eyes snapped back to mine. "You a moonlighter? You don't look like anybody who's full-time delivery."

"Looks aren't everything."

"Some say that," she said. Her blouse had fallen open again, but she turned away and shut the door as soon as she pulled two bills from the stack in her hand and passed me eleven dollars for the nine ninety-five plain pie.

A minute later Bobby was on my cell again. "Once everybody's gone I'm going to put on a ski mask, walk inside, and fuck Rumbaugh up," he said.

"He'll know it's you."

"I don't give a fuck."

"Yes, you do," I said, but he'd already hung up.

I dropped off two more orders, waiting for Bobby to call again, but when he didn't, I punched in his number and started right in. "You want to fuck him up, you need a plan that doesn't include going to jail."

Bobby mumbled something about his rather being in jail than knowing Rumbaugh wasn't in the hospital, but I headed him off. "Okay," I said, "here's the plan. You stop off at The Wave and make sure people who know you see you having a beer there until past 10:30. Not just 10:30, Bobby. Past, so people remember something like that."

"An alibi? You're not as smart as you think you are, Russ. Rumbaugh'll be gone."

"No, he won't. He said he was staying tonight to do the books. He'll be there near to eleven. He won't remember the exact time or anything working in the back where there's no clock. I'll even bullshit with him for a few minutes to make sure it takes him longer."

"Okay."

"Wear that ski mask, Bobby."

All that was left was the other make-up order, a trailer set on blocks on what looked to be a strip-mine reclamation. "Finally," the man who answered said. "I'm starved. Come on in while I get the money together." His face looked to be seventy, or maybe what had married him to that trailer in that spot had added ten or fifteen years. There was a bed and a small television, two pillows propped against the wall. I knew right off the other rooms had to be empty.

He handed me seventeen dollars and fifty cents instead of the twenty-two fifty he owed on the pizzas. I looked at the five a second time before I held it out. "You need this to be another ten."

"Bobby always has a coupon he lets me use. I don't get the paper or anything, but he cuts his out and keeps it for when I order." I looked at the five again. "Bobby has a ton of them. He'll give you one to make the difference." He laid the box on the bed, opened it and took out a slice as if he'd forgotten about me. He took a bite and smiled. "I'd tell you Bobby's a saint, but I bet you already know that."

"It's beginning to dawn on me."

"He knows I can't tip, and yet he cashes coupons for me like I was a high roller. You tell him same time Saturday."

"You can call and make sure."

"I ain't got no phone. You just tell him."

Outside, I sat in my car and looked up through the windshield. There were hardly any lights in the area, and the moon looked so clear and bright I thought you might be able to see people if there was a crowd of them all in one place, like at a football game. They'd be a tiny dot, but they'd be there and you'd know, even if you had to imagine every one of them for their looks.

I thought of Bobby's story about the three moons. What if they had lasted? Before too long, somebody, for sure, would have compared them to beautiful sisters thrown up into the sky by some sort of jealous god. They would have taken on the faces of women that men would kill for. And then the floodlight on the garage flicked on, and I saw the man standing on his porch looking my way. For a second I thought he was going to come ask if I was all right, whether I had car trouble, but I saw he was holding a fresh slice in his hand, bringing it to his mouth to take a bite. He was working on the three-meat one, saving the plain for tomorrow. Pepperoni, sausage, and meatball—he took another bite but didn't move, and it occurred to me that when he finished that slice he had to do something because he couldn't just go back inside empty handed to where that small television was waiting without being sure I wasn't about to come back for the five dollars.

I waited until he'd taken four bites so he'd know I wasn't nervous about anything before I turned the key and finished the loop that wide span of driveway allowed me, watching the man in my mirror for a second or two. The light didn't go out until I reached the highway.

I had time to go home, change clothes, and find the Spiderman mask Janelle had given me once because bugs freaked me out. After that, there was nothing left to do but drive to Mineo's and hurt Rumbaugh before Bobby showed up. I was going to take the cue stick butt end I'd put under my seat my second night out, following Bobby's advice, and walk in swinging. I remembered the weight of that half stick, aware I was sweating. Spots on both sides of my rib cage felt fragile. My left temple grew hot where my pulse throbbed.

The place would be empty by 10:15. It wouldn't take me more than a minute. I'd have to steal the cash from the register, which was so little it would be like severance pay. I wanted to save Bobby from hurting Rumbaugh. And I admitted I would take some pleasure in it, self-sacrifice sounding noble just then, a better phrase than nothing-to-lose.

Such a coward for myself, but I thought I could stand up for someone else. And though I didn't know what Bobby deserved, there was a chance it was enough to risk myself for. I'd count my swings to ten and stop. There were limits. And stopping meant he might still be conscious as I walked outside. He'd have time to come after me with a knife or even a gun. That was fair. It made me relax a bit, believing that maybe it was a good thought after all, that I wasn't preparing to do anything but take what was mine.

Bobby would walk in bare-faced and wearing his Mineo's shirt like the doofus he was, and that would save him. He might even have a shot at hero if Rumbaugh needed a doctor. When I showed up tomorrow and said I was going to quit because I was moving, that would be nothing but the truth, and Rumbaugh would have to keep Bobby on, especially if I gave him the $33.75 from the register cash. I could afford it. I planned on selling my furniture, everything but the tv and the stereo so I could take Joplin and move where she wouldn't have anything to make her crazy, some place furnished where everything smelled like a hundred strangers she didn't care even the tiniest bit about.

The Selfishness of Bravery

The week of my sixteenth birthday, every teacher at James Buchanan High School talked as if the world was about to end. Instead of listening to three days of talk about the War of 1812, we heard about first-strike capability and how that was one way the United States could end the Cold War. Instead of discussing *Walden*, we talked about the morality of using H-bombs. Instead of more ways to identify the first thirty elements of the periodic table by mixing and matching them, we were told about the U-2 spy planes and how important chemistry and physics were now that wars could be won by scientists.

I had a late birthday, meaning nearly everybody who was a junior had a driver's license, some since late in their sophomore year. The cutoff was December 1st, but I didn't know anybody with a November birthday except Bonnie Sellers, who had been born on Thanksgiving and was my date for the junior prom, which was always the last Saturday in October, even when it fell exactly on Halloween.

"There's a line in the sand now," Mr. Karwoski, the history teacher said on Wednesday. "We still have weapons' superiority," Mr. Price, the chemistry teacher said for the third time that week. And Miss Rossi, in her first year of teaching English, said, "Every boy and girl in this room should pray."

That Wednesday was my birthday, and by the time school ended it felt as if this might be my last. Maybe Aunt Peg thought so too because she'd made two pepperoni and anchovy pizzas from scratch, even grating the mozzarella on some old metal contraption she'd found in a drawer where everything we never used in the kitchen was stored. She seemed exhausted, her feet up on the couch. "The cake is store bought," she said. "The pizza took the oomph right out of me, but that pepperoni is the cat's meow."

Aunt Peg had moved in with my sister Diana and me almost seven years ago after our parents died in a plane crash. She was thirteen years older than our mother, and all the extra weight she'd been carrying for sixty-one years had worn out her heart. Diana was in college, and Aunt

Peg, about once a week, would tell me to "hurry up and get there" because her swollen ankles and heavy breathing were telling her she didn't have much more of staying on her feet in her. "You two will have what's left of the insurance money and this house all paid for," she'd said before Diana had gone off to Penn State at the end of August.

Birthday or not, the pizza was a nice change. We'd started having tv dinners every night after Diana left. Aunt Peg would give me the little sliver of meat from hers and act like she was on a diet, but now she said, "I do like a good pizza. Two slices won't kill me, and if they do, I'll die happy."

Right then, with all the talk about doomsday and the taste of anchovies and pepperoni in my mouth, it sounded like the right attitude. And then, for her present to me, Aunt Peg handed me the keys to my father's 1955 Fiat Spider, which had been parked in our garage 99% of the time for seven years. "That car needs a driver," she said. "I'm too old to learn, and your sister's afraid of it. It's too pretty to go to waste."

At that particular moment I knew the meaning of "bittersweet," because I'd driven that beautiful red two-seater up and down our street for the past year since Diana had shown me how to drive on the old Chevy our mother had left behind, but now, a few weeks from getting a license, I might go up in a mushroom cloud before I ever drove that car farther than the Miller's house where our street dead-ended a quarter mile from our driveway.

IN HISTORY CLASS, on Thursday, Mr. Karwoski told us the United States military forces were at DefCon 2, a place we'd never been before. The class sat there staring at Mr. Karwoski as if he'd just levitated until Linda Crosby said, "What does that mean?"

"We're ready," Mr. Karwoski said. "We're prepared."

He sounded so much like he wanted to go to DefCon 1 that I waved my hand. "Why do you think anybody would ever drop the bomb?" I said, but my voice sounded soft and squeaky like I was having an asthma attack like Sharon Grammes, the girl who'd needed a nebulizer half an hour after I'd walked her into our sophomore spring dance.

"Hiroshima and Nagasaki," Mr. Karwoski said, pumping his right and then his left fist in short jabs as if he was putting exclamation marks after those names. "And Pearl Harbor," he added, giving his fists the old one-two again, his tone like the one Aunt Peg used when she gave reasons why she'd never have a dog in the house.

By lunch time there was a rumor the prom would be canceled. "Postponed," Miss Rossi said near the end of English. "There's a right word for everything."

"Canceled is the right word," Jimmy Daniels said, and two girls began to cry.

Ten minutes later, while my bus was filling up, I talked to Bonnie who, I noticed right away, had changed her dark brown hair. It was shorter, teased a little on top, but she had small, separated bangs now, and an upward flip of hair across her ears, everything held miraculously in shape by the hair spray that every girl carried in her purse. "Your hair looks great," I said, and I thought she glanced at my flat-top as if she was disappointed I hadn't altered myself for the prom.

"I heard you had a fight with Mr. Karwoski."

"I asked a question is all." I waited for her to say she'd heard I'd lost the fight, but she just said, "Call me at eight so we can really talk. I'm glad you like my hair."

ON FRIDAY, ALL our teachers said the Russian ships had slowed down before they reached Kennedy's blockade, some, it looked like, even turning back. The halls got noisier. The principal announced over the PA that the prom was on, and everybody in the room who had a date cheered.

Saturday, though, Aunt Peg said she'd heard a rumor that a spy plane had been shot down over Cuba, and the television news she turned on said there was an unconfirmed report the Russians were still arming the missiles in Cuba. "Too late to cancel that prom now," Aunt Peg said. She was lying on the couch waiting to help me figure out how to dress. "How far is it from Cuba to Pittsburgh?" she said when I walked into the living room with clothes on hangers.

"Just over a thousand miles."

"Have they taught you how long it would take for a missile to get here? Is there a way to figure that?"

"Not long," I said, holding up the hangers. The junior prom didn't require a tuxedo, just a coat and tie, and I had two of each to choose from. "The darker," Aunt Peg said, "and the gray tie." It took her five seconds to decide for me.

When I told Aunt Peg I needed to ride the bus to the flower shop before it got too late, she shook her head and said, "Nobody rides a bus on prom day. If I can squeeze into that that new car of yours, you can drive us to Dick Trowbridge's greenhouse and save yourself some money to spend later."

"On the road?" I said as if there were some other way.

"It's closer than that shopping center," she said. "Let's find out if that pretty thing likes going farther than our dead end and back before you drive your sweetheart all the way to Pittsburgh."

I had to call Jack Bayne before we left, tell him I didn't need to double with him and Sue Savich in his father's chrome-covered Chrysler. "The Spider?" he said. "You don't even have a permit." He sounded jealous, like he wished Sue and Bonnie would take the Chrysler and meet us there after we drove around for an hour like Italian playboys.

"Dick Trowbridge is an old friend," Aunt Peg said after she watched the road for half a mile as if she had anything to do with keeping the car on the asphalt. "He'll have something nice."

I kept my eyes on the road. I made sure we were right on the speed limit. "I paid for the registration," she said. "It's been waiting for you, but it hasn't been inspected since 1955, so don't you be doing anything to get yourself stopped."

"I'm being careful," I said.

"We'll take care of the inspection when you get your permit if we're all still around, but your sister has to bring the Chevy back home for your test. Those state cops will fail you if you show up looking like a hot shot. And look here, we made it all the way to Dick's in one piece."

Dick Trowbridge had two greenhouses, but we walked straight through the first one before he paused just inside the second where the temperature seemed to soar and it felt like it might rain. "Show us what a young man needs for a special night," Aunt Peg said.

Trowbridge stood near a row of exotic looking flowers. "What color is her dress?" he said.

"I have no idea."

"No matter," Trowbridge said. "White will do. A wrist corsage so you don't have to be fussing with pins."

"Mini calla lilies," Trowbridge said, passing a gift box with a corsage lying in a bed of green tissue paper to me. I understood that Aunt Peg had called Trowbridge before we'd watched the news, that this wrist corsage was the only one in the greenhouse. "And here's a full-sized one for your boutonniere."

I held the flower in my hand, inspecting it as if I was afraid it could hurt me. Aunt Peg laughed. "I'll pin it on your coat before you go out the door. Don't you worry about it."

By the time we reached the car, Aunt Peg was panting. "I'll hold these for you," she said between gasps. "You don't need to be looking at flowers while you drive." Her hands full, she settled so heavily into the passenger seat I imagined the seams of the leather splitting. "Whoo boy," she said. "It's a good thing nobody's taking me to the prom. I'd be a wet blanket."

We were half way home when she leaned forward and opened the glove compartment, and I looked over. "You keep your eyes on the road, young man," she said. "I'm just making sure that little card's in here instead of in a drawer at the house."

"That, and Dad's Beretta," I said.

She slid the pistol out. In her hands it looked large and evil. "Your father kept this in here, but then I expect you looked one day and there it was."

"Yes."

"So you know he kept it loaded in case there was trouble?"

"It probably doesn't even work anymore."

"Let's hope you never need to find out. Your father was such a desperado when it came to his things. Him and his being prepared. He was such a Boy Scout and yet it didn't make any difference at all."

"Maybe it did. You don't know."

"All these things from other countries. I used to ask him why he bought from foreigners, and he'd just say 'Peg, some things are made better somewhere else.'" She laid the gun back inside, careful not to bump either end against the sides of the glove compartment. "You have yourself a time tonight," she said. "Those bombs will fall or they won't."

BONNIE'S DRESS WAS powder blue. I slid the wrist corsage over her hand while Mrs. Sellers snapped a picture with a Polaroid camera. "So we can see the two of you right away," she said, motioning us to stand close together, but she had to wait a minute between each one while we stood beside each other like the figures I'd seen on cakes at a couple of cousins' weddings. "Jerry," she kept saying. "Come out here and look at your beautiful daughter. The war won't start without you."

After the fourth picture, Mr. Sellers came out of the room where they kept the television. A den, Bonnie called it. He looked bleary and tired, wearing a sleeveless undershirt and holding a half empty bottle of Stroh's. "Aren't you the prettiest girl ever," he said, kissing Bonnie's cheek.

I could hear somebody talking about Cuba and the Russians, something about how there were experts who believed the missiles might already be armed, that the Russians didn't need any of the stuff that was on the boats that turned back to be able to fire. One of the voices declared that some of Kennedy's advisors thought Castro was crazy enough to welcome launching a nuclear strike. "You have the time of your life," Mr. Sellers said. Curls of dark chest hair showed above the top of his undershirt. Light flickered through the open doorway for a moment, and then he closed the door.

"He's been watching all day," Mrs. Sellers said. "Nobody knows anything. They just talk and talk and talk, and he sits there listening like being the first to know would make any difference." She opened the door for us and held it. "Look at that car he's driving, Bonnie," she called as we walked away. "You're a Cinderella who can stay out past midnight."

"Your aunt owns this car?" Bonnie practically whispered as I started the engine.

"My father's. Well, hers, I guess. She gave it to me for my birthday."

"You passed your test already?"

"No."

"So you're driving us without a license?"

"Not even a learner's permit. We're like desperados," I said. "But don't worry. I've been driving this for a year."

"Up and down your driveway?"

"My street," I said, and she laughed.

"It's really cool, but I wish it had a radio."

"You don't need a radio when you're driving a car like this," my father had said more than once, but what I told her was, "It's a good night not to have a radio."

THE PROM WAS at the Hotel Webster Hall in the part of Pittsburgh where there were four colleges that I knew of, the biggest building, Pitt's Cathedral of Learning, towering up like a skyscraper almost right next door. "We're right in the bullseye," said Jimmy Daniels, who was waiting by the cloakroom when we walked in.

I didn't answer. I checked Bonnie's coat and took her hand, leaving Daniels and his doom fever behind. Jack and Sue had saved us two seats at a table, but Bonnie and Sue went off to what they called the powder room before we'd even settled in. "You see Miss Rossi's low-cut dress?" Jack said. "You could go to jail for what it makes you think."

I took a look at Miss Rossi who, for sure, didn't look like a chaperone where she was standing near the gym teacher Mr. Barrone. "Or if the cops pull me over," I said because Bonnie and Sue were on their way back.

"I know you," Jack said. "You'll keep it slow and straight."

The band didn't have any guitars, and the bass was a stand up. There were horns and two saxophones and thank God, drums, and all the men were wearing dark suits that made them look older than anybody's father. But they played songs we recognized like "Mr. Blue" and "Sealed with a Kiss."

There was green punch in a huge frosted bowl and plenty of chips and pretzels. We sat at a table where each place had a thin plastic glass filled with what I tasted and found out was carbonated cider. JBHS Junior Prom, 1962 was frosted onto the side. "It's called a flute," Bonnie said, but she didn't touch hers.

AFTER A HALF dozen slow songs, the band cranked up "The Twist." Bonnie seemed surprised when I started twisting, but she kept up. Miss Rossi ended up beside us, twisting like crazy while Mr. Barrone shuffled a little, his eyes fixed on the top of her dress. After a minute, the band started doing a call and response from a different Twist song called "Dear Lady," my favorite, the singer shouting "Get up a' off your chair" and the horn section calling out "Dear Lady." It sounded old fashioned, like something one of the big bands my father had listened to would do. Like Louie Prima, I thought, the name coming to me as I worked my feet and arms. And then the band took up again, the singer belting out, "'Cause doctors agree, so I've been told, do the Twist and you'll never grow old" before they switched, over the singer's cackling laugh, to "Monster Mash." I skidded my way into the Mashed Potato and Bonnie, without moving, said, "Where did you learn that?"

It was wonderful to have her marvel, but I couldn't tell Bonnie I'd spent nearly every Saturday night since high school began dancing by myself in my room, the door locked in case my sister decided it would be hilarious to throw it open and surprise me.

I was happy and sweaty and tried slurping punch from the glass dipper into my flute, spilling it on my hand as Bonnie laughed. Her arms were bare except for the lilies. I wanted to tell her she was beautiful, but settled for "You look really nice in that dress."

"Thank you," she said, which didn't prompt a next line. I swallowed the mouthful of punch I'd dumped in the flute, and Bonnie carried the cup I'd filled for her back to the table.

We didn't dance for the next three songs, but when the band started "The Way You Look Tonight," a song my father used to sing along with when he played the record, I was on my feet and Bonnie followed. She pressed against me this time, and I dropped both arms around her back, holding her and swaying from side to side without even bothering to move my feet. We just stood there when the song ended, and though I knew it wouldn't happen, I wanted the band to play the same song again.

AFTERWARD, WE WERE supposed to follow Jack and Sue and six other couples to a nightclub in Monroeville so we could sit at another table and drink Cokes and listen to Bobby Vinton, who was from somewhere near

Pittsburgh and had a number one song called "Roses are Red."

"Let's look inside the Cathedral first," Bonnie said. "They have all those Nationality Rooms there."

"It won't be open," I said.

"Maybe it is. If it's all locked up, we can find Monroeville by ourselves."

To make her happy, I tugged on the heavy front door, and I nearly lost my balance when it swung open. There were lights on, but as soon as we walked inside, a security guard rose from a chair and strode toward us as if he meant to throw us out.

"Prom night?" he said.

"Yes," Bonnie said.

"Hard to have fun tonight," he said. He glanced around as a bearded man in a light brown jacket clattered down the uncarpeted stairs. The guard nodded as the man left. "Busy night here," he said. "Professors arranging things. You know. They have me here until one o'clock." He looked at his watch. "Forty more minutes and then, Cuba or no Cuba, I have to chase everybody."

"Are the Nationality Rooms open?" Bonnie said.

"No," he said, but I could see him looking her up and down, and when she said, "Could you just open one for a minute?" I knew he was adding up the minutes he had left, how they would be more pleasant if he could spend some of them near a pretty girl in a prom dress.

"Okay," he said. "I'll open my favorite, and you can pick one more that's close and that's it. Ten minutes and you're gone."

He opened Italian. "You know who that is up there?" he said, pointing at a bust on top of a wooden cabinet. "Dante," he said, before either of us could answer. "Have you read him?"

"Not yet," Bonnie said.

"Look at this," he said, opening the wooden doors, a blackboard behind them the way our old television had come inside a set of doors.

"Da Vinci," Bonnie said, reading from the wall paneling. "Galileo, Marconi. I know all of these people."

I didn't say anything. The room was so extraordinary I thought I was in a castle, and five minutes later I let Bonnie pick the German room, which was right next door. There were quotations from Goethe and Schiller on plaques, another list of famous names, and Bonnie asked me, "Why do we know all the Italians but I never heard of the Germans?" as if she knew I didn't recognize them either.

"I don't know," I said, but the guard had put one hand on Bonnie's arm and was guiding her toward a row of stained glass windows.

"Grimm's fairy tales," he said, mentioning one name I recognized, but I noticed he didn't take his hand away when they stopped. "Rumplestiltskin," he said, "and here's Cinderella, the girl of my dreams."

His hand began to rub her arm, moving just a few inches. Bonnie seemed entranced. I took a few steps, reading the marker. "She's Ashenputtel in German," I said, and the guard dropped his hand.

"These are all so gorgeous," Bonnie said. "I want to come back and look at every room."

"It would take all night to do it right, sweetheart," the guard said, and there was a moment when all three of us stood there in silence, eyes forward, before another set of footsteps made the guard turn away and say, "I have to lock up in a few minutes. You kids need to move along."

"I'm STARVED," I said. It was all I could think of, a half hour later, to keep the night from ending as we drove north on Route 8 toward Bonnie's house after we decided to skip Bobby Vinton.

"So am I," she said, "but what's still open?"

"A diner. I remember one's out a little farther by the turnpike exit."

A little farther meant nearly ten miles, but I was happy to keep driving until we passed the interchange and saw the Venus Diner right there where I remembered it, only two cars in the parking lot but lights on the sign that said "Open 24 Hours."

Two men wearing plaid flannel shirts over dark t-shirts sat at the counter drinking coffee and smoking, so I picked a booth and we waited for the waitress to bring us menus. "Here you go, kids," she said. "Prom get you hungry?"

"Yes," Bonnie said, but she was looking at the fork the waitress had put in front of her. "This has egg stuck on it," she said, handing it back.

"That happens," the waitress said. I could see the men looking our way, listening. "I'll bring you a new one with your order."

Bonnie and I scanned our menus, and the thought of that egg made both of us order pancakes. "Gotcha," the waitress said, and she disappeared into the kitchen.

The men raised their voices then, as if they were staging an argument for us.

"Nuke those cocksuckers," the man who wore a cap said. "Shoot first. It's the only way."

The bare-headed man nodded his head as if he'd been convinced. "That fat fuck Khrushchev," he said. "That fucking cocksucker."

The waitress pushed through the swinging door. "Tone it down, boys," she said, and both men looked our way. The man with the cap stood up and said, "You kids should go fuck someplace before it's too late." I thought the men could tell Bonnie was still fifteen, that her age made them stare at her as if that was the perfect age for all the things they wanted to do to a girl.

"Enough, boys," the waitress said, "or I'll have to ask George to come out here."

The men went back to smoking. The pancakes arrived. Bonnie had a clean fork. It was sliding past two a.m., we were eating breakfast, and just then I was happy we'd gone to the Nationality Rooms and the Venus Diner, that all the men looking at Bonnie made her more beautiful.

We took our time eating. I pushed the last few bites around in syrup and waited for the men to leave, but finally, when there was nothing else to do that didn't make me look afraid, I dropped a few bills on the table and walked Bonnie to the door.

We weren't halfway to the car when I heard the door open behind us. "Hey, cutie," the cap-wearer called, and the other, as we approached the Fiat, said, "Don't it figure, in a foreign car. A Guinea one at that. Hey, schoolboy, it don't matter what your Daddy's car is. The bomb don't check the make and model."

The men were surprisingly thin. I'd never thought of threats wearing bodies similar to mine, but the danger was in their faces, the stubble and the slicked back hair part of a costume that amplified what was in their eyes and mouths. Something predatory. As if there were bars between them and us, and now it had dawned on them that a gate had been left open.

"Cutie," the cap wearer said again. "Come go for a ride in an American car."

I dropped my keys, and Bonnie moved closer to me as I bent to retrieve them. "There you go," one man said. "Now you're cooking."

The door was finally open. Bonnie scrambled inside. She was crying and my arm dropped around her shoulders and her head rested against my chest. I took a breath, relieved, but as I slipped the key into the ignition I could see the men approaching the car from the front, closing up the distance, laying their hands n the hood as if they expected me to pop it open so they could check the oil.

I reached across Bonnie, opened the glove compartment, and pulled out the Beretta. Bonnie sat up, staring, and I stepped out of the car, pointing the gun my father had left there almost eight years ago. I hadn't told Aunt Peg on the way back from the greenhouse, but he'd not only shown it to me one day, he'd taught me how to hold it and shoot it before he told me if I ever touched it, I'd never ride in that car again. "It's for emergencies," he'd said, and this was one.

"Whoa there, Jesse James," the bareheaded man said.

I swung the gun in a small arc from one to the other. They lifted their hands off the hood, but when they didn't step away, I said, "You two go fuck yourselves someplace" and fixed the gun on the cap-wearing man.

"You'd never shoot," he said, his voice softer now.

"Only if you get closer."

"Not even then," he said. "And we'd have that car and that girl and have us a night of it."

My mouth was suddenly so dry I was afraid to say anything else. I tried to keep my eyes on his face in order to read what would happen next, and then I saw the waitress step outside, the cook beside her. "Hey," she said, and the word broke whatever spell all of us were under. I reached behind me, found the door, and dropped into my seat, the Beretta pointed at the roof, then switched it to my left hand as I turned the key to rev up the Spider.

I didn't look back. I drove a mile without either of us speaking, the gun still in my left hand, before I saw a set of headlights come up so fast in the mirror that by the time Bonnie turned in her seat to look the car whizzed by. "He must be going 100," she said.

I checked my speed and saw it was seventy-five, the Spider acting like it enjoyed it. Bonnie seemed to be following the disappearing taillights; and I started to slow. "It's like *On the Beach*," I said, "when Fred Astaire wins that race near the end when everybody's already starting to die."

I let the car settle in again at fifty-five, the speed limit. Bonnie was still staring, but she said, "What happened to everybody?"

"All the fallout from World War III killed everybody, even in Australia."

"Oh," Bonnie said. "When?"

"1964." I was surprised she hadn't ever heard of *On the Beach*. The novel had been so popular, *The Pittsburgh Press* has run a condensed version as a serial when it first came out. She looked out the side window, her breath clouding the glass, and I let us drop back to fifty, heading south toward her house,

"What do you think we'll be doing tonight?" Bonnie said as we pulled into her driveway.

"It's still prom night," I said, although I knew what she meant. "Tomorrow night we have homework. Chemistry and trigonometry." Both of us were in accelerated science and math, chosen, when we started seventh grade, to keep up with the Russians.

Bonnie smiled, and for a second I thought she hadn't meant anything at all asking about how Sunday might end. "I wish I could get out of all that. All those numbers and Greek letters. Everything I want to do is in English."

She slipped out, and I followed. "I thought the fast car was the Venus creeps," she said.

"More likely than Fred Astaire," I said. "That was my father's gun back there."

"He's been dead a long time, hasn't he?"

"He thought if he owned things other people dreamed about he'd need to defend them."

"That would be hard, wouldn't it? Always looking for something awful to happen?"

"And then it did."

"I didn't know you then. But my parents talked about it like you lived next door."

She looked up, and so did I. It was past three a.m. This had been the longest night of our lives, and now there wasn't anything left to do to make it more than a few minutes longer. Bonnie said, "I'm freezing," and I took it as a signal she was ready to go inside.

I kissed her once more at the door, but when she opened it, her mother was sitting in a chair, a shaded floor lamp on behind her as if she'd stayed up reading a book. "Come on in, the both of you," she said, and when she stood, I saw she had a glass in her hand. "Go on downstairs where you'll be comfortable," she said. "You kids make yourselves at home."

I'd never been in her basement, but if I'd been blindfolded and didn't know we'd gone downstairs, I would have thought we were in a huge living room. The walls were paneled; the floor was carpeted. And besides the chairs and a couch and a table designed for card players, there was a bar with a tap for beer and a shelf of bottles.

"Wow," I said. I thought about turning on the television, but it seemed like a terrible idea. We sat together on the couch, and I listened to the footsteps above us until they stopped, and then I leaned into Bonnie again, and she pressed against me.

"It's like we're starting over," she said.

The door opened. Mrs. Sellers started down the stairs. "I need a refill," she said. "You two pay me no mind." She stood behind the bar and looked our way as if she was inspecting us. "I'll tell you what," she said, "as long as I'm in your way, let me make each of you a drink. One cocktail never hurt anybody."

It was nearly three thirty. She wobbled a little in a robe over what looked to be a lace trimmed negligee. "Some outfit for a bartender," she said. "Bonnie's brothers would never let me peek under their covers, but her father is upstairs asleep in his underwear. I told him he should look decent just in case, wear those pajamas I bought for him last Christmas"

She finished making the drinks by dropping two maraschino cherries in each one. "This is called a Manhattan," she said. "Mostly bourbon. The extra cherry will make it sweeter for you." She hooked a thin orange slice on the side of each thick glass, handed them to us, and plodded upstairs..

We sipped those drinks, which didn't taste sweet enough for either of us, but they gave us something to do, sitting apart, the words gone out of us. Twenty minutes later, Mrs. Sellers returned. "If I make you all a second drink, can I show you a movie?"

"Mom," Bonnie said, but Mrs. Sellers was already wheeling a projector out from where it had been stored behind one of the two overstuffed chairs..

"It's not from when you were a baby or anything like that," Mrs. Sellers said. She flipped the tube for the screen to horizontal, unfurled it, and snapped it in place above the tripod it sat on. "Hold on while I make the drinks."

More Manhattans. I drank off half of mine while she fiddled with the projector. I'd never drunk anything but a few half glasses of beer Aunt Peg set in front of me when she wanted just a little more than one bottle, and now I felt light-headed and wondered if Bonnie, maybe sixty or seventy pounds lighter than I was, felt giddy.

When the film began, Bonnie groaned because there she was in a one-piece flower print swimsuit with two boys, one younger, one older. "Look at you and those brothers of yours," her mother said, and as she stood between them on a dock, I did, figuring her for about eleven.

I thought Bonnie would tell her to shut it off, maybe even get up and shut it off herself, but she let her eleven year-old self pose on the dock, wave at the camera, even blow a kiss with her open hand cupped below her mouth like Marilyn Monroe in a photograph I'd seen somewhere.

Her brothers hopped into the lake. They splashed each other, and then the camera went back to Bonnie walking farther down the dock before she leaped into the water.

There was more, the camera sweeping along the shore to where Mr. Sellers stood fully dressed. A few minutes later, though, Mrs. Sellers seemed to sag. "That's all there is of you here," she said, speaking toward the screen, but then she ran the film backward, something my uncle did at family reunions so everybody could laugh, and we all watched without making a sound as Bonnie emerged from the water and landed on her feet; her brothers returned to the dock, and then that kiss as if Bonnie was slapping herself in the mouth.

Mrs. Sellers let the film run all the way back to the beginning and the room went dark. "Don't you wish you could do that sometimes?" she said, and when nobody answered, she said, "I'll leave you kids alone, but the bar's closed, you hear?" She wobbled up three stairs before pausing and turning, her hand clutching the railing. "Goodbye" she said and held her gaze on us for a few seconds before she turned and disappeared up the stairs.

"What now?" Bonnie said, and it was so much a signal we stood at the same time, and the next kiss was just like dancing with our lips together, hers parting until our tongues met like both of us had been practicing. "You can touch me if you want," she said, which paralyzed me, my hands locked against her sides a few inches from her breasts. I kissed her again, felt her heart racing through the pressure of my hands, but they didn't move.

When she stepped back, Bonnie said, "I want to sleep down here." I swallowed hard. "Will you stay until I change and get a blanket and pillow?"

I heard the furnace kick off and on while I waited. All I had to do was move my hands over her body and the rest was up to her. And then I told myself I was afraid she thought I'd earned something at the diner, or worse, that I expected it.

While Bonnie was gone, I thought about the Hotel Webster Hall, how we could have walked a few more blocks and gone into the Carnegie Library if it was open, too, at one a.m. Three years ago, I'd ridden the bus into Pittsburgh. I knew how to transfer to one heading out to Oakland because that's how Aunt Peg and I went to a couple of Pirate games at Forbes Field every summer. The library was right there out past the left field wall, and though I'd never been inside, I knew somebody would help me find the old newspaper stories about the plane crash. That's what I counted on, somebody who knew how to find answers to whatever question you had. She didn't have to know the answers, just where to find them.

"I remember that crash," she said. "It gave everybody something new to worry about."

I didn't say anything, and she hooked up the microfilm, and it began to spin through the last three months of 1955. She stopped it at October 31st as if she could feel the right date through her fingers. She slowed it down, crawling through November 1st, the day it happened, and stopping on the front page of *The Pittsburgh Press,* November 2nd, the plane crash story that said "Passengers included local couple."

"You writing a report for school?" she said.

"No."

"Well then," she said. "You just be sure to rewind it when you're done and return it to me."

I didn't explain that my parents had been passengers the first time anybody had set off a bomb on board a plane while it was in the air, some asshole wanting to receive his mother's insurance money, but I went back and asked her for 1956, the last three months. "I know how to work it," I said, so I was alone when I found November 1st and the photograph of me standing with Diana above a caption that said, "Tragedy's Children." By then, Aunt Peg had lived with us for a year, keeping us from the orphanage.

I felt tired and sad. People were cruel. The Venus Diner jerks could break into Bonnie's house and someone like Mr. Sellers wouldn't be able to stop them. You needed a gun like my father. You needed to have the nerve to shoot it.

He should have taken it on the plane, I thought, which made no sense. He should have noticed some nervous guy saying goodbye to his mother and and been able to tell he'd packed a bomb in her suitcase, which was as impossible as world peace. I felt like I had when I heard the news, nine years old and grinding my teeth until Aunt Peg had given me a package of chewing gum, saying "Don't hurt yourself."

Bonnie returned in pajamas. She carried a blanket and pillow. Her breasts were loose under the soft fabric, and there was a moment when she bent down and kissed my forehead that the top billowed out like an invitation to push my hands up under it, but I held my breath until she said, "Thank you," and turned toward the couch where she lay down and pulled the blanket over herself.

"You think Cuba will get worse?" she said.

"We'll hear sirens if it does."

"It would be better if we didn't. I don't want to know there's one minute left before everything blows up."

I thought we would talk more, say something we needed to say as Kennedy and Khrushchev decided whether this Sunday was the day that had been speeding toward us since 1945. When, after a minute, nothing that mattered came out of me, I said, "I hope you had as good a time as I did." Bonnie didn't answer, and I thought I'd made a fool of myself until I realized she was asleep.

I didn't leave. I watched her sleep and wondered, if there was a sudden, brilliant light, whether covering Bonnie's sleeping body with mine would be shelter enough to save her, turning so sentimental I thought about watching the old home movie of Bonnie again, having her wake up to the image of her blowing a kiss. When the sky stayed dark and quiet, I had time to decide that it would be more merciful not to disturb Bonnie, that I'd been foolish even to imagine the selfishness of bravery.

As it grew light, I stood at the window to watch the eastern sky. I couldn't remember ever seeing a sunrise. I'd been dragged out of bed for years around the time the sun came up in winter, but I'd never looked outside until it was time to walk to the bus stop, checking for how deep the snow was or whether it was raining. By then, the sun was up.

Just before eight o'clock, I heard stirring upstairs, the floor creaking, and knew I should leave before her parents dressed and checked on her. Neither of them would be drunk now. They were churchgoers, and there was no explaining my being in the house with their daughter at eight a.m. Still I kept watch. The sky remained quiet. Bonnie's eyes stayed shut, her face so beautiful in the natural light that I knew what I wanted to tell her—I felt grateful to have spent the night with her.

And there was more I'd say if this Sunday let me, if speaking aloud and honestly still mattered when she woke and found me eating a second breakfast with her parents, her father in a suit, her mother dressed for church and blessing me with eggs over easy, bacon, and toast, all of the silverware beside my plate sparkling and clean.

Running Through Directions

"Pastor Shaffer," his wife, Diane, said in her member-of-the congregation voice, "you had a little girl eat her milk carton during church social today."

Alex Shaffer, just back from Sunday afternoon hospital visits, nodded. "You mean she took a bite out of it," he said. "Kids do that."

"Nobody's called you yet, have they?" Diane said.

Shaffer laid his cell phone on the table. "Not one call all afternoon," he said. "It's been a pleasure of silence."

"They will, Alex. She ate the milk carton like an apple."

"No, she didn't."

"You're right. It wasn't quite like an apple because she ate everything. There wasn't a core left over."

"Well," he said. "A sick little toddler she'll be."

"This girl is ten years old, Alex. Evelyn Vaughn is her name, and she sits in church every Sunday. You've seen her. She's always with her mother."

Shaffer saw that Diane was working on a set of her fourth-grade class pictures dated two years earlier. Sayresburg Elementary School, Grade 4, the largest picture was captioned. Two of the boys in the snapshot she'd just positioned wore broad-brimmed hats and identical outfits of blue and black. They stood watching a playground soccer game, neither of them looking at Diane's camera. "Maybe she's modeling the Amish. They rely on folk medicine. You don't see any of them in the hospital."

"What?" Diane studied the photo as if she'd never noticed the two boys.

"They use the same medicines as animals," Shaffer said. "Roots and leaves. Paper's made from trees."

"In twenty-four years, Caleb and Zachary are the only Amish I've ever had. Hardly any come to public school. They were sweethearts."

"They hang a stocking filled with hot potatoes around the neck for a cold."

"That's good." Diane turned the photograph of the Amish boys over and sighed. "You can stop, Alex. This girl just needs a talking to."

"They carry a raw potato in their pockets to prevent rheumatism."

"You sound like an ass, Mr. Potato Head," Diane said. "You should talk, you and your paper bag."

Shaffer settled into a chair to glance at the newspaper. Thirteen hours earlier, he'd sat up from sleep with shortness of breath. A heart attack, he'd thought, feeling the tightness in his chest. He'd taken rapid, shallow breaths, each of them ending in a whistle that sounded like it was tuned to the Conelrad frequency for the heart.

He'd shaken Diane's shoulder, waking her. "I'm in trouble here," he'd said, and as soon as she sat up, he'd panicked, his breathing so shallow it went silent.

"All right," Diane said. "Relax."

He'd heard his wife getting dressed and knew she'd decided to drive him to the hospital. A place of miracles, he'd thought, going cold and clammy, yet somehow shuffling to the car without tumbling face down on the driveway.

He'd walked into the emergency room as pale and shaky as if he were dripping blood from multiple stab wounds. "I think I'm having a heart attack," he'd forced out, just audible.

A woman who had the look of a senior citizen volunteer evaluated him. Her name tag said, "L. Swartz," no sign of M.D. She listened to his heart and took his blood pressure. She disappeared and returned after precisely one minute on the clock positioned directly in front of Shaffer, so well-timed he assumed her absence was an elementary medical test. "Put this over your nose and mouth and breathe," L. Swartz said.

A brown paper bag. Thirty-five years ago he could have carried his lunch inside it and left it sitting on a shelf among thirty others in the cloak room until the fourth grade teacher gave the class permission to retrieve them. Swartz wasn't even writing his symptoms down.

"There won't be any oxygen," he squeaked, beginning to clarify how she'd mistaken his need for treatment with a request for euthanasia.

L. Swartz, her silver hair so tightly permed it looked as if it might snap, said, "That's the idea." He took the bag and held it in his lap like an airplane barf bag. No doubt she had attended the University of No Explanations, but he was prepared to drop dead before he'd raise that bag to his face. "Try it a minute," she counseled. "You'll see."

He could hold his breath for a minute, Shaffer decided. Even with his heart under siege. He could die here and Diane could get a lawsuit settlement that would guarantee she could quit teaching and enjoy the rest of her life in comfort. When the real nurse, the one this crazy old woman had locked in the closet after stripping off her uniform, began to thump the door with her bound, bare feet, a security officer would rush in to rescue her and discover Rev. Alexander Shaffer had succumbed to a lunatic's diagnosis.

He took a deep breath and stuck his face in the bag. "Breathe," L. Swartz said. He flexed his chest and relaxed it twice, still holding his breath. "Naturally," she tacked on, and before thirty seconds were over he inhaled in spite of himself. He exhaled, then inhaled again. He kept it up for another minute before he yanked the bag away and stared at the woman as if he were about to knot his fingers around her throat.

"Feel better?" she said.

He took a breath and evaluated. He took another and nodded.

"Fear makes us see our symptoms like children. You're forty-four, Mr. Shaffer. The odds in your favor are still good. Use the bag for another minute. You're doing fine." L. Swartz walked behind a partition, and a small child began screaming. Whatever was wrong with that child had nothing to do with lungs and air. He breathed in the bag for another minute, felt so enormously better he began to appreciate the wisdom of witch doctors who scattered the bones of small animals to diagnose.

Ten minutes later, settled beside his wife in the car, Shaffer said, "I never once thought of prayer. Isn't that odd?"

THE FOLLOWING SUNDAY, Diane walked into Shaffer's study before the service and told him Evelyn Vaughn was wearing a dress of red and white stripes. "A kind of flag," she said. "It makes you think there might be stars on the back." Shaffer exhaled and tapped the hymnal he always carried as he followed the choir up the aisle. "Take a look when you get the chance," Diane went on. "See what you think."

Just before he read the scripture for the day, Shaffer noticed a swaying of red and white, a girl rocking from side to side in a way that, in spite of himself, made him think "hypnosis." He looked down at Ephesians. He read slowly and evenly, and when he glanced up from time to time, he knew exactly where to look so he wouldn't see even a glimpse of red and white.

During the anthem, when he had five minutes to prepare himself for delivering the sermon, Shaffer counted pews. Evelyn Vaughn was eleven rows back, exactly half way between the chancel and the nave. When the choir soared into the first of two choruses, he watched as the girl lifted one of the small devotional booklets from the hymnal rack in front of her. Before she tore the first page from it and stuffed it into her mouth, he remembered there were fifty-two pages of Bible verses and short meditations, one for each week, that there were fourteen sheets of paper, counting the cover.

He thought she was staring at him as her mouth moved, about to spit the soggy paper into her hand and smile, but she swallowed, then tugged another sheet from where he knew it was stapled and pushed it into her mouth. He listened to the choir a moment, trying to gauge how much longer their anthem would go on, whether she would swallow the whole booklet by the end so he could present his sermon without stopping to check on her progress.

He fought the impulse to walk down the steps of the chancel, march back the aisle and grab that booklet from the child's hand. How would he ever stand up and preach afterwards? What would he do if the child fought back or the mother reared up and clawed at him?

Four pages she'd finished by the time the anthem ended. He delivered his sermon to the right side of the congregation and followed the choir back the aisle during the recessional, looking closely at the girl as he approached her, checking her mouth and hands, neither of which held anything.

Through small talk with eight parishioners Shaffer kept his eye on the mother and daughter as they crept toward him in the receiving line. When the woman finally extended her hand, he said, "Good morning, Mrs. Vaughn" and kept himself from looking down.

"Not these three months, Pastor," the woman said, "what with Mr. Vaughn packed up and gone."

Shaffer glanced down at once at the girl, who was busy rapidly touching her fingertips together one by one in sequence, forming a sort of steeple and then undoing it before touching them again. "Oh? I'm sorry to hear that," he said.

"It's nothing to be sorrowful about," the woman said, and then she was gone, taking one of her daughter's busy hands and pulling her toward the stairs that led to the street.

The next woman in line held onto Shaffer's hand, watching the Vaughns go down the stairs before she spoke. "I have to tell you, Pastor, I just witnessed something I hope to never see in this church again. That child needs talking to."

"Oh?" Shaffer said, suddenly lightheaded.

"Could I have a moment of your time in your study?" she said, and Shaffer knew he had a problem.

THE FOLLOWING SATURDAY morning, holding the newspaper open in front of her, Diane asked Shaffer to ride along to an Amish orchard where apples with no pesticides were sold.

"Sure," he said. "I need to think about something humans eat."

"You've had nearly a week, Alex. Mrs. Vaughn has a phone."

"This can't go on. I felt like preaching with my back to the congregation." Diane sighed, "Why paper? At least the Amish have their reasons. They eat yams as a contraceptive." When she sighed again, he went on. "Yams, Diane. Think about it."

"You should eat that bag that nurse told you to keep. See if it prevents another heart attack." He thought about telling her he'd also read about people who had ignored their symptoms because they thought they were just anxious, but he couldn't remember any names or what they'd said.

"Anxiety," he finally said. "I create the symptoms I'm most afraid of."

"It's not a good thing for a minister to have an ego that rules his vital organs. It makes it look like your faith is weak." She paused, snapping the paper taut in her hands. "Listen to this before we go. 'Wayne Snow charged with soliciting three men for prostitution with a minor at his residence.' It has to be his daughter, Robin."

"I know who Robin Snow is. You had her in class three years ago. She'd be thirteen or fourteen now, but in your album, she'd be ten or eleven. You must have ten pictures of her. You must have shown them to me twenty times. How'd they catch the father?"

"Over a period of four months, beginning in June,' it says here. The police must have watched or something. How long do you have to let a girl get sold before you can arrest somebody? Think of it—she'd be just out of eighth grade, Alex."

"At least when the Amish finish eighth grade they become full-time farmers."

"I liked you better when you thought you were dying," Diane said. "It says here that allegedly the father had sex with Robin, too."

Shaffer decided to shut up. He didn't need to be an asshole just because one girl ate paper during church. On the front page, he noticed, was a story about a local school bus driver becoming a cross dresser on the job. There was a photo. The man reminded him of *Tootsie*. He was homelier than Dustin Hoffman, and the photo suggested he hadn't shaved before climbing onto the school bus in a dress. "Let's go get those Amish apples," Shaffer said, walking to the door. "I won't say one more judgmental word. A minister's not a judge."

Diane stayed seated, testing him, Shaffer thought at once. "If he isn't," she finally said, folding the paper into something that resembled a fly swatter and slapping it on the table, "he should go sit in a pew."

Shaffer kept his vow of silence right past the turn off to the Amish farm. In less than a minute he found himself on a narrow two-lane that threatened to turn to packed dirt or a rain-gutted test of tires.

"You can take the next left," Diane said. "You don't have to turn around."

He slowed, knowing the road was unlikely to be marked. "The Snows live out here," Diane said. "In a trailer. The father gave me directions once. 'So you know where to find me,' he said."

The road looked bleak enough to support a full spectrum of horrible behavior.

"Robin Snow," Diane blurted. He saw a trailer set back on what looked to be a reclaimed landfill. A few spindly pines struggled for space near stands of sumac. The rest of the land around the trailer was bare, tire tracks running through shale and mud. Nothing revealed a name but the box number she remembered from a class card. He downshifted to second gear. "Raped by the father," Diane said. "Sold by the hour to his friends." She asked him to park on the shoulder. She seemed to be memorizing the details while Shaffer watched for the man who lived there, out, according to Diane's summary of the article, on bail. By now, Wayne Snow, his name in the morning newspaper, would be holding a rifle by the small, front window where he studied the shitheads who saw the world as a television show.

Wayne Snow wouldn't know, sighting down the barrel from 200 feet away, that his daughter, four years before, had turned in homework to the woman in the parked car. He wouldn't care if she'd taken her tests and carried report cards home to an earlier version of himself, a father who attended open house, sitting in her desk among the visiting parents.

A jug-band breath of wind started humming at Shaffer's cracked window as a white Camaro veered toward them and parked so close, nose to nose, they seemed to dip in its turbulence. When Shaffer shifted to reverse, certain it was time to stop gawking, Diane said "No." He paused, understanding this was not Wayne Snow. The driver of the Camaro stepped out and checked his watch, shading his eyes to stare toward the trailer as if running through directions. Shaffer imagined he was matching Box #73 to word-of-mouth advertising, checking the time at which he'd agreed, nights ago, to arrive. It was entirely possible, Shaffer thought, that this man didn't read a newspaper or listen to a radio or watch the television news.

The man wore his thinning hair pulled back into a ponytail. He was sporting a badly faded t-shirt that read *Can the Juice*. Shaffer had seen those shirts hanging in windows along a New Jersey boardwalk years before Robin Snow had been born. The face of OJ Simpson rose and fell slightly as the man breathed.

"Oh Christ," Diane murmured.

"It can't be," Shaffer said. "It's only 9:30." But he couldn't think of a worthwhile reason the man was standing across the road from Box #73.

"Look at him. Tell me he's not here to get laid."

"She can't be inside, Diane."

"You don't have to fight. All you have to do is ask this pervert about Wayne Snow's arrest. He'll take the hint and hightail it."

"Really?"

Diane stared at him. "Yes, really," the words forcing him out of the car. He took a stance with the door open, his body behind it, but he looked directly at the mailbox that read 73, waiting for the driver to decide what would happen next.

All the conviction oozed out of him. He listened for his wife to say his name and the words, "Enough. Let's go." He sensed the man in the OJ shirt sizing him up, making a decision that ended with, "This wimp needs his ass kicked."

"Draws a crowd, don't it?" the ponytailed man said, but Shaffer kept his eyes on the mailbox. The stranger, when he spoke again, said, "Don't need a license I'm aware of for pussy hunting," spewing the words directly into Shaffer's left ear, telling him, no doubt, he'd better have a hell of a good reason to argue about a man's constitutional right to live-action pornography.

"Piss on you, fella," the man said then, and Shaffer, terrified, had to turn, his hands curling into fists. To his joy, the man slid into his Camaro and backed up a car length. *Appeasement*, Shaffer thought, hoping.

Diane tapped the inside of the windshield and motioned him inside. "Let's get the apples," she said. "I'm sorry I made you stop."

THE NEXT MORNING, after he watched Evelyn Vaughn, sitting in row five dressed in all blue, eat paper throughout the anthem, he lost his place three times during the first five minutes of his sermon, looking up and then down so quickly, his sentences swam into nonsense. He read for five minutes without looking up, and then, confident because the last section of his sermon was an anecdote about food, the pleasures of bread in all its flavors--rye, whole wheat, garlic, sourdough, onion--he delivered his metaphor about love and diversity to a space just above the heads of the congregation so there was no chance he'd notice a flash of blue.

"I need to speak with you immediately," he said to Evelyn's mother when she came through the receiving line. "Excuse me," he said to the two married couples left in line behind her. "There's an emergency."

As soon as the three of them were in his study, Shaffer started right in. "I know you've been attending this church for several years, but we have a problem here with Evelyn's behavior."

"What?" The mother shook her head and looked at her daughter. Evelyn was beginning to touch fingertips again, so rapid and so certain he thought she would make a wonderful video game player.

"The paper," Shaffer tried.

Evelyn's mother brightened. "Oh, that?" she said. "It wasn't none of your books this time. I'll pay for your little book. What's that run, a dollar or some such?"

"The money's not an issue."

"I carry paper with me now. You know, the blank kind, so I can give it to her when she sets her mind on it."

"She does this elsewhere?"

"Only when she's nervous or bored. She sometimes goes weeks without doing it, and then something kicks it off again. You know, Pastor, some talk out loud and some wiggle. She uses it like gum, I'd say."

"Well, it's not coming just from me," Shaffer began, and then his words trailed off because he wanted to address her by name, and calling her Mrs. Vaughn, he was certain, would lead to stories of her awful marriage.

"Do you know what, Pastor?" the woman said, looking at Evelyn while she raced through five repetitions of fingertip-touching. "She stops when you're talking. What do you think of that?"

"There are other ways to deal with this besides giving her blank paper."

"She's not about to be swallowing pills, Pastor. Then she'd be somebody else."

"Give this some thought," Shaffer concluded, and when his words hung in the air, the woman smiled.

"Jean," she said. She watched his face. "Go ahead," she added. "It's okay to call a woman by her first name. I'm not exactly Mrs. Vaughn these days, am I?"

She guided Evelyn to the door and paused for a moment. "I've never seen you with family, Pastor. Are yours all grown?"

"I don't have children."

"Well, now," she said, and then she turned and disappeared.

Before he moved from where he'd been standing, Diane stepped inside Shaffer's study. "What did you say to her?" she asked at once.

"Mrs. Vaughn told me she brought her own paper this week. She made sure I knew she wasn't costing the church a penny more for damaged books."

"What did you say to the girl?"

"Nothing. She sat there the whole time playing finger games."

"You need to test yourself more," Diane said, sounding so sad Shaffer believed she'd made a judgment about him she'd been waffling about for twenty years.

FRIDAY AFTERNOON, AS he always did, Shaffer wrote his sermon, a meditation on "Blessed are the merciful." When he read it aloud to himself, listening to the cadences of his sentences, it sounded so insincere that he went to his files and retrieved a sermon on "Blessed are the poor" that he'd delivered six years ago, long enough that no one would remember. "Let's go out," he said to Diane. "Some place where I can eat beef and French fries and get free refills of ginger ale."

By seven o'clock, half way through dinner, Shaffer wished he was sitting farther away from the noisy foursome nearby. "School tax," he heard a man's voice say. "There's a punishment."

"Now we have a cross-dressing bus driver," another man said. "What's next? Our taxes pay for him to get his dick cut off?"

He heard the two women laugh. One said, "I'd feel better about paying to sew some balls on the teachers, the things they let the kids do anymore."

Everyone laughed again, and Shaffer, when he turned to evaluate the two couples, saw one of the women staring at him, and he recognized her and the others as members of his congregation, the two couples who had been waiting behind Evelyn Vaughn in the receiving line last Sunday.

Fifteen minutes later, when the two couples stood up to leave, the woman who'd been staring said, "Hello, there, Pastor. Getting material to illustrate God's word on the evils of alcohol for the rest of us?"

Her husband laughed as if she'd said something hilarious. "Zip it up, Marilyn," he said. "Don't bring the Lord's name into this."

"Jesus, Frank."

"Ministers have to eat," Shaffer said, thinking at once that he sounded so dreadfully timid he deserved this woman's contempt.

"What do you think, Pastor? Aren't there children who need something more than a talking to?" She swayed slightly, and then looked at Diane as if gauging how she might counsel him when this conversation ended. "If you had children, Pastor, let me tell you," she finally said, and then her voice trailed off as if he was supposed to fill in the phrases that followed.

The two couples marched away, the woman who hadn't spoken

suddenly shrieking with laughter. Shaffer tapped his fork on the table. "That girl will eat a ream of white paper by Christmas," he said. "She's made me a joke."

"Don't make yourself an ass, Alex."

"That's what I'm becoming," he said. "That's one thing you can count on."

"Ok, Alex. Let's at least not waste our food."

"You sound like a mother," Shaffer said. "That's the tone you would use if we had kids and they were sitting here with their plates half full."

"We can talk later when you're settled," she said, and worked her fork full of pasta, intent, Shaffer thought, on what looked to be about six more bites.

Shaffer tapped his fork again, and then, noticing the sound, laid it on his plate. "Remember the doctor we went to the summer we were married?"

"Dr. Cianci?" Diane said at once. "Sure."

Her instant recall flustered Shaffer a moment. "Was that his name?" he said. "I was just remembering him as the doctor whose office was decorated with praying hands."

"He was Catholic," Diane said between forkfuls.

"He talked to us as if we were kneeling for Communion. He offered solace for desire and praise for abstinence. He prescribed the rhythm method. I wanted to tell him what I was studying to be."

"We thanked him and looked for another doctor who'd write up an order for birth control pills," Diane said, "which kept us in the dark for the next five years about how things would turn out for us."

"I'm thinking we could have managed just fine with blasphemy," Shaffer said. "We didn't even need Cianci's faith."

"We're not the only childless couple," Diane said. "Finish your ginger ale if you want and let's leave."

Shaffer lifted his glass and then set it down without drinking. "There was a pregnant woman in Cianci's waiting room as we left. She was younger than you and had four kids who hadn't started school."

Diane shook her head. "She told us the praying hands on Cianci's posters were the same as the ones on a set of dish towels she owned. 'Identical,' she said. 'So holy.'"

Shaffer felt his lungs locking up. And then, not wanting to struggle in front of Diane, he settled himself and concentrated on controlling his breathing as if his head was covered by a paper bag.

HOURS LATER, WHEN Shaffer touched Diane as she lay in bed, she didn't move or speak. He lifted her nightgown, drawing it up her back, and still she stayed inert. His fingers entered her, and he held his breath. And then he withdrew them and pushed himself inside her from behind. "Oh," she said, and he closed his eyes before he leaned forward and thrusted. He could hear the whistle in his breath as he shuddered through his climax, and for the second time that evening, he concentrated on slowing his breathing.

At 1:38, according to the clock radio, Shaffer sat up silently, measuring the seriousness of his symptoms—shortness of breath, chest pain. When he decided he'd strangle if he stayed in bed, he stood as if his feet on hardwood could charm away the pillow-on-the-face of fear. If he was having a heart attack, he was going to die believing he was fine.

He dressed himself and waited for his lungs to calculate his need for faith. He saw the brown bag he'd brought home from the hospital lying on the dresser. When Diane didn't stir, he lifted it carefully and carried it into the living room.

Shaffer concentrated on survival to convince himself that he needed nothing but the common sense of calm and the brown bag for panic. Shaffer breathed in, breathed out, listening between breaths for any sign that Diane had woken, and when he felt himself beginning to recover, he smoothed the bag and closed his eyes to pray.

IN THE MORNING, Diane said nothing about either attack, reading the paper as if it was filled with prophecy. "Any news about Wayne Snow?" he said.

"Nothing."

"How did Robin Snow act when she was in your class?"

"You mean what kind of weirdness she showed? She drew pictures on her arms with her pen."

"Like tattoos?"

"Like she was in kindergarten. Like she had the coordination of a fourth-grader and the mind of a five year-old."

"Tell me about her," he said. "Every detail you can remember."

SUNDAY MORNING, WHEN Shaffer turned to face the congregation after climbing the chancel steps, he saw that the Vaughns were sitting in the first pew directly in front of the lectern from which he delivered his sermon. The girl was wearing her red and white striped dress again, but someone had cut her hair, hacking the black strands of it down to a sort of military crew cut that was so uneven he decided she must have done it to herself.

The girl didn't budge during the scripture reading. She sat so perfectly still through the anthem that Shaffer let his lips form the "Amen" at the end. He imagined the congregation beaming with approval, the two couples from the restaurant, now sober, regretting their indiscretion.

Before he began the sermon, Shaffer had enough confidence to glance down at Evelyn, and for a moment he thought she was chewing paper, but her mouth moved as if forming words. And then, to his horror, he was convinced she was repeating, "Help me," as he looked at her. Shaffer looked out at the congregation and spoke his old words about the downtrodden and their eternal reward. When Shaffer looked down at Jean Vaughn as the sermon ended, she was staring up at him as if she expected his gaze, and in that second, he thought her expression signaled disappointment.

MONDAY MORNING, THE paper carried a full page of letters-to-the-editor about the cross-dressing bus driver. If Wayne Snow had sold his daughter for a bushel of apples, there was no mention of it.

Shaffer wore his collar. He had afternoon shut-in visitations, but for now he told himself he was driving into the country to enjoy the first turning of leaves before he started work on the quarterly budget accounts. He thought of buying an Amish pie from the stand by the farm they'd visited the day they'd parked by Wayne Snow's trailer. A surprise for Diane, he thought, and the idea cheered him.

Even this early, a young girl was standing under the small shelter. He chose a shoo-fly pie, something so rich both of them could enjoy the guilt of gorging themselves. When he handed her the nine dollars, a gust of wind nearly pulled the batch of one-dollar bills out of her hand. "Close," he said, smiling, and a second gust tightened her dark dress against her body, the shape of her breasts and thighs forming so suddenly Shaffer's eyes held on them for a moment before he wheeled around and dropped back into the front seat of his car.

Instead of turning back toward town, he followed the road he'd used with Diane. In less than a minute he saw the mailbox labeled Box #73. His hands tightened on the wheel as he slowed, dropping into second gear. When the makeshift driveway was a few car lengths away, he felt the same urge he sometimes did when he approached a pornography shop, the thought that all he had to do was give himself up to his imagination, pull in, park, and walk toward whatever pleased him.

He shivered as the trailer receded behind him, and then he accelerated, telling himself he'd passed some sort of self-graded test. But when, after he'd looped into Amish country again on the way back to town, he drove by two girls walking along the shoulder, both of them appearing to be barely teenagers, and their dark-clothed bodies were transformed into something a man would pay to use. When he passed the Amish food stand, he kept his eyes on the hood of his car, but he could hardly breathe.

Shaffer entered the church and checked his messages, pleased not one of them was about Evelyn Vaughn. This thing will pass, he said to himself, wandering into the choir loft, standing above the chancel and looking at the rows of empty pews before he dropped his gaze and noticed what looked to be a note on the lectern.

Something from the janitor, he guessed, annoyed that the man wouldn't think to attach the note to his study door. A moment later he saw that he was wrong. "You saw that I answered your prayers," the note began, "but you have no mercy in you. Goodbye, Jean."

An inch or so below "goodbye" there was a PS. "And don't think I didn't remember all you had to say about the poor from way back before."

Below that, another inch down as if she'd remembered at the last minute, she'd printed, "not God" followed by a long arrow that looped up to point at, "I answered."

Shaffer leaned on the lectern with both hands, lingering on the word *Goodbye.* As soon as he knew he was relieved, he felt like throwing up. He had underestimated the look on Jean Vaughn's face. It wasn't disappointment. It was dismissal.

Shaffer grabbed the budget folder and carried it to his car. He could work on it at home, he thought. Or he could not work on it at all. Three miles later, he was driving alongside a series of Amish farms. He passed a buggy. There was a straight stretch right after the next curve, and Shaffer accelerated, closing on a blue pickup that suddenly veered left and lurched as if it would roll over. Shaffer braked as the truck bounced down, its tires grabbing, and Shaffer pressed hard on the brake pedal as he saw a second horse and buggy still skidding sideways.

The blue pickup stopped a hundred feet down along the shoulder. The driver, instead of backing up, opened the door and yelled "Shit" before slamming his boots to the asphalt and jogging toward where Shaffer was kneeling by the body he'd seen pitched onto the pavement.

When Shaffer saw her face, he thought she was a teenager. Sixteen, he guessed, and he looked around to see if he'd missed someone, the buggy driver, a man, or at least an older brother, because he'd heard the Amish didn't let girls drive by themselves.

The horse was bicycling slowly near the center line, unable to rise. The sky, Shaffer observed, was cloudless. It was 10 a.m., late enough for the sun to be in nobody's eyes,

The driver of the pickup hovered. "She dead?" he asked, sounding exactly like somebody who'd decided this girl had fractured her skull or ruptured an essential internal organ.

"I hope not," Shaffer said.

"Busted up bad, I'll bet. What the hell? She came right out of nowhere."

"Wave somebody down. Call 911." Shaffer checked the girl's mouth, saw her tongue wasn't in the way of her breathing, but if she had a pulse he couldn't find it.

The man stared at Shaffer's collar. "You a preacher? God help me, this ain't my fault."

Shaffer straddled her body and locked the fingers of his hands together, bent into her chest and counted the compressions—one, two, three, four, five, he muttered, and blew air into her mouth as he held her nose.

"You know CPR?" the driver said. "Thank God."

"Wave somebody down," Shaffer shouted. He pressed down hard— one, two, three, four, five. He blew air again. He'd taken the lessons years ago, signing up because he'd volunteered to coach junior soccer. The instructor had called the rubber dummy Mike Muscles. One by one they'd performed the ritual in front of their classmates. How many times had they counted? There was a chance, he knew, that his technique was wrong.

"Goddamn it to hell," the driver said then, "that horse should have known better than to trot out of that dirt lane."

He could save this girl, Shaffer thought. As long as he remembered correctly what he'd learned, settling into a rhythm, keeping things going until professional help arrived.

"God damned Amish," the driver shouted. "A girl like this here ought to be in school this time of day." Shaffer didn't look up. One two, three, four, five, he repeated. When the pickup driver stepped on a piece of glass, it popped, but Shaffer didn't even flinch.

WILDFIRE

LOU STOLTZ, OUR landlord, said, "You water these plants of yours, right?" but he didn't wait for us to answer. "Sure you do," he went on, "so why didn't you water the trees standing right there beside them?"

Lou Stoltz was pissed because he'd received three letters from Forest Services and a threat, in letter number three, of a hefty fine for not clearing underbrush and dead trees that would fuel a wildfire sweeping across the hill behind the half of the big double my sister and I rented. As far as I could see, there wasn't much question that such a fire would engulf all that tinder and Lou's double with it when it came, what seemed more likely than ever with all the other fires in the area springing up the past few days, most of them within an hour's drive from where we stood twenty miles from downtown Los Angeles.

Lou had come directly to our side of the double because he knew not to expect our neighbor Jason to be home. Jason, whose last name we hadn't learned since he'd moved in about the same time my sister Jenny had two years ago, apparently paid his rent in a timely way, but he slept under his roof maybe one week a month, sometimes less. For quite some time now, Jenny and I believed that Jason needed a permanent address in case of whatever illegal shit he was doing required the appearance of domesticity.

There were trees all over the hillside, but the four Lou was concerned about stood in a row just on the other side of the fence he'd been forced to put up years ago to shield the patio from coyotes and other nuisances. His complaining suggested those cypress technically belonged to him, and all of them had been dead for three years, smart-bombed by some relentless, unseen pest.

Nobody would water full-grown trees, and no amount of water was bringing them back, but Lou was the kind of asshole who needed a scapegoat for his neglect. He took the hose we had coiled in a corner of the patio and hoisted it over the fence and turned on the tap. "There," he said, as if he expected some sort of backdating to recover green. "Now, for Christ's sake, take care of them."

No surprise, the Forest Service showed up at dawn the next day to clear the vacant lot next door, waking us after we'd spent a couple of after-midnight hours listening to the party next door let us know Jason was home. Since I'd moved in nine years ago, the Service had never been anywhere close, but by late afternoon that hillside was clean and tidy, like you could sit over there and not look like you were homeless or some sort of pervert loitering around among the waist-high underbrush and a scattering of fallen trees.

It was understandable, the Forest Service tending property and being short-tempered with assholes like Lou. Instead of December rain and a break from high alert, California firefighters had their hands full. After dinner, for the past few days, Jenny and I had watched the fires on the television news, the nearest one about ten miles away over by the Getty Museum. The Skirball Fire, they were calling it, after the Jewish Cultural Center near the 405 by Bel Air. A cooking fire had started it, they said, and that revelation had already stirred up a lot of anti-homeless trash talk on the news sites that were covering that fire and several others like it, including what was becoming an enormous one farther north called the Thomas. If the Santa Ana winds kept blowing the way they had been, nothing looked to stop that one but reaching the ocean.

"Enough," Jenny said, going outside, and I had to agree. From my bedroom, I watched her water our plants, mostly succulents that handled the inevitable droughts well. She was sparing. Precise, it seemed, as if she'd read up on just what those plants required. She used a sprinkling can and never glanced at the dead cypress trees, but before she was finished, she turned toward the head-high fence that separated our patio from Jason's.

A woman's voice had said something through the fence. I listened hard, but there was no making out what the faceless person, either a cleaning lady or one of Jason's girlfriends, was saying. Jenny laughed once, then spoke softly, so I relaxed, giving me time to notice that all of the cypress trees behind Jason's patio were green. A minute later there were footsteps on our side stairs, the ones that neither of us ever used except to haul garbage down to the street for pickup.

"I didn't bring the noise," the woman who appeared said at once. "Jason says he loves company when he's home," substituting an apology for, "Hello."

"Brassy," I thought, my father's old expression crawling up from some landfill of discarded language. The woman was dressed the way defense lawyers sometimes cite to defend their rapist clients. "She-was-asking-for-it" clothes—cleavage, bare midriff, shorts that reminded me of the ones worn by the Dallas Cowboy Cheerleaders. "Painted on," I thought, more old-timey I couldn't shake. If sexual violence had ever entered this woman's life the way it had my sister's, she was treating the aftermath differently, something else, besides her outfit, that made me guess she was a prostitute, someone who had built up her immune system for feeling violated.

JENNY HAD MOVED in a week after her rape and hadn't worked for six months until she signed on as a teacher's aide at the elementary school. I'd switched into the smaller bedroom when she'd asked to stay for a while. "It's not the size," she'd said, "it's how easy it looks for somebody to break in from the patio. I'd be staring at those sliding glass doors every morning and night. I know it's locked, but it doesn't feel like it is. It's so private back there, it's terrifying."

I had a security bar put in to double lock that sliding door. I had a dead bolt added to both doors. We settled into lives that didn't seem lived in. It was as if everything surrounding us was reported like the fires. We're like spinsters, she said once, truth in that, and she compounded it by dressing like a schoolmarm. She wore glasses instead of her contact lenses. Her blouses all looked a size too large. When she seemed to sense me thinking, *Fear disguised as modesty*, she said, "I'm thinner now. I don't party. I don't pig out on bar food." As if you could transform yourself with glasses, a high neckline, and a few lost pounds. Like you could be Clark Kent in a dress.

Later, when I asked, Jenny said the woman's name was Cassandra, and she'd called over to offer her opinion on Lou Stoltz—"The worst kind of cheap, fucking asshat."

"I told her Lou looks like that pig that's been on the news," Jenny said, "the famous sex harasser, the ugly one. You know what Cassandra said? 'Jason looks like one of the handsome ones.'"

Jenny laughed for the second time in an hour. Cassandra was better than Xanax. When I didn't reply, she said, "You were too embarrassed to come outside and meet her, weren't you? You and your comb-over. I saw your hand go right up to it when the breeze kicked up. You're squeamish when women are spirited."

"Spirited is a push," I said.

"What's that, some kind of accountant's talk? You work in a room full of men, don't you? And numbers don't argue."

For a moment, I thought about what our mother had said to me when I was about to start high school a year before she'd left. "You always liked numbers," she'd said. "I used to think that was cute until you moved in with them."

"Numbers don't argue. They win," I said, but Jenny was pouring herself a glass of wine.

"Let's order in some Chinese," she said. "Let's eat some of that tangerine chicken and hate on Lou Stoltz and that firetrap behind the fence."

BEFORE THE CHICKEN and rice arrived, I stood in the kitchen doorway and listened as the foreman of the Forest Service work crew told me they had a file on Lou Stoltz that went back seventeen years. "This guy," he said, "you can pretty much count your chances of him doing the right thing at point zero zero."

"Amen to that," I said. Lou was the sort of landlord who, when I'd called to tell him the roof was leaking, none of the four numbers he'd given me connected to a working phone. Now I had his email, but he didn't respond.

"Stoltz has other neglected properties," he said. "He knows we have serious eyes on him. A rash of wildfires has a way of prompting some heavy arm-twisting." He nodded toward the empty lot for emphasis.

I hoped they'd fine him big time, but then again, I was afraid that would make him raise the rent. Jason, the unscrupulous next door, wouldn't squawk, but me who'd lived here nine years and taken care of plumbing and electrical repairs without a squawk, would have to pick up the slack in silence, too.

But what made me despise Lou was he knew my sister had moved in with me because she'd been raped, and he still talked to her like a thoughtless moron. He referenced pieces of ass and outstanding racks every time he came around to talk about Jason's women like he was a friend of mine. When Jenny was close by on the patio, he'd say, "Guy's talk," looking her way and shrugging. "My bad."

The rapist, at least, had been caught. He'd lawyered up with the usual I-dropped-her-off story, the one about being punished for being a good Samaritan, but he'd had an MO by then, two other victims ready to testify and, finally, a DNA match to nail his coffin shut.

I'd driven her to work for a month, leaving the apartment half an hour earlier than usual. I'd arranged for a teacher I knew to drive her home so there was only an hour each day when she was alone. Lately, she'd been walking both ways, a half mile of traffic-clogged streets, but now Jenny had read about how prisoners from where her rapist was incarcerated were cheap-labor firefighters, and when the Thomas fire had widened, she started to believe they'd need so many firefighters that he was getting paid a dollar an hour to be a hero.

"I don't think a violent criminal would be allowed," I said, intent on the news as we started in on the Chinese.

"You don't know that," she said, and then brightened. "Maybe it's a good thing he's out there. Maybe he'll burn."

I was at the gym doing my three-a-week workout the next afternoon when Jenny came home and saw the three kids sitting at the table we had on the patio. She never went out back if I wasn't there, but three kids, all strangers, got the best of her, and she opened the sliding door and saw a stranger sawing down those four dead cypress trees that Lou's watering hadn't resurrected. "My God," she said when I got home. "I didn't know what to think him standing there with a chain saw and knowing he couldn't be Forest Service, not with three kids there, each with a coloring book and sharing a box of crayons."

"'Those are mine,' he said, like I was thinking of taking them inside and locking them in a closet. 'Lou sent me after he got another letter. I'm his brother.'" "'Bullshit you are,'" was what I thought, no resemblance at all, and not a peep from the three kids. 'I couldn't get a babysitter,' he said. He'd finished three trees and hadn't had one fall on the house, so I thought maybe he knew what was up about tree cutting. But you'll see, when you go out there, that the stumps are high enough to catch you in the crotch."

I followed her out back and, sure enough, there were four waist-high stumps, so maybe that guy had been Lou's brother after all because who else would leave things in a state like that?

Not to mention there was a stack of logs by the side steps and a teetering pile of dead branches on the other side as if Lou's brother had arranged things according to avoiding tossing stuff on his kids. "I told him it's like he broke into our house," Jenny said, "and he laughed and told me he'd tell Lou how we didn't appreciate all the trouble they'd gone to for us."

The news showed a commuter's video of the Skirball Fire taken that morning on the 405. The hillside across from the Getty was a holocaust of flame. The traffic was snarled. The 405, shortly after, was closed. "Wow," I said, when a photo of the empty highway was shown. "When was that ever empty? It looks like a site for a *Walking Dead* shoot."

Jenny tensed. "It looks like a place rapists would love."

The evening began to tip. The next news was about a firefighter being killed. He wasn't identified yet, and Jenny said she'd keep checking online. The Thomas Fire had exploded. The Santa Ana was relentless.

Just before eleven o'clock, dressed for bed, Jenny told me she'd done a search to see if any prisoners had ever died fighting fires "A tree fell on one," she said. "One other was chewed up by a chainsaw. Just those two."

Lou showed up late the next afternoon, returning, I was sure, to receive some thanks, or better yet, see if we'd cleared off the patio. Twice disappointed, he turned mean. "That there on the other side of the fence is for the Forest jerks. On this side is what's called collateral damage that needs attending to."

"And both unfinished business," Jenny said at once, surprising me.

"Stumps don't spread fire and there's folks who come and take shit away if you give them a call."

"Those aren't stumps."

"You got a different name for them you want to spit out?"

"Hideous."

"That's not a name. That's an attitude. It'll go away once you get this mess gone." He picked up a branch and swished it back and forth like a swashbuckler. "Your brother's name is right there on the lease," he said, taking a step my way, the branch extended. "That's all I'm saying."

Jenny stayed quiet. I sorted through responses. Lou satisfied himself by dropping the branch in a clear spot on the patio and left by the side steps.

"It's his responsibility," I said, as if that settled it.

"In another dimension," Jenny said. "In somebody's fantasy."

I kicked the branch toward the pile, and she laughed, dry and forced. A cackle. She was already examining the hillside as if she'd noticed something more interesting than acquiescence. "What's that stuff all over the hill called that's always brown and dry-looking like it was born to burn?" Jenny said.

"Underbrush."

"It has a name. There was green here last winter when it rained a lot."

"And the hill filled up with underbrush after it got hot and dry again."

"Chaparral," she said. "Does that sound right?"

"The guy who got killed. He wasn't your rapist. He wasn't even a prisoner."

"I know," she said, "but I wonder if there's somebody who's happy that guy's dead."

"You can't think like that."

"I can't do what I want, but I can think what I want," she said. She paused, taking a breath, but I didn't fill in with a judgment, and she went on. "I knew who that dickhead was, but I didn't know him. He didn't jump out of the bushes. He gave me a ride. I might as well have been six years old listening to him say my daddy had asked him to pick me up after school."

"You're not the one that needs to be hard on yourself," I said.

"You know what I keep thinking? Somebody, somewhere, sometime, must have offered a ride like that and done what he promised."

"It's like believing in God because the minister says so."

"What? Really? Don't go there. This actually happened."

"Sorry," I said. "Faith is the world's oldest lie. We just learn that in different ways."

UP EARLY THE next morning, I had time to step out onto the patio. I hefted one of the logs. It felt awkward more than heavy. Clearing the patio was doable as long as I was careful and patient, lugging them down the side steps one at a time so I didn't take a tumble. I carried one, and then another down to where my car was parked and laid them in the back seat. I took a shower and told myself it wasn't crazy to look for a place to dump them.

By the time I was dressed, I expected Jenny to be gone, but when I looked into the bedroom, she was standing before the mirror examining her face. She was dressed, but I noticed her school ID hanging by its lanyard from the edge of the mirror. In her photo, she'd turned her head slightly as if someone had spoken from her left and she was listening.

"I kept telling myself that as soon as he was in jail I'd be okay, but that's never happened. And now there's a chance he might be freed to act the hero."

"Did you know that when the firefighting prisoners get out of jail, they aren't allowed to be real firefighters?"

"That can't be true."

"Because they're convicted felons." I felt good saying that, like it was the best possible news she could hear. And maybe it was because she opened the drawer where she kept her underwear, slid her right hand under a stack of panties, and retrieved a small handgun.

"I figured this was secure right there," she said. "I've had it since the week after I moved in and so much time by myself." She laid it on the dresser, the barrel pointing toward the mirror. "Say something," she said.

"Have you fired it?"

"I went to a range and practiced. It's not enough to just know the basics."

"Like going to the gym."

"It's not any kind of miracle," Jenny said. "It's just a step."

"It might get you killed instead."

"That's a choice I'll deal with," she said. "What I don't want ever again is a rerun." She seemed to be gnawing the inside of her lower lip. I thought of telling her she looked frightened rather than fierce, but let it go.

"I take it to school," she said, "even though nobody's older than eleven and the teachers are all women except for two old guys."

I thought of a child opening her purse. I thought of some teacher discovering that she carried a gun into an elementary school building, how quickly an aide would be dismissed. "I told myself I wasn't taking it today. And then I couldn't make myself go."

"After today, school's over until January," I said. "Let's go someplace for a couple of days. Let's go to Joshua Tree," I said, the name swirling up like sparks.

"You've never once mentioned Joshua Tree since I lived here. You don't even play your old U2 CD anymore."

"It's thirty years now. I wore those songs out."

"Dad always acted like the release date was a family birthday, like it was almost my twin because I was born the day after."

"He wanted to stay at The Harmony Motel because U2 stayed there, but it was full," I said. "I remember it was little. We can try it again. I'll check to make sure it's even still there."

"Okay, but first bring those two logs back up—we're not maids."

"Where did that come from?" I said.

"Cassandra said you looked like a pussy carrying those logs. She laughed."

"Somebody has to clean up," I said, but I felt sweat under my armpits and on my forehead. I reached up and brushed my comb-over to keep it from sticking.

"I'm not riding in a car with those bodies in the trunk. Anyway, Cassandra gave me an idea." She looked excited, like we were planning a heist. "Toss everything over the side fence where it's not as high because of the hillside. Cleaning up will be all on Lou if it's dumped on just-cleared land. The forest service will see it that way."

"And Lou will do what?" I said, but Jenny tossed a branch and then another over the side fence, then stared at me until I lifted a log. It took an hour to move that mess.

By the time I'd taken a shower, Jenny was ready with her overnight bag. "Cassandra said she'd sweep up while we were gone," she said, but what made me smile was she'd put in her contact lenses. "I thought I'd wear them for a change," she said. "And I have this swimsuit I bought way back and never wore. The Harmony has a pool, right? Dad had us wait outside while he looked at photos in the lobby and asked which rooms U2 stayed in like he'd had the good sense to make a reservation."

"He asked a maid to open a room door for him. He gave her money. How much do you think he gave her? A couple of bucks, tops?"

"Tops, for sure," Jenny said, "but she let him stand inside so he could tell us how it was to maybe be in Bono's room."

I pulled out into traffic, relaxed now that we were leaving the debris behind. "Mom told me later that she'd bet that maid just opened a messy room and figured he couldn't slow her down unless he threw up on the floor. Why would the maid give a damn about U2?"

"And while he was in that room, we saw the naked woman at the pool. In the middle of the day when nobody was around and she saw us and just waved like she was wrapped in a robe. Mom was smoking by the car, so there we were getting an eyeful. I always wondered what she thought of two kids watching her."

"It's like a story where we don't know the ending," I said. "Like it has those dots at the end of the last sentence."

"Ellipses," Jenny said. "There's always a word for everything."

"Maybe she didn't have a bathing suit and it was so hot she just said, 'Fuck it, I'm all in.' Maybe that's all that was."

"I never put that at the end of any version I imagined. Not once."

"Me neither," I said, and she laughed and I thought maybe some small thing had been repaired for a while. Then her face clouded and she said, "You thought she was showing off, even though you were what, ten? You thought she was something for you to enjoy."

"I didn't even know what a woman looked like underneath everything."

"But later you finished that story the way you wanted."

"You don't know what I did."

She was angry now. "You think you're so mysterious. No kids, no pets, no parents—we have all this freedom, and all I can think is how badly we've used it."

I kept my eyes on the road. "You know I'm right," she said, and then turned to look out the side window as if the road to 29 Palms was full of scenery that had to be absorbed.

THE HARMONY WAS little, that was for sure. Six rooms plus a cottage that turned out to be named for Jack Kerouac. And just as she'd promised, she changed as soon as we were checked in, put on a robe, and went out to the pool without even asking me if I was interested.

I watched from the doorway. She stood by the ladder for a minute, then two. Finally, she undid the robe and let it slide off. Her suit was a modest two-piece, and her body looked the way I remembered it from when she was in college—athletic, toned, beautiful. A man who didn't know her, I thought, would think she had a choice of lovers. Or that she was unattainable.

She turned and saw me. "I can feel eyes on me."

"You're right," I called out. "I'm guilty."

"Not you," she said. She seemed to be scanning the length of the motel. There was only one other car in the lot. In a few seconds, I thought, she'll cover up and come inside.

"I'll come out and sit while you swim."

My offer seemed to anger her. "Absolutely not. Just watch from inside."

She swam for half an hour. As if she were testing herself, she walked across the lot with her robe open. "There were people everywhere back then," she said. "Other kids like us with Moms who kept saying to stay on the park trails when you could hardly see the difference between what's allowed and not."

"I thought there'd be tourists here," I said. "Families. It's creepy with nearly empty."

"Creepy? For you? What are you afraid of?"

"That he ruined you."

"That's a magician's answer," she said. "That's a diversion so I look in the wrong direction."

THE NEWS THAT night told us Skirball was contained. Two days ago, we'd watched that fire on the news, and it looked as if there was no way it wasn't going to the other side of the 405 and up the hill to the Getty. But now one side of the 405 was blackened and charred and Getty's side was green. "Look at that," Jenny said. "It's like the Getty people paid God to stop the fire. Everywhere else it jumped highways, but not there."

"Up at Ojai," I said, "the town was surrounded and still dodged the worst. It's topography, wind, and a lot of luck."

"It's beyond a lot of luck," Jenny said, as we watched videos of the

Thomas fire. Ventura looked like Hiroshima. The houses in the town weren't scattered up in the woods. They were all in orderly patterns along roads, yet whole neighborhoods were leveled. It looked as if everything that could burn was destroyed, and all the trees in the "before picture" were a deeper shade of green than anything on the hillside beside our apartment. "It looks like hell on the morning after," the newscaster said.

"I hate to hear people describe the fire as "hell," Jenny said. "Hell isn't real. That fire isn't imaginary. You'd have to ask that firefighter who died what that fire was like. What it's like to be consumed. I bet he wouldn't say it was like being in hell. In hell, you're tortured, not destroyed."

She grabbed the remote and ran through channels until she found the PBS station. "That's enough about the fire," she said. "It makes me think about Lou and the fucking hose. I bet he's never saved a thing in his whole life."

We watched a woman talking about the astonishing weight of birds. Sometimes, she said, the eyes of birds weigh more than their brains. Sometimes their bones weigh less than their feathers.

"That asshole who fucked me," Jenny said, "he was heavy. He felt like dead weight on me." And then both of us went quiet, letting the expert go on about how light birds could be.

"IT FEELS COLD," Jenny said, as we set off early to hike through the park. "It's hard to believe it will be over 90 today."

"And it's nearly Christmas. They shut this place down after ten a.m. almost every day in the summer, even sometimes, now, in the spring and fall."

"It looks like this place already had its fire and nothing ever grew back except the Joshua Trees."

"It's just different."

"For sure, it is, if looking dead counts."

When a man walking alone began to overtake us, she clutched her purse, and then let it go after he'd passed. "I thought I could leave it behind," she said before I could say anything. No one else alone came near, just one family with children and two other couples. None of them spoke to us.

"I thought this place was popular," Jenny said.

"Maybe people think it's way too hot even though it's winter."

"Or they think it's boring. After ten minutes, you've seen everything there is. It's all the same everywhere you look."

"But it's fascinating what some living things can stand."

"Yes," Jenny said. "It's like an enormous condemned building that won't fall down." She turned herself in a circle as if she meant to see everywhere at once. "Maybe they're what will outlive everything if they could stand it out here all these years."

Two women walking together caught up to us. Young. Fit-looking. "Hi, there," Jenny said, smiling, as they passed.

"It's good to see you better," I said.

Her expression hardened. "Better than what?"

"I don't know. Better than last week. Better than back then."

"Than after the rape."

"Yes."

"As far as you can tell."

"Yes."

Jenny seemed to be evaluating the landscape. Whether it had earned her attention. She opened her water bottle and took a sip. "So," she said, screwing the cap back on, "show me the album-cover tree. It fell down, didn't it?"

Somebody, I remembered, had sawed off a piece of the trunk as a souvenir a couple of years ago, but the remains were easy to identify because they were surrounded by signs and photographs and trinkets. None of it looked like it had been there for more than a couple of weeks. "Somebody must come out here and remove stuff," I said.

"Maybe," Jenny said, "but what do they do with it then?"

When I didn't answer, she said, "Of course."

FOR THE FIRST time in weeks, the sky clouded up as we drove through 29 Palms and started back to Los Angeles. It was only 3:30, but I turned on the lights, and Jenny noticed. "You remember how Dad used to not put his headlights on until it was so dark nobody could see us?" she said. "And there was that one road we used a lot that still had three lanes. It was so scary there."

"That day we went to Joshua Tree it started to rain on the way back. It rained almost the whole way home," I said.

"It absolutely poured near the end. We got off the 10, and it was like we'd never been in our neighborhood before."

"And Dad didn't have his lights on because he said it wasn't night and we weren't going fast. I thought Dad was going to pull over we were going so slow. And still he kept the lights off."

"Dad sat there in front of the house laughing like he thought it was the funniest thing ever we were all so terrified. 'You all look like refugees,' he said.'" I gave her a smile, but her expression didn't change.

The rain didn't start, but the clouds thickened. I concentrated on the road and Jenny stayed silent. I had time to think about our father, how I could hardly remember another time he had laughed out loud like that.

The only woman I'd had sex with since moving into the apartment lived with me for two years right before our father died, the cigarettes catching up with his lungs the year he turned fifty. He'd visited once a month, the two of us picking him up from where he lived in Glendale. He spent his time watching television. There were reruns of Lawrence Welk on the PBS station, back to back in the early evening on Saturdays, the champagne music makers switching from black and white to color, sometimes on the same night, the men growing sideburns, the Lennon Sisters becoming women. "You kids enjoy yourselves," he'd say, whether or not we were going out or staying in, as if he wanted to watch by himself.

Our mother had been gone for thirteen years by then. "She moved on," was all he ever said when I'd asked a month before he went into hospice.

"That's it?" I'd said.

"You ought to know," he'd said. "You lived there. You were a teenager by then, old enough to get it." He'd coughed then, beginning one of those spells that went on for a minute or two while I thought he might stop breathing altogether. When he'd caught his breath, he'd stared at me like I was on trial. "I wasn't surprised," he'd said, "if that's what you're getting at."

He waited for another two weeks, his last visit, before he said another word about the past. "Always," he said, "the worst thing is loneliness," and settled for that and not another word.

I understood he meant to let me know we had something in common, the secrecy of humiliation. Two months before, the woman who lived with me had told me I was "predictable." That she was moving on while she still felt something for me so she wouldn't have to leave because she felt nothing whatsoever. By now it had been almost five years without parents or a woman.

I turned off the lights a mile from the house. It hadn't rained, but it was so close to full dark I had to slow down to speed-bump pace. Jenny didn't say anything. She was sitting up though, alert. By the time I'd parked, both of us could see the smoke behind the house being reflected by a moving light that turned out, when we'd climbed the stairs, to be from Lou's phone.

Casandra was on the patio, too, dressed the same as she was the first time she'd climbed those stairs, only in different colors, cheering for a different franchise. She'd added a sweater for the chill, but it was unbuttoned and wide open. The smoke was swirling up from the patio's fire pit I hadn't used for months because of the drought. The patio was spotless because she'd been burning all the little twigs she'd swept up, but Lou wasn't showing appreciation for her work.

"The fuck you all doing here?" he said.

"I had the hose right here," Cassandra said. "I sprayed the roof before I lit the fire. I had this."

Lou turned his phone on her, swinging up past her cleavage to her face. "You stupid bitch," he said, and then he swung the light toward me. "And you, you dumb fuck, heaving all that shit over the fence like that's some sort of funny shit?"

"Something had to be done," Jenny said. "You said you wouldn't pay to have it moved, so we did the moving."

"Jesus," Lou said, but he kept the light on me.

"Fuck explaining," Cassandra said. "Fuck that spitting into the wind bullshit. The Forest Service will come or it won't."

"They'll come, all right," Lou said. "If I got a call, they got a call."

"Who called?" Cassandra said. "Jason didn't call. I didn't call. Jenny didn't call."

"I own another house here."

"Of course, you do," Cassandra said.

"Yeah, and just like I did for Paul Bunyan here, I gave those people my number when they moved in a month ago."

"Good," Jenny said. "I'll get your number from them We have some calls we need to make."

Lou swung the light over Jenny's body twice as if examining her loose sweatshirt and her baggy sweatpants to get an estimate of what her body might look like. She started to clutch herself in a way that made me focus on the purse she held in one hand.

I didn't move. I didn't call out. My mother, before she left, had told me she had never heard me raise my voice. "It worries me," she'd said, and then twittered a nervous laugh before she'd added, "because your father is exactly like that, and it's kept me up some nights, his quiet. It sounds like indifference."

I watched Jenny's fingers fluttering over the purse and wondered whether Lou, asshole that he was, would put his hands on her, whether, in turn, she would be capable of firing that gun. I took a deep breath and readied myself.

Cassandra stepped between them, so close to Lou, the light went right to her pushed-up cleavage. "I did all this work," she said, "not them, and now you need to back the fuck up."

"You think I'm a fool, that it?" Lou said, his voice settling back toward uncertainty and on its way, I thought, to cowardice.

"The house didn't burn down. Nobody got hurt."

She reached over the fence and picked up a branch that had caught against the fence and let its tip switch back and forth on the patio stones as if she were blind and feeling for problems. When she lifted it, Lou took one step back, then caught himself and straightened. "Your brother must have a truck if he does this sort of work. It can be loaded in no time."

I half-expected Lou to grab that branch and yank it away, but he just inhaled loudly and said, "I'm not here to be told."

"You know what I think?" Cassandra said. "If I could burn down just Jason's half of this house, I'd do it."

"You think you're funny?" Lou said, but his voice stayed measured. "The two of you getting it on or something? You look like you're ready, but your teasing bitch there keeps it covered like she wouldn't give it up."

Lou swung the light back onto Jenny, but she dropped her arms and let him play the beam over her body. Cassandra slapped the branch against Lou's shoes. "Fuck you all," Lou said, but he walked away and down the stairs without turning his head.

I stayed outside long enough to watch Jenny and Cassandra hug, then stand close together chatting. Jenny seemed excited. Not joyful, but for certain, ordinary, something sustainable. When Cassandra was gone, I thought, replaced by another temporary woman, Jenny might not wither.

I went inside, noticing that Jenny had left a book opened face down on her bed. She was reading again. I'd never been a reader, but lately I'd not only stopped listening to U2, I'd stopped listening to all music, even in the car, and though I watched movies, I drank beer during them, retrieving fresh cans without hitting pause, using the bathroom, finding a fresh bag of potato chips and chewing noisily through dialogue. What was I going to do when Jenny left and returned to her life? For just a moment, I caught myself wishing that she would stay terrified and helpless, someone who needed me. Or, at least, a presence, a voice.

ACKNOWLEDGMENTS FOR *THE SORROWS*

"The Selfishness of Bravery"   *Ascent*
"The Complete Stats"   *South Dakota Review*
"Pussy"   *South Dakota Review*
"The Chronological Library"   *Florida Review*
"The Sorrows"   *Santa Monica Review*
"Climbing to the LaBiancas'"   *South Dakota Review*
"Running through Directions"   *Cimarron Review*
"Filthy"   *Santa Monica Review*
"Wildfire"   *South Dakota Review*
"Side Effects"   *South Carolina Review*
"Queen for a Day"   *Pleiades*
"The Habits of Insects"   *Beloit Fiction Journal*
"What's Next?"   *South Carolina Review*

CPSIA information can be obtained
at www.ICGtesting.com
Printed in the USA
JSHW020505100120
3501JS00001B/5

9 781622 883110